FURIOUS

OTHER TITLES BY T.R. RAGAN

LIZZY GARDNER SERIES

Abducted

Dead Weight

A Dark Mind

Obsessed

Almost Dead

Evil Never Dies

WRITING AS THERESA RAGAN

Return of the Rose

A Knight in Central Park

Taming Mad Max

Finding Kate Huntley

Having My Baby

An Offer He Can't Refuse

Here Comes the Bride

I Will Wait For You: A Novella

Dead Man Running

FURIOUS

A FAITH MCMANN NOVEL

T.R. RAGAN

f THOMAS & MERCER

Published by Thomas & Mercer, Seattle

www.apub.com

Amazon, the Amazon logo, and Thomas & Mercer are trademarks of .com, Inc., or its affiliates.

ISBN-13: 9781612184500

ISBN-10: 1612184502

Cover art by melteddashboard.com

Cover design by Rex Bonomelli

Printed in the United States of America

Human trafficking is a form of modern-day slavery. Victims include adults and children, men and women. Anytime a person is coerced through fraudulent means to provide a service, it is a violation of human rights. Those most affected are children who come from places of instability, abuse, and homelessness, making them easy targets for gangs and traffickers, often forced or manipulated into street prostitution. Without an adult to look after them, without a mentor to look up to, these children miss out on an education—a chance to develop valuable life skills. By the age of eighteen, many of these kids find themselves alone, trapped in an endless cycle of poverty and exploitation.

The Faith McMann series is dedicated to those people who work tirelessly to raise awareness and increase understanding and who struggle endlessly to supply services and help survivors of human trafficking. You are all heroes.

For information about trafficking:
www.traffickingresourcecenter.org.

ONE

Thank God it's Friday. That was the thought running through Faith McMann's mind as the tires of her Camry rolled over the road toward home. Being a fourth-grade teacher could be exhausting. The best thing about her job was the children—looking into their eyes when they had an "aha" moment. The worst thing was everything else, including the overwhelming load of paperwork piled on the seat next to her: student assessments, evaluations, and homework to grade.

Faith kept her hands on the wheel and her eyes on the road, watching for the neighbor's Chihuahua, since the dog had a tendency to dart out and head straight for her front tires. She then glanced in the rearview mirror at her children. Lara and Hudson, only fifteen months apart in age, were in the backseat singing along with Brittany of Alabama Shakes.

"Hold on," they sang at the top of their lungs, hanging on to the last syllable until they were out of breath. They leaned toward each other, their heads touching. Her son caught her peeking, and he blushed. They were both growing so fast.

Lately Hudson had become fond of negotiating, whether it was bedtime hours or how many vegetables they put on his dinner plate.

His mop of brown hair and his green eyes made most people comment on how much he resembled his dad. That much was true, but her son had the same boundless energy she'd had when she was that age. He loved running sprints and playing soccer, always on the move.

Lara, on the other hand, was the quiet one . . . much like her father. Those two liked to plan and analyze. They would both opt to jump off a bridge rather than run the length of the driveway or exert too much energy simply for the sheer pleasure of doing so.

It was three o'clock on Friday afternoon, warm for November. Her husband came home early on Fridays, and his black GMC was parked out front. Hudson would be turning nine tomorrow. Craig didn't know it yet, but so far fifty people had responded yes to the birthday party e-vite she'd sent out. They were going to need a lot more hot dogs and hamburgers, which meant she needed to make a quick run to the grocery store. But first she would drop the kids off at home. If she brought them to the store with her, she'd never get anything done.

Faith waved at Beth Tanner, who lived in the second house on the left. Beth was an enigma of sorts. Nobody seemed to know much about her, and yet she'd lived in that same house since before Faith's family moved in twelve years ago. As Beth watered her hydrangeas, she kept her eyes downcast, pretending she didn't notice Faith driving by.

As she made a right onto her driveway, her shoulders dipped when she noticed that Craig had yet to cut the lawn for the party tomorrow. She pressed the button next to the sun visor. The garage door rolled open. She put the car in park and said, "Tell Dad I'm running to the store and I'll be right back."

The kids unlatched their seatbelts, jumped out of the car, and ran through the garage and into the house before the song ended. Faith sang along until the last verse, then sat there for a moment and soaked in a little peace and quiet. Working full-time and raising two young kids tended to make moments like this rare.

Her cell phone buzzed. It was her sister. "Hey, what's up?" Faith asked.

"I'll tell you what's up," Jana said. "Steve is driving me nuts! I quit drinking, I stopped devouring cake and cookies, but now he won't let me lift anything heavier than a milk carton. This baby is going to be born stressed out if he doesn't chill."

Faith smiled. Her sister was a drama queen. "What time will you be coming tomorrow?"

"Oh, my God, I forgot about the party."

"You have got to be kidding me," Faith said. "You were supposed to make six dozen cupcakes. Do you know how much I still have to do before—"

Her sister's laughter cut her off midsentence.

Faith sighed when she realized Jana had been joking about not making the cupcakes. "That's not funny, Jana."

"You're such a dweeb. How could I possibly forget to make six dozen cupcakes when you've reminded me every single day for the past two weeks?"

"I don't know, but I have to go."

"Wait—Have you told Craig the news?"

"No."

"Why not?"

"He's been busy with work—and, you know, bills stacking up, new tires for the car, busted water heater last month. I haven't found the right moment to tell him about baby number three."

"He'll be thrilled. Don't wait too long, OK?"

"Don't worry, I won't." Faith disconnected the call and was about to head off for the store when she remembered the grocery list hanging on the refrigerator. She left her purse in the car and climbed out.

Weaving around toys and bikes, she headed through the garage door into the kitchen, where it looked as if a tornado had swept through the house. Kitchen drawers had been left open. Papers and broken dishes were scattered across the floor.

Her heart raced. *What is going on?*

Just as she was about to call out her husband's name, she stepped into the family room and saw Craig on the floor, bound and gagged.

A man she didn't recognize hovered over him.

The scene before her made no sense.

Her heart pounded in her chest, making it difficult to breathe as her gaze darted around the room.

And then she spotted them.

Lara and Hudson sat together on the couch. Their hands had been duct-taped behind their backs. More duct tape covered their mouths. Another man stood close by, watching over them.

Time stopped as she tried to figure out what to do. Craig always said they should buy a gun, but she didn't want to keep one in the house. Eyes wide, she looked at the knife drawer. *Grab a knife? Or run and alert the neighbors?*

The two men exchanged a glance. Their eyes said it all.

She turned and ran.

If she could get inside the car and lock the doors, she could honk the horn or drive the car right through the wall and into the house if she had to. That might get one of the neighbors' attention.

She flew through the back door leading to the garage and screamed at the top of her lungs before someone grabbed her from behind, twisted her around, and brought her face up close to his.

"Where is it?"

"I don't know what you're talking about," she said as she struggled to get free.

He sneered. His eyes were bloodshot, filled with desperation. He smelled of stale tobacco. Strong arms held her in place. She thought of every show she'd ever seen on getting away from an assailant, but fighting him was useless. "Let us go!" she cried.

He shook her hard enough to make her teeth rattle. "You have five seconds to tell me where it is!"

This time when she screamed, she dug her heel into his foot and tried to twist out of his grasp.

He slammed her to the ground. Her head hit the cement floor, and her world turned black.

———

When Faith opened her eyes, it took her a few seconds to realize she'd been dragged back into the house. She was on her side, facing her husband. She'd been restrained. Duct tape over her mouth. Ankles bound, hands taped behind her back. She tried to look over her shoulder to see the kids. It was no use.

Craig stared at her, his expression intense. He looked relieved to see her conscious.

Please don't let them harm my children. Oh, God, no.

She felt the vibration of heavy footfalls against the wood flooring. She tried to lift her head as a third man entered the room from down the hall. "There's nothing here," he said. "Kill them both. Make it quick."

"What about the kids?" someone asked.

"Bring them."

She squirmed, tried to scream and wriggle free. *My babies. Don't you dare touch my babies!*

The man who had been hovering over Craig, the one with the closely shaved head, leaned forward. Her gaze fell on the marking tattooed on his neck. A symbol of some sort.

Her head ached; her brain felt fuzzy. And then she saw the knife in the man's hand. A hunter's knife—sharp, serrated, deadly.

Craig's gaze remained on hers, his eyes telling her he loved her. She knew the look. She'd seen it a hundred times before.

No. No. No. You can't die. We're having another baby. This isn't real. Everything will be all right. I know it will. This is not happening.

She saw a flash of steel and then one clean swipe across his neck. That's all it took.

Ggggrrggg . . .

The noise coming from Craig's throat was too much to bear.

"Hurry it up!"

Blood, dark and thick, oozed from Craig's wound. His eyes wide open, a mirror in which to watch as the same blade sliced quickly across her throat at an awkward angle. She felt the icy chill of the blade as it cut across her flesh. Not a clean swipe. He was in hurry. She tried to breathe through her nose, but she had a difficult time getting air into her lungs. She was suffocating on her own blood.

Lara. Hudson.

Two

The bright lights prevented Faith from opening her eyes. Whenever she tried to take a breath, she panicked and choked. Her airway was constricted.

Machines beeped all around her.

She tried to say something, but no words would come forth. Her throat was dry, scratchy. Her head pounded. And then she recognized her sister's voice as Jana brushed her hair.

Somebody was crying.

The baby she was carrying . . . had something happened to her baby?

As she faded in and out, she caught glimmers of shadows and people. Mom was somewhere close, reading to her. Her cheerful tone contrasted with the excruciating pain.

The room reeked of antiseptics and sadness.

The beeping stopped. Finally. For the first time in forever the room was blissfully quiet. Death was coming. Its loving arms wrapped her in warmth and filled her with peace.

Mom stopped reading.

Dad hovered close. His smooth jaw touched her cheek as he whispered into her ear. "Don't give up without a fight. You've been a fighter since the day you were born."

The blood swooshing through her veins slowed to a crawl.

Why was she here? It was the oddest sensation, not remembering. And even stranger was the fact that she knew she was dying, and she was glad.

"You can't leave us, Faith," Dad said. "You've got to think of Lara and Hudson. They're out there somewhere, and they need you."

———

Faith shot up in bed and sucked in a deep, shaky breath.

She'd been having a dream—a nightmare.

It took her a moment to remember she was no longer in the hospital. She was home.

How long had she been here? She looked at the calendar on the bedside table. Today was November 16—ten days since the attack, three days back at the house. Or was it four? The clock's neon numbers told her it was five thirty in the morning.

The days had all blurred together. With a steadying hand on her chest, she waited until her heart stopped racing and the dizziness passed.

Panic attacks—she'd been plagued with them since returning home. When they struck, they woke her in a blinding rush and made breathing a chore.

Her fingers went to her throat, where she could feel the thick keloid scar that ran across the lower part of her face and neck. The blade, she'd been told, had sliced her carotid artery and stopped just shy of her jugular vein. According to nurses and doctors, she had beat incredible odds. If not for her neighbor Beth Tanner's quick thinking, she wouldn't have survived.

After nearly a week in intensive care and then a few days being weaned off machines, she'd returned to a house that no longer vibrated with life. The walls were cold and hollow, the pictures lining the mantel sad. Every creak startled her. Her parents and siblings took turns watching her disintegrate, molting before their eyes. People had been coming and going. She didn't know who. She didn't care. Her former self, vibrant and exploding with life, had quickly been shed and replaced with a pale, thin shell of grief and sadness.

She could hardly eat or drink.

At the hospital, after being brought out of a drug-induced coma, the heartache was numbing—a vast hole of nothingness tucked beneath a layer of physical pain. Knowing that Craig was gone forever and her kids were missing was too much to bear. The misery and despair touched her very core: blinding, deafening, debilitating. Easiest just to wrap herself in a blanket of grief and never get out of bed.

The psychotherapist she'd talked to on her last day at the hospital told her the memories of that day might come back not all at once but instead in tiny pieces. He had prescribed her medication, but she didn't take it. She *wanted* to see the images when and if they returned. *Needed* to see every bloody detail.

She vaguely recalled the police coming to see her on her first day home—too soon. She'd tried to answer their questions, but her mind had been a giant blank slate of nothingness. The harder she'd tried to remember the sequence of events and what the men looked like, the more distorted the images became, everything melting into a bloody mess. Although she had no recollection of the detectives leaving, she did remember two FBI agents paying her a visit the next day. She'd wanted to help them. She needed them to find her children. But again, the harder she'd tried to focus on their questions, the more difficult it became to breathe until she was gasping for air, leaving Mom to usher them from the room.

Friends and coworkers stopped coming by once they saw the state she was in. No need to bring casseroles and meatloaf since the freezer was full and she had no appetite. The phone calls stopped, too, which was a relief because she had nothing to say to anyone.

Faith pushed herself upward to a sitting position.

Something strange had happened last night.

The images from *that* day had started coming back with a vengeance.

And that wasn't all.

She'd experienced an odd sensation. For most of the night, her mind had flickered, as if fireflies were darting around inside her head, trying to find a way out.

At the moment, one tiny speck of light remained.

If her sister were there, Jana would immediately latch on to the idea that the light had something to do with hope and optimism, but Faith knew it had nothing to do with sanguinity. Not even close.

This speck of light was bloodthirsty.

The pinpoint of light was real. So real she could taste it, metallic and bittersweet on her tongue. It was also dark and cold, and it had fangs that refused to let go. She pushed the covers aside. When her feet touched the wood floor, an odd sensation swept through her, almost as if her body and mind were no longer hers.

She walked to the bathroom, stared at her reflection in the mirror. For the first time since she'd returned home, she let her gaze roam, at a slow and measured pace, over the jagged red scar that started at her left ear and continued on a drunken sideways path to her chin before free-falling down and across her neck to an inch below the right ear.

Beth Tanner had heard her screams, after all, and she'd called the police. She was a retired ER nurse and had known what to do. According to Mom, Beth had used two fingers to pinch the artery and somehow managed to stanch the flow of blood.

Faith continued to look intently at her reflection.

She blinked.

Eyes, dark and hollow, stared back at her. *Don't turn away,* her eyes seemed to be telling her. *Look at me. Look closely.*

These eyes were no longer the sad, woeful eyes of yesterday or the day before that. These eyes were on the brink of insanity. She leaned forward until the porcelain rim of the sink pressed into her stomach. In that instant, Faith knew what the flickers of light meant.

Every muscle inside her body twitched. Electric.

Anger, red and raw, nipped at the inner regions of her skull, its gnarled fingers repeatedly flipping the "On" and "Off" switches inside her head.

She could feel it. Hell, she could see it.

It wanted her attention, and it wanted out. The thing rattled her bones and knocked on her chest, telling her it was time to *wake up* and find her kids. Her legs wobbled, forcing her to hang on to the veiny gray marble countertop for support.

No more crying.

Tears weren't going to help her find her children.

Tears would not bring her husband back.

No more lying in bed like a worthless corpse.

Your children need you!

She knew suddenly what needed to be done. Every time bits and pieces of that day came to mind, she needed to snatch them up and put them to paper.

Quickly.

She stripped off her clothes, took a clean towel from the rack, then went to the shower. Ignoring the tightness in her chest and the light-headedness she felt with every dizzying step, she turned on the water and stepped into the stall.

The water was icy cold. Goose bumps sprouted.

One time since her return home, Jana had attempted to wash her hair while she lay curled in a fetal position in bed, but this was the first time Faith had stepped into the shower. Her hair was matted to her skull. She picked up the shampoo bottle, struggled to open the lid, then drizzled its contents over the top of her head. The nerve damage to her left side made it difficult to reach for the soap, so she used the soapy suds from the shampoo to wash her body.

The water went from freezing to scalding in a matter of minutes, turning her skin pink by the time she turned off the faucet and stepped out.

Her jeans were loose around her hips. The T-shirt fell across breasts that had shrunk to half their former size. She lifted her right hand and used her fingers to comb through her hair, then made her way to the kitchen, a room that used to mean happy chaos but now meant nothing at all.

She ignored the section of the hardwood floor in the family room that had already been replaced with new wood planks. Bloody or not, she would've known the exact spot where she'd watched Craig die.

Her family hadn't wanted her to return to this house of nightmares, but she'd refused to listen. When her children found their way home, Faith would be there waiting.

She opened the kitchen drawer, found a notepad and a felt-tip pen. Then she found her laptop and turned it on. Taking a seat on a stool, she made a short list of possible suspects, anyone who popped into her head. Next she researched pedophiles and known criminals in the area. Finally, as she tried to summon the images she'd seen last night, images of the day her life was destroyed, she began to sketch. For the first few minutes, the particulars flowed from mind to paper without too much effort, but she was running out of room. She needed a bigger canvas.

She glanced from the pad of paper to the living room wall, then hurried to the garage, where she ripped plastic lids from containers stacked high. One at a time, she moved through the contents until she found what she was looking for.

For a few seconds, she stood motionless, staring at the art supplies, and her heart twisted. Visions sizzled and flashed like bolts of lightning inside her brain. So clearly she could see her children. Smiling, laughing, glue and glitter everywhere.

Think of something else, Faith. Anything. She concentrated on the blood traveling through her veins, pulsing, carrying oxygen to her cells. Because now was not the time to think about when she'd used the paints and glitter.

Put the memory away! Eat it. Swallow it. Save it for another day.

Once she had her bearings and found a way to breathe again, she carried the art supplies into the house and got to work.

Time held still until hours later when the front door flew open.

Faith's sister, Jana, swept into the room like a gust of wind, then merely stood there, her eyes wide, her chest rising and falling with each ragged breath. "Faith. Oh, my God, you're OK."

Faith kept painting. The visions from that day were still there but fading fast, like a filmy ghost sliding back into the walls. She concentrated on each stroke of the paintbrush.

"We've been calling the house all morning. Why aren't you answering your phone?" Jana turned toward the living room wall. Her mouth fell open. She shifted her weight from one foot to the other. "What are you doing?"

Faith painted faster in an attempt to tune out her sister's voice. Another minute or two; that's all she needed. She couldn't stop if she wanted to, but then Jana placed a hand on her shoulder. Faith whipped around. Paint splattered across the front of Jana's pea-green long-sleeved sweater.

Her sister's gaze, now fixed on Faith's feet, traveled quickly upward, stopping midface. Their eyes met. Jana attempted to cover a gasp with her fingertips before she dropped her hand and said, "You've got to start eating. You're wasting away."

Faith turned back to the task at hand.

"That's not paper," Jana told her. "In case you didn't notice, you're painting on the living room wall."

Faith had always had a flair for artwork, dabbling in charcoals and oils during her college years and later watercolors, but what was happening at the moment was an out-of-body experience. She'd been at it for more than three hours now. Her arms were beginning to feel the weight of her efforts.

"Is that a tattoo on the man's neck?"

Doing her best to ignore her sister, Faith took her time with the elegant scroll of the symbol she'd seen in her dream. The images were gone now. Jana had swished away the last remnants of her vision, leaving only wisps of fumes like those left behind from the exhaust pipe of an old car.

She set the paint-filled pan on the floor and stepped back to take a look. On the left side of the wall she'd painted the two men she'd seen when she first walked into the house. She hadn't painted the third man since she never did get a good look at his face. They'd all been dressed in dark clothes. On the right side of the wall were the dozens of notes she'd written earlier, ripped out of the notebook and stapled in place.

She walked to the chair, Craig's favorite recliner, the one the kids fought over whenever he was gone, and plopped down, exhaustion pushing heavily on her shoulders. Her sister was on the phone talking to Mom or Dad, letting them know everything was OK. After she finished her call, Jana went to the kitchen, returned with a cold glass of water, and handed it to her.

Obligingly, Faith took a few sips. Her lips were dry to the point of cracking. Her tongue soaked up the moisture like a dehydrated sponge. She hadn't thought to drink or eat.

Her sister took a seat on the couch next to her. "Mind telling me what's going on here?"

Using the back of her hand, Faith wiped the hair out of her face. "I've been having visions," she said. "I need to remember everything about that day and get it on paper, or the wall."

"I don't think you should torture yourself that way."

Faith took another sip of water, letting it trickle down her throat before she looked at Jana and said, "I'm going to find Hudson and Lara."

A long pause settled between them.

"You need to talk to the police. Detective Dillon Yuhasz is working your case. He came to the hospital to talk to you, but you were pretty out of it. And when he came to the house, your answers to his questions were jumbled and confusing. He told us to give him a call once you were feeling better. You're their main witness, Faith. Now that events of that day are coming back to you, you need to talk to them."

"How about right now?" Faith asked.

Jana looked her over, then shook her head. "I'll give Detective Yuhasz a call and arrange a meeting for tomorrow morning."

Faith nodded and reached for the pen and paper she'd left on the coffee table. After writing Detective Yuhasz's name at the top of the page, she added another suspect to her list.

"What are you doing?"

Faith handed her the notebook.

"You have your neighbor Mr. Hawkins on your list of suspects," Jana said. "Seriously?"

"He used to offer the kids cookies."

"That's because he's a baker."

Faith narrowed her eyes. "He's *too* nice."

"You always liked him."

"But I never said I trusted him."

"Steve Murray? What the hell is my husband doing on this list?"

"I crossed him off."

"Jesus, Faith. This is crazy. I think we should get you to the doctor. He said that the memories might return and cause you a fright, but I don't think this is what he was talking about." Jana gestured around the room. "I'm worried about your state of mind."

"My kids are missing. Everyone is a suspect, including Steve. Get over it." A bout of nausea hit her. She laid her head back on the chair.

"You look pale," Jana said. "I'll get you something to eat."

Faith waved her off.

"How are you ever going to find your kids if you don't stay nourished?"

Jana was right. She needed to eat, take care of herself, so she could go after these people and bring back her children. "OK," Faith said.

"How about some soup?"

Faith nodded, and Jana tossed the notebook on the table and went to the kitchen, where she searched through cupboards for a pan. "I noticed you have the word *pedophile* on the list," Jana said as she went through the pantry. "What's that about?"

"There's a website that lists the names and addresses of pedophiles living all across the country. Any pedophiles living within a ten-mile radius of this house are going on my list, along with anyone I've ever known who looked at me cross-eyed."

"You're not planning on knocking on their doors, are you?"

"Of course I am."

Jana wagged a can opener at her. "The police have already interviewed the neighbors and potential witnesses. At least hold off until you've had a chance to talk to the detective about the investigation."

It wasn't long before Jana brought her a bowl of tomato soup along with a spoon and a napkin. "Here you go. Eat up."

Faith's gaze fell on her sister's stomach. She reached for her own belly. She had lost her baby. At eight weeks, the doctor had told her it had been too early to know the sex.

"I'm so sorry," Jana said.

Faith brought the spoon to her mouth, every motion robotic. Lingering grief threatened to bring her to her knees. She had to fight it, needed to get stronger. She couldn't taste a thing, but she ate until the bowl was empty.

Jana sat across from her and used her sleeve to wipe her eyes.

"Do you want more?"

Faith nodded as she looked around the room worriedly.

"What is it?" Jana asked.

"Craig," she blurted. He was adamant about being cremated in the event of his death. "Do you have his ashes?"

"I do. I didn't want to say anything until you had a chance to get back on your feet. Do you want me to make memorial service arrangements?"

"No. Not yet."

"When?"

"I'll do it after Lara and Hudson are back home. They'll need closure. They need to be there, too."

THREE

Miranda and five other girls, all between the ages of ten and sixteen, sat on the cold wood floor in a circle, filing and polishing their nails, doing their best to ignore the intermittent whimpers coming through the vents. One of the other girls in the house, Adele, had disobeyed Mother . . . again. Big mistake. Mother had rules and they were not to be broken.

Miranda had been at the farmhouse for eighteen months now. Adele had been there for about a year. Adele didn't like her new name. She told anyone who would listen that her real name was Samantha Perelman and that she'd been abducted while shopping for groceries with her mother. Every time she told the story, she was beat. When Adele had first been brought to the house, she'd looked like a wide-eyed, fresh-faced teenager with pale skin and long dark hair. It wouldn't have surprised Miranda to see Adele's face on the cover of a glossy magazine. She was *that* pretty.

But that was then.

Now she looked scary thin and out of touch with the world, her eyes blank, her face without emotion.

Initially Adele had fought Mother on everything. Once she'd gotten hold of a knife and tried to take Mother down, but one of the boys who worked at the farm heard the commotion and managed to stop Adele from stabbing Mother in the chest. She would have done it, too. Adele wasn't afraid of anyone. At least she didn't used to be. At first it had seemed she'd rather die than be forced to comply with their rules. She was outspoken, and she often talked to the other girls in private about how they could escape if they all worked together. She plotted and planned, and she gave Miranda hope.

But then Mother had overheard Adele telling the girls about her plan to escape through the window in the basement, the only window in the house that wasn't covered with iron bars. The window was quickly boarded up from the outside, and Adele was separated from the rest of them, locked away at night. They rarely saw Adele any longer.

Miranda sighed as she helped Jean with her toenail polish.

Jean was the newest girl. She was also the youngest in the house. She was so quiet that it was easy to forget she was in the room.

She wished she could say the same for Felicia. Eleven years old with curly red hair, Felicia started to cry. Miranda grabbed a T-shirt from atop the dirty cot behind her and tossed it her way. "Hurry. Wipe those tears. If Mother comes in here and sees you crying, you'll be whipped."

"Or worse," Denise chimed in, "she'll make you spend an hour with one of those boys." She moaned and shivered, pretending to be orgasmic, making the two older girls laugh.

The boys she referred to were Jasper and Phoenix. They did most of the work around the farm. They fed the chickens and goats and milked the cows. They also trained the girls on how to please a man, which was ridiculous considering they couldn't be much more than eighteen, if that. Miranda often ended up with Jasper. She'd hated him in the beginning, but after months of fighting him and everyone else in the house she began to crave his company. Now she went to him willingly. Phoenix was another story. He was a disgusting pig, and every time he touched her, she thought she might be sick.

Denise blew on her nails before she asked, "Did you know that they're not really training us?"

"Then what are they doing?" Miranda wanted to know.

"Mother can't afford to pay them, so she gives us to them for payment for all the chores they do around here."

"That's a lie," Miranda said.

They all looked at Miranda, surprised by her reaction.

Denise lifted an eyebrow. "You're not falling for Jasper, are you?"

Miranda didn't answer. The truth was she did have feelings for him, but if what they were saying was true, that meant Jasper had lied about his feelings for her. He'd never once mentioned that she was a form of payment for services provided to Mother. The idea of it made her sick to her stomach. He said she was special and that he cared for her.

For the hundredth time since being brought to the farmhouse, she wondered if anyone was looking for her. There were no telephones, televisions, computers, or radios allowed in the house. No way of knowing what was going on in the outside world.

She'd been so stupid for believing a woman she'd only just met. But Caroline had been well dressed and friendly. She knew just what to say—promising her a better life. Thrilled by the idea of making enough money to help her mom, Miranda had gone with the woman.

Caroline's car had been a clunker, old and rickety with worn seats and trash littered about, which should have been her first clue that something was wrong. But ever since her mom had lost her job and they'd been living on the streets, she'd developed a bad cough and Miranda had been worried about her. Desperate for a better life, she'd swallowed her fears and doubts and climbed into the car.

They had driven for hours, maybe days. It was hard to tell because after she drank the soda Caroline gave her, she kept falling asleep. By the time they arrived at the farmhouse, she felt groggy and weird and had no idea where she was.

The powder-blue two-story house was in the middle of nowhere, surrounded by acres of tall dry grass where cows grazed and roosters crowed. The windows were frosted, or maybe they had been painted; it was hard to tell. They were also secured from the outside with metal bars.

The woman who greeted them, a slender female with frizzy hair and a cruel expression etched on her face, handed Caroline an envelope and then took hold of Miranda's hand and pulled her toward the house. Miranda hadn't fully realized she'd been duped until she heard the squeal of tires and watched Caroline speed off without telling her when she would be back to pick her up.

Panicked, Miranda told the woman she'd made a mistake and needed to go home. Her mom needed her. When she tried to run, the woman grabbed her by the hair, dragged her into the house, and secured the door with a chain and a combination lock. She didn't waste any time letting Miranda know that Rita Calloway no longer existed.

Her name was now Miranda Hall.

She bit and kicked, fought the woman and anyone who came near her. She was locked inside a closet. Days later she was branded with the letter *H*.

When she refused to eat or take a bath, she was beaten with a stick. She didn't care. She wanted to go home. Every time she tried to escape she was tossed back into a closet and left alone in the dark. Not only did she fight the woman in charge, she fought the two boys who worked for her. She also refused to talk to the other girls in the house. She hated them all. For weeks she waged war with everyone in the house. And they stopped giving her food and water.

In the end it was her intense thirst that lost her the battle of wills. She'd wanted water more than she'd wanted death. As the cool liquid quenched her thirst and soothed her sore throat, she knew her life would never be the same. No more fighting. No more crying. No more praying for her mom to save her.

Rita Calloway truly was dead.

Four

Faith rummaged through the hall closet for something to dump the contents of her purse into. Craig had given her the purse for Christmas. She couldn't look at it without feeling sick to her stomach. She found an old backpack and transferred her belongings into it.

She glanced at the clock. Mom would be arriving at any moment to go with her to meet with Detective Yuhasz.

At the same time a key rattled in the front door, she heard the news reporter on television talking about arresting a child killer.

The smile on the killer's face during the court proceeding was chilling.

The Florida man had brutally murdered his girlfriend's young boy. Worse yet, according to the reporter, the girlfriend had helped him hide the body. Faith pointed the remote at the television set and turned it off. "Sick. People are sick."

As she did every moment of every day, she thought of her kids. She refused to believe that Lara and Hudson were dead. If the men who had taken her kids had meant to kill them, they would have done it right then.

The door opened. Mom stepped inside and looked around. She fixed her gaze on the wall where Faith had recorded memories of that horrific day. "Oh, my. Jana mentioned that you had been painting . . . but I had no idea." Mom took a moment to look Faith over, clearly struggling not to comment on her appearance: pale and thin, for starters. Hollow eyes framed by dark shadows.

Faith had seen her reflection. She knew.

The lights within were flickering again, worse than yesterday, like dangling electric wires whipping around in strong, wet winds. Faith was feeling anxious and more than a little annoyed by everything and anything when Mom wrapped her arms around her and said, "I love you, sweetheart."

For a moment Faith rested her head on her mom's shoulder and just breathed. It felt good.

When she straightened, Mom said, "There's a media van outside again. Maybe it's time you talked to them."

Faith peeked through the blinds. Balloons and flowers lined the fence all the way to the main road. At the end of the drive was a news van from a local Sacramento station that hadn't been there earlier.

"You've been too sick to pay any attention, Faith, but your tragedy has made national news. There are people all over the world who have been mourning Craig and rooting for you to pull through, praying for Lara and Hudson's return. Maybe you should go out there and talk to the media, ask their listeners for help in finding your kids."

"I don't know what I would say to them."

"Tell them what's in your heart. Tell them we need their help . . . the more people we have looking for Lara and Hudson, the better."

Faith straightened as an idea came to her. "I'll be right back."

Faith walked out of the house and made her way up the driveway. Before she reached the street, both doors to the van opened. A young man with his hair pulled back in a ponytail scurried to the back of the van to grab his equipment. "Mary, get over here!"

Mary—late twenties Faith guessed—jumped out of the passenger seat, smoothed the wrinkles from her blouse, grabbed her microphone, and rushed to greet Faith.

They shook hands.

"Are you recording?" Faith asked.

"Not yet. Jim," she said. "Are we on?"

"I got it," he said as he adjusted the strap around his body, then angled the lens their way. "Shoot."

"How are you holding up?" Mary asked.

"Just taking things one moment at a time," Faith said, and that was the truth. "I want my children returned to me. That's all that matters."

Mary cleared her throat. "It's a shocking story. I'm sorry for your loss. The entire world has been praying for you and your family."

"Thank you."

"Your children have been missing for eleven days now—"

"Would you and Jim mind coming with me?" Faith interrupted. "To the house?"

Faith nodded. "I'd like to show you and your viewers something."

Mary's eyes widened. She gestured wildly at Jim to follow as she hurried to Faith's side and walked with her toward the house. "Is it OK for Jim to keep the camera on?"

"Yes, please do." They walked the rest of the way without speaking. Faith opened the door and entered the house. She waited until the cameraman caught up to them before she said, "This is my mom, Lilly Gray." Faith turned to the painted wall. "These are the men who took my children."

"Get a close-up," Mary instructed. "Did you paint this yourself?"

Faith nodded. "The visions come and go, but for a few hours I saw them so clearly in my mind I knew it was important that I get their images on canvas, or in this case, onto the living room wall. I don't want to forget their faces," Faith said. "There were three men, but I only saw the faces of two of them. If anyone has seen either of these men, please call the police."

Mom was off to the side rifling through her purse. After a moment she held up a picture of Lara and Hudson that Faith hadn't seen. It was a recent photo taken of the two of them with their grandpa, all three of them holding ice-cream cones and smiling at the camera. "This is Lara, ten and a half years old," Faith said when she realized Mom had lost her voice. "She recently won a local spelling bee with the word *flibbertigibbet*." She forced a smile. "I can hardly pronounce it, let alone use it in a sentence." She pointed at Hudson. "This is my son, Hudson. We were about to celebrate his ninth birthday when he was taken. He recently started the third grade. His teachers say he's unusually curious and acts older than other kids his age and that sometimes he—"

Faith lost it then. Head bent, she couldn't stop the tears from coming.

Mom stepped forward and wrapped her arms around her. A half a minute passed before Faith managed to gain control. She stood tall and said, "Lara and Hudson are out there somewhere. Please. If you recognize these men or know anything about why or where they might have taken my children, please call the Placer County Sheriff's Department." She looked into the camera once more and said in a clear voice, "Lara. Hudson. Mom is going to find you both and bring you home. I won't let anyone or anything stop me. Stay strong."

Mary looked at the cameraman. "That's a wrap." She handed Faith a card with her name and number. "If there's anything I can do to help, let me know."

———

Sitting in her mother's Kia Spectra headed for the sheriff's department, Faith glanced at her mom and noticed that the lines in her face appeared deeper, her hair grayer. She'd aged five years. It dawned on her in that moment that Mom, the woman who had driven her to school each day, wiped her tears, and braided her hair, was suffering, too. Faith would have preferred going to the police station alone. She didn't have the energy to worry about anyone else, but still, she had to say something. "Thanks for coming with me."

"Of course," Mom said. "Anything you need. Dad and I are here for you."

"How's Dad doing? Shouldn't you be with him?"

"He's strong as an ox—he'll be fine. He wanted me to be with you today."

Faith nodded, wishing Mom would drive a little faster. Something closer to the speed limit would be nice. She scratched her arm, the side of her head, then drummed the tips of her fingers against the car door as she looked out at a blur of trees and road signs. The fury she felt within would not subside, contrasting greatly with the love she felt for her mother. She closed her eyes until the quiet settled over them like dust motes, which couldn't be easy for Mom since she and Jana were talkers—the type of people who liked to fill every nook and cranny with words. Minutes felt like hours until they finally merged off the freeway.

They walked through one of two glass doors leading into the building. To the left was what looked like the dispatcher room with a large sliding-glass window. Up a short flight of stairs and to the right was a desk with a sign-in sheet. A frazzled-looking woman held the phone to her ear and took notes. Another woman in uniform handled five tasks at once. One hand flipped through a file; the other jotted a number on a pad of paper. She used her foot to shut the file cabinet. The phone rang. She picked it up and put the caller on hold, leaving a flashing red button in its wake.

Faith cleared her throat.

"What can I help you with?" the woman asked.

"I'm Faith McMann. We're here to see Detective Yuhasz."

Recognition lit up her face. "Detectives Yuhasz and O'Sullivan are expecting you. Come with me."

They were led past rows of cubicles to a desk at the far back corner of the building. Chaos abounded. Reports were being taken, phones ringing, everyone talking at once. According to the nameplate on the desk, the detective's name was Ryan O'Sullivan. He stood and extended a hand to Mom as he told her how nice it was to see her again. O'Sullivan was tall and lanky with dark-framed eyeglasses and thin, straight hair. He turned his attention to Faith. "It's good to see you up and moving around. I'm sorry for your loss, and I want to assure you that we're doing everything in our power to find your children."

"Thank you."

He nodded. "Detective Yuhasz will be with us shortly, and then we'll move into his office. Elaine Burnett, with the FBI, is on her way."

Faith hadn't realized she would be talking to the FBI at the same time, but she wasn't complaining. Having both the detectives and the FBI in the same room would make things easier, since she had questions for all of them.

"Can I get either of you anything to drink?" the detective asked.

They both declined.

He moved piles of papers dotted with sticky notes out of the way. Tall stacks of files remained. Faith couldn't take her eyes off the folder with *McMann* scribbled on the bottom left-hand corner. He gestured for them both to take a seat.

Faith pointed at the folder. "Can I take a look?"

He clicked his tongue. "Sorry. Open investigation. I can't let you review the file, but I'll do my best to answer all your questions."

"I would like to know if anyone in your department talked to my neighbors."

"Yes. We went door-to-door and collected brief statements."

"How about the pedophile living on Oakwood right around the corner from my house?"

He made a note. "I'm sure someone has looked into it, but I'll get back to you on that." O'Sullivan set his pen down. "Maybe it would be helpful if we wait until Detective Yuhasz is ready to go so that we can catch you up on the investigation process and everything we've done so far."

Her eyelid twitched. "Did you search Mr. Hawkins's house?"

"Mr. Hawkins?"

"The neighbor to my right. He's a baker."

"For the duration of your stay in the hospital, your house was a crime scene. I can personally assure you that an intensive and thorough investigation was done. Every available resource has been mobilized. For the first ten days an officer was stationed at your home in case of the return of your children or a demand for ransom was made. All bases were covered. Nonpolice personnel such as scout groups and fire rescue units gathered to help with ground searches."

"It's true," Mom chimed in. "There were at a least a dozen officers working double shifts during the first ninety-six hours."

Faith felt jittery and anxious as if she'd had too much coffee. She wanted answers, and she wanted them now. Just because she'd been out of commission didn't give them all an excuse to twiddle their thumbs. "Was someone able to check inside Mr. Hawkins's house?" she asked again.

O'Sullivan shook his head. "We would need a warrant to do so."

"OK," she said, scooting her chair closer to his desk. "Now we're getting somewhere. Let's get one."

"Searches cannot be performed based on mere suspicion."

Mom gave Faith's arm a gentle squeeze.

O'Sullivan looked over his shoulder, obviously relieved when Yuhasz signaled that he was ready for them. "Looks like Detective Yuhasz is ready to go."

They followed Detective O'Sullivan into the office. Faith had met Detective Yuhasz in the hospital and then again at home, but she'd been flying high on painkillers and her memories of the attack had been blurry and jumbled. She wouldn't have recognized the man in front of her if she'd passed him on the street. The smell of his cologne was overbearing. He had a wide grin. Her mom gave him a hug, everyone acting as if they were old friends.

Short-cropped hair left Detective Yuhasz with sharp, angular spikes that Faith imagined would be painful to touch. Like petting a porcupine. He was a few inches shorter than Dad, who stood well over six feet. For his age, which she guessed to be close to sixty, Yuhasz appeared to be in decent shape. His muscles strained against the cotton sleeves of his button-up shirt.

They all took a seat.

Just as O'Sullivan pulled up a chair, Agent Burnett, a tall woman with dark hair tied back in a knot, joined them. Introductions were made while another chair was brought into the room.

"I'm glad to see you're doing better," Detective Yuhasz said to Faith. "Your parents told me in the hospital that you were a fighter, and it's clear they were right." He retrieved a recorder from his top drawer. "Your sister said your memories of that day have returned. Is that right?"

"I've been having visions, yes. Some things, like the men's faces, came to me all at once, while other things are coming back in bits and pieces. I'm still a little foggy."

He clicked on the tape recorder and said, "If it's OK with you, I'm going to record our conversation."

"That's fine," she said.

He pushed his notebook to the side. "First off, I'd like to thank you both for coming today." He then stated, by name, each person who was gathered in the room. "I know this can't be easy. You've been through a very traumatizing experience, but we need you to tell us everything you remember about the day of the attack."

The police had analyzed the crime scene. They had seen the bloodshed and talked to neighbors and potential witnesses. She'd hoped to come here today to discover who was responsible for Craig's death. And find out where they thought her kids might be.

She inhaled, tried to rein in her frustration. *Stay calm and stick with protocol,* she told herself. "Should I start at the very beginning, before I arrived home?"

He nodded.

"OK . . . well, after school was let out," she began, "the kids met me in the classroom and we drove home just as we did every weekday." She paused, remembering the kids singing along together, their happy faces and sweet voices. Her chest tightened.

"Are you OK?" Detective Yuhasz asked. "Would you like some more time before we get started?"

"No," she said. "I'm good . . . um . . . I remember waving at the neighbor, Beth Tanner. The kids, Lara and Hudson, were in the backseat singing along to a song on the radio. As I came down the driveway, I noticed Craig's GMC parked in the driveway." A sharp pain sliced through her skull. She squeezed her eyes shut until the ache disappeared, then opened her eyes. "The lawn hadn't been mowed. We were planning to celebrate my son's birthday the next day, and I had yet to tell Craig that fifty people had RSVP'd." A crackle and a hiss, and an image appeared in her mind's eye. The GMC parked on the grass. Tire tracks. Craig didn't like anyone driving on his lawn. He always went out of his way to mark the sprinklers with little red flags. "His car was parked at an angle," Faith blurted as the image came to her. "The tires were on the lawn," she said. "Did you check the driveway for evidence?"

Yuhasz frowned.

Mom leaned forward and said, "Her doctor warned that she may or may not recall everything at once."

He nodded. "Please continue."

Faith proceeded to relay in excruciating detail exactly what happened after she arrived home—step by step, every bloody detail that she remembered. How she sat in the car talking to her sister while her family was being bound and gagged, her shock at seeing strange men in her house, and her attempt to run away. By the time she finished, Mom was sniffling.

Detective Yuhasz handed Mom a tissue, but he kept his attention focused on Faith. "You had never seen those men before?"

"No. Never."

"Do you have any reason to believe your husband might have known them?"

"No."

"Were you and your husband having problems—marital, financial, or otherwise?"

"We were happy." She swallowed. "I was pregnant, but I hadn't told him."

"Why not?"

"Because I wanted to surprise him." She didn't feel the need to tell the detective the entire reason she'd waited . . . because money was tight and she was waiting for the right time. "You've been working on the case for over a week now," Faith said before he could ask another question. "You must have some idea of who might have taken my children."

"Patrol officers were assigned door-to-door searches asking people in your area if they had seen anything or anyone who didn't belong.

They talked to teachers and parents at the school where you work. Polygraphs of all family members and close friends of the family have been obtained."

Faith felt the blood drain from her face. She had no idea. She looked at her mom. "Jana never mentioned taking a polygraph."

"It's standard procedure," Detective Yuhasz told her. "It's best if we positively eliminate the possibility that anyone close to Lara and Hudson had anything to do with their abduction."

"Can I ask you a few questions?" Faith asked.

He nodded.

She turned toward Agent Burnett. "You must have some idea of who might possibly be involved in the murder of my husband and the abduction of my two children. Would it be possible for me to see a list of suspects?"

"No," she said without pause. "Such information is protected from public disclosure, in accordance with current law and Department of Justice and FBI policy. It also serves to protect the rights of people not yet charged with a crime."

"So you do have a suspect?"

"I'm not at liberty to say one way or another."

Faith turned back to Detective Yuhasz. "Have you located my husband's SUV?"

"Not at this time."

"How about fingerprints or DNA?" She rubbed her temple. "Have you found anything at all?"

"No matches so far."

"So you did find fingerprints?"

"Footprints."

"What about motive?" Agent Burnett cut in.

"It's not clear. Home invasion gone bad or something more . . ." Yuhasz stated rather than questioned, peering at Faith as if he thought she might know more than she was letting on. "Was Craig McMann hijacked and forced to drive home for a reason, or was this a random act of violence?"

"I was hoping you would tell me," Faith said. "Am I a suspect?"

"No, of course not. We just need to ask the hard questions, see if anything jogs your memory."

"Have there been other break-ins in the area?" Faith asked.

Yuhasz shook his head. "Bikes, jewelry . . . nothing like this."

There was a knock on the door. A police officer entered the room, handed Detective Yuhasz a note, and left. Yuhasz read it over and then looked at Faith. "It says here that you invited the media into your house this morning."

"That's true. I did."

"Apparently whatever you said on camera has inspired a frenzy of activity. Our phones are ringing off the hook."

She grabbed hold of her mom's arm. "Maybe someone recognized one of the men from my painting."

"Detective O'Sullivan and I have been meeting with the media at regular intervals, keeping the public updated. In the future I would appreciate it if you could go through me or Detective O'Sullivan before you decide to do any impromptu interviews."

Faith stiffened. "My kids have been missing for eleven days now. Every second that passes is one second too many. If we're on the same side, there's no reason whatsoever that I can think of that you should object to my getting the word out." She leaned forward and tapped a finger on his desk. "You must have something by now . . . a suspect or two . . . some idea of what happened that day and why those men took my children."

The detective looked at O'Sullivan. Their expressions were unreadable, which merely added to her frustrations. "If we're going to find my children," Faith added, "we need to keep their faces in the forefront of people's minds."

Detective Yuhasz rubbed a hand over his prickly head.

"Faith," Detective O'Sullivan cut in, "we know you've been through a lot, but you can't simply jump into these things."

Faith looked over her shoulder at O'Sullivan. "I talked to the media and I asked for help. I didn't jump into anything."

"Faith," Detective Yuhasz said, speaking to her as if she were a child. "We're merely asking you for your cooperation so we can utilize all resources and do our job to the best of our ability."

She felt as if she were in the twilight zone. As far as she could see, they had all been picking their noses while she was fighting for her life. "Clearly, your staff is stressed and overworked," she said, ignoring the hand her mother placed on her forearm. "You've got officers at the front desk using both feet and hands and still unable to answer incoming calls, and I refuse to sit home and twiddle my thumbs while I wait for you and your men to find my children." She tapped a finger on his desk again. "I'm not going away until someone gives me a name of a possible suspect."

Yuhasz opened his desk drawer, reached inside, and handed her a brochure. "You might want to talk to someone at NCMEC, the National Center for Missing and Exploited Children. I believe they offer counseling."

The door opened, and Detective Yuhasz was called away before she could give him a piece of her mind and tell him exactly what she thought about that.

FIVE

Miranda held a damp cloth to Jean's arm. At ten years old, Jean was five years younger than she was. The girl had just been branded, and it was the first time Miranda had seen her cry.

The tattoo man, whom they called Fin, had done a number on Jean. He said it took longer than usual and he'd had to go deeper because she was so young. That way he wouldn't have to do it all over again in a few years. All the girls got a swirly letter *H* tattooed on their upper arms at some point after being brought to the house. With all the fancy twirls it was hard to tell if it was a letter at all. Miranda didn't believe Fin's story about having to be so rough on Jean. Neither had she liked the way he'd looked at the girl while he was working. If she hadn't been hovering over him the entire time he worked, he would have made a move; she was sure of it.

Being the oldest in the house and having been there the longest now that some of the girls had been moved to another house or onto the streets, Miranda knew a few things about this place—things that made it difficult to sleep at night. Things she refused to talk about.

The younger girls were to be minded 24-7. Miranda was in charge of watching over Jean. Girls under twelve years of age who had never been touched were treated like gold. Sure, they got slapped around and had their hair pulled like everyone else, but they got to eat first, were allowed to sleep in while everyone else did chores, and they didn't have to go upstairs for training sessions on the weekends. They were innocent. And there were plenty of filthy johns out there who were willing to pay a lot of money for innocence.

Miranda had been a virgin when she was brought to the house, but she'd hated Mother and told her she'd been fucked by every man her real mom ever brought home. Only Jasper knew the truth, since he had ended up being the one to take her virginity. He'd been scared to death when he saw the blood, slapped her when she smiled with the knowledge of what she'd done. "If Mother found out," he'd said, "we'd both be beat . . . or killed."

At night when Miranda closed her eyes, it was becoming more and more difficult to remember what her mom looked like. If she focused really hard, she could see the dimple in her mom's cheek and smell the sweet perfume she used to wear when Miranda was small. She worried that if too much time went by she might not recognize her if they passed each other on the street.

The sound of tires rolling over gravel caught her attention, making her forget all about her other life. Handing off the damp rag to Jean, she let her take care of the red welt on her arm for a minute so she could stand on the chair and peer through the window. The white filmy glaze on the glass made it difficult to see clearly. But she could make out the silhouette of a car and the shadow of a man as he climbed out. She wondered who it was. Most of the time the girls were taken to the johns, driven to some seedy hotel room or an apartment like the one she and her mom used to live in before they were kicked out onto the streets. Every once in a while, though, a wealthy man or woman came to the farmhouse to pick out a girl for themselves.

She thought back to her first "client," as Mother liked to call them. She'd never been so afraid in her life. The hotel room wasn't so bad. No horrible smells. Even the carpet was nice. He appeared to be a regular guy, a businessman you might see working at his desk in a bank. He seemed so normal and friendly she asked him if he would help her escape. Told him she was being held against her will. He said that if she did everything he asked of her, he would help her. But in the end, he didn't help her at all. She overheard him tell Mother everything she'd said. He was concerned she might be trouble. He was a respectable, hardworking man, and trouble was the last thing he needed. And so Miranda was taken to the barn where Phoenix used a sock full of rocks to teach her to keep her mouth shut.

"Is someone here?" Jean asked, her voice shaky and small.

"Yes," Miranda said. She looked away from the window and back at Jean, glad that the girl had yet to be touched. Jean was younger than most, and apparently Mother's boss man was holding out for big money. If she ever got the chance to escape, Miranda decided, she would take Jean with her.

The bells at the front entry rang.

Miranda jumped from the chair, wiped away more tears from Jean's eyes, and then grabbed hold of her small hand. "Come on," she said, tugging. "Mother wants us."

Jean was a good girl. She always obeyed and did whatever anyone asked of her. She hardly said a word. But a lot of girls were quiet when they first arrived. Sooner or later, Jean would start talking about her other life. And if and when she did, she'd pay for it. Mother had all sorts of rules and different forms of mistreatment for every blunder. Every punishment she thought of was designed to be painful and invoke fear.

"Come on, girls," Mother said, clapping her hands. "Everyone gather around. Hurry, hurry. Take a seat."

There were fifteen girls, everyone seated close together. Three of the walls in the main living area were lined with mismatched couches that were used only for this sort of occasion. Mother insisted that her girls, as she liked to call them, sit together, side by side, backs ramrod straight, knees together, whenever she held a meeting. Adele was nowhere to be seen, and that worried Miranda.

No sooner had they taken a seat than a heavyset man walked into the room. The tips of his shiny dress shoes stuck out beneath the hem of his pants. He had a large nose and rosy-red cheeks. He took a good long look at the younger girls, asked a few of them to stand up and turn around, but in the end he chose Trudi. She was fourteen, pale-skinned, and blue-eyed. Mother often referred to her as a cash cow. Trudi didn't care. She liked it when the rich men chose her. She would always return to the house days later with stories of how she'd dined on fat, juicy steak, sipped sparkly champagne, and slept beneath silk sheets. Miranda knew it was ridiculous, but more than anything she wanted to be picked. Just once. Not because she wanted to eat steak or sleep under silk sheets, but because she knew that being the chosen one might be her only chance to escape.

Six

Faith picked up the phone on the second ring. "Hello?"

"Is this Faith McMann?"

"This is she."

"My name is Corrie Perelman."

The name sounded vaguely familiar, but Faith couldn't place it. She said nothing, merely waited for the woman to continue.

"My daughter, Samantha Perelman, went missing one year ago today."

Faith remembered the news story. Samantha Perelman—taken when her mother asked her to run to the dairy section and grab some milk. Surveillance tapes from the grocery store had shown a man whose face was mostly covered by a baseball cap as he led the teenager right out the front entrance of the store. The outside camera had been smashed, leaving the authorities without further leads. Despite the video footage, the abductor had yet to be identified. For months, it seemed, the entire state had been on high alert, everyone keeping one eye on their kids and the other on neighbors and friends, paranoid and afraid. But like most life events, the passing of time had a way of making even the most newsworthy of stories slip away like a forgotten dream upon waking.

"Are you still there?" Corrie asked.

"Yes," Faith said as a wave of hope washed over her, wondering if the woman had news about her kids or information that might lead to finding them. "I'm here."

"I don't mean to intrude. I've left a message with Detective Yuhasz, letting him know I want to help in any way I can and offer you my full support."

Deflated, Faith managed a weak, "Thank you."

"If there's anything I can do, anything at all, please let me know."

Her muscles constricted. If anyone should know how she felt, it was this woman. And to get one more call that would lead nowhere was almost too much to bear. "That's very kind of you," Faith said, "but unless you have information that could possibly lead to the whereabouts of my children, I don't know what you could possibly do for me."

Faith instantly regretted the hostility in her tone, but the woman either didn't notice or didn't care.

"If you have time," Corrie Perelman said, "I was hoping you wouldn't mind if I stopped by."

So they could share their stories and grieve together? Faith wondered. "As you can imagine," Faith said, working hard to keep her voice steady, "I'm incredibly busy at this time, Mrs. Perelman. I'm sorry. Again, unless you have any idea of where I might find my children, I can't meet with you."

"I understand. If you change your mind and you want someone to talk with or perhaps attend a support group meeting with me, please know that you can call me at any time." She gave Faith her number.

Awkward silence ensued.

"My husband and I will be thinking of you, praying for your children's swift return."

The call ended, leaving Faith in a panic at the thought of some-day being that person in charge of a support group, spending her days calling the grieving parents of missing children to offer support.

———

Determined to keep Lara and Hudson at the forefront of the detective's mind, Faith made the daily trek to the police station. Once again she followed her mom through the double doors and up the short flight of stairs. The officers at the front desk waved them both in without bothering to make them sign in.

The pinpricks of light inside Faith's head had grown brighter, sharper. At times she wondered if she might be losing her mind. She hardly slept. Instead her nights were filled with memories of time spent with Craig and the children. Last night she hadn't been able to stop thinking about the time they'd gone to the water park.

The sun warmed her back as she watched Craig and Hudson return from a trip down the biggest water slide. Hudson's smile was a mile wide, but then he frowned and asked, "Where's Lara?"

Faith spun around.

Lara was gone—disappeared in the time it takes to snap your fingers.

Without a word, Craig set off in search of their daughter while Faith stayed with Hudson. Time held still, and Faith forgot how to breathe. Minutes felt like hours until she saw Craig in the distance holding Lara in his arms.

"Look who I found?" Craig blew air bubbles into the soft flesh of her neck.

Lara giggled.

They never talked about the incident again, but Faith remem-bered the emotions as if it had happened yesterday. Mostly because every second of every day since her kids had been taken felt exactly as if she were replaying those few terrifying seconds over and over again.

Faith and her mom passed by O'Sullivan's empty desk. A few days ago, Yuhasz had been out, so she'd talked with O'Sullivan instead. She'd left him photocopies of the pictures she'd painted on her living room wall, hoping they might be able to find a match within one of their criminal databases.

Yuhasz signaled for them to come inside.

Faith had barely sat down before she bombarded him with questions. "What did you think of the pictures I left with Detective O'Sullivan? And that tattoo . . . any ideas about what it could mean?"

He pursed his lips as if he were about to whistle but instead blew out a stream of air. "What pictures are you talking about?"

"The pictures I painted of the men I had seen. The pictures I left with O'Sullivan. The same images that have been all over the news."

"I've been out. Let me get the file."

"Have you been working my case or not?"

"I'm working several cases. Yours is certainly one of the priorities around here."

He left and returned with the file.

"You haven't talked with O'Sullivan?"

"We're scheduled to meet this afternoon." He opened the file and looked through the pictures and notes she'd made, but she sensed he was merely placating her. "I'll make sure this all gets scanned and logged in."

She could hardly believe how lackadaisical they all seemed when it came to her case. She tried to rein in her frustration. "Have you learned anything new about the three men who attacked my family?"

"According to your neighbor, there were two men."

Every muscle in her body tensed. "Are you fucking kidding me?"

Her mom stiffened beside her.

"I just told you there were three men," Faith went on. "I saw them with my own eyes when they were slitting my husband's throat."

"Watch your language, ma'am."

"Ma'am?"

"Faith," Mom said, but Faith ignored her.

Somebody called Yuhasz away from his desk. He looked at Mom with apologetic eyes before he stepped away. The detective liked Mom. No wonder he'd gone out of his way to give her regular updates while Faith was in the hospital.

"I don't like him," Faith said.

"He's a good man. He's doing everything he can to find Lara and Hudson."

"Like what? Tell me one thing he's done that has produced results. Just one damn thing."

"They're working with the FBI and the National Crime Information Center," Mom said. "Routine patrols have been set up throughout the county with no plans to stop."

She sounded like the rest of them, robotic and brainwashed. "They didn't talk to Craig's coworkers at his office," Faith said. "I called Joe yesterday, and he said he never got a call from the police. Don't you think that's odd?"

"If that's true," Mom said, "I'm sure it's some sort of crazy oversight. Detective Yuhasz has been on the force for thirty years. He knows what he's doing."

Frustration consumed her. "You like the man, don't you? That's why you keep coming here with me, isn't it?"

Mom pushed herself out of her chair so fast it wobbled. She pointed a shaky finger at Faith. "Listen here. I don't like what you're insinuating. Your family has been putting up with your mood swings because we can't begin to imagine what you're going through, but you've gone too far."

"My husband was murdered and my kids are gone!"

"You don't think I know that?" Mom grabbed her purse. "Don't let them win, Faith."

"Who?"

"The men you painted on your living room wall for God's sake!"

"If you think I'm going to sit at home and do nothing while these jokesters look for my kids, you're crazy."

"Nobody is telling you not to do everything possible to find your kids." Her voice quavered. "Those are my grandkids. You don't think I care about what happens to them? My God, Faith. Look at yourself. When was the last time you slept? You're not well. You need help."

Seven

Tears, blood, and snot ran down the side of Hudson's face.

It was hot and stuffy. He could hardly breathe. He and ten other boys were stuck at the bottom of a metal shipping container. No doors. No window. No fresh air.

Hudson had never been so scared in his life. He kept hoping Mom and Dad would show up and take him home, but he didn't think that would happen since he'd seen them tied up on the floor when the men took him and his sister. He couldn't think about his parents without crying.

In the beginning he'd tried to keep count of how many days had passed since he'd been taken, but he'd quickly lost track.

A stream of light sliced through the top of the container. That's how he knew it was daytime.

Memories of that awful day kept coming back to him, and when they did, he squeezed his eyes shut and tried to make them go away. He and Lara had been stuck in the back of Dad's car for a long time before they were moved to another car. His dad's car was then pushed over a hill into a lake. It had been dark when they took Lara away.

She'd screamed and kicked, but she was small and they were big. When Hudson tried to help her, one of the men smacked him and made his nose bleed.

After that, they drove forever before Hudson was finally let out of the car, handed a small paper bag, and thrown into the metal box. He landed hard and the kids inside rushed him and grabbed his food and water. It didn't take long to realize he needed to fight back if he wanted to survive.

Every kid in the container had been beaten pretty badly. One of the boys had become so sick, Hudson still didn't know whether or not he'd survived after a group of men came and took him away.

Some of the boys talked about how they had escaped before, only to be caught again. The containers, they said, were merely holding bins used to keep the boys out of sight until they decided what to do with them. One kid had been beaten so badly, his arm didn't look right—sort of twisted the wrong way. When one of the younger boys cried, the older boys were easily annoyed and they would kick the kid or threaten to shut him up for good. Sometimes the older kids seemed to be as bad as the men who had taken them to begin with.

When the night came and the little sliver of light disappeared, he'd shut his eyes and dream about the times he'd gone camping with Dad, Uncle Colton, and Grandpa. Those were some of the best times ever. They would sit around a fire while Grandpa told them war stories. Hudson's favorite story was the one about the time Grandpa and seven of his men fled enemy camp after being captured. While the guards were eating, he'd grabbed their rifles and escaped. With only the clothes they were wearing, Grandpa led the men through dangerous terrain—up steep cliffs and down a treacherous gorge. One of the men in his unit had a busted leg, and they took turns carrying him over streams and through the woods. It was hot, and they covered their bodies and faces in mud to keep from getting burned.

For weeks they ate bugs, pink berries, snakes, lizards, and squirrel. Grandpa liked to talk about how they used the palms of their hands to scoop water from the river and how good it had tasted.

Stuck in that metal bin for too long, Hudson fantasized about drinking cold water from a river. He could almost taste the water trickling down his dry throat.

"They're here!" someone cried.

The boys all jumped to their feet.

The top of the bin opened, and when Hudson looked up, he squinted into the daylight.

One by one they were pulled out, then blindfolded and separated into groups. Their hands were duct-taped behind their backs before they were shoved inside a bus or a van; he wasn't sure. The engine rumbled and the vehicle sped off, bouncing over uneven ground and making them bang against one another every time the driver turned a corner.

His mom used to tell him that if anyone ever tried to pull him into a car, he was supposed to run. Run as fast as you can, she would say.

The next time they opened the door, that's exactly what he planned to do.

EIGHT

Faith finished placing the cloth napkins and silverware just so, then stepped back to examine the dining room table. Usually they spent Thanksgiving with Faith's family at her parents' house, but this year Craig's parents had decided to fly all the way from New Jersey to visit during the holidays.

Not being the best cook, Faith had awoken at four o'clock in the morning to get the stuffing made and the turkey in the oven. The homemade biscuits weren't nearly as fluffy as the ones her sister made, but they would have to do. Looking fabulous in slacks and a nice sweater, Craig walked down the hall toward her and kissed her on the cheek. "The table looks great, honey."

Faith leaned into him. "I put too much salt in the stuffing, and the biscuits are hard."

"You're worrying too much. It'll be great. Once Mom and Dad taste your mashed potatoes and gravy, they'll want to visit every Thanksgiving and we'll—" He took a sniff. "What's that smell?"

Faith smelled it, too. She headed quickly for the kitchen, where she saw black plumes of smoke pouring from the oven.

Craig ran to the kitchen, slipped on a pair of oven mitts, and tried to save the turkey while Faith ran to open the sliding door to let the smoke out.

The doorbell rang at the same time the fire alarm went off, filling the house with a deafening screech. Faith's shoulders sagged when she saw that her in-laws had arrived early.

Hudson ran to open the door and let them in. When he saw Grandma standing there holding two pies, his eyes lit up. "It's OK, Mom. We can all be thankful again because Grandma brought pie for dinner!"

There was a knock on the front door. Sighing, Faith pushed herself to her feet. Jana and her husband, Steve, had insisted on picking her up on the way to Mom and Dad's for Thanksgiving dinner. Steve was at the door. Before she knew what he was up to, he stepped inside, wrapped his arms around her, and held her close. She could feel the beat of his heart against the side of her face. He'd been her best friend throughout college and like a brother to Craig. The thought of never being held in Craig's arms again caused her to swallow and pull away.

He stepped back. "It's so good to see you up and about."

"Thanks," she said. They stepped outside. She locked the door and followed him to the car, where Jana was waiting. Faith climbed into the back of their Ford Escape. Steve drove. Before he made a left onto Auburn-Folsom Road, heading toward Loomis, Faith said, "You guys didn't have to pick me up."

Jana snorted. "You never would have come if we hadn't."

She couldn't argue with that, so she didn't. "How's Dad?"

"The doctors are saying he suffered a ministroke due to high blood pressure. Dad doesn't like anyone making a big deal about it. He's having a bit of trouble with dizziness, but he refuses to use a walker."

The thought of losing her dad was too much. A few days after she was brought home from the hospital, Dad had begun having leg pain and difficulty speaking. For the next few hours, he'd lost the ability to move his arms. Mom had rushed him to the emergency room. They'd kept him overnight, but he was allowed to return home the very next day.

"Tears in Heaven" by Eric Clapton played in the background on the radio. Jana quickly reached for the knob and turned it off. "Have the police made any progress?"

"None so far . . . at least that I know of."

"I'm sorry," Jana offered.

"Agent Burnett with the FBI was at our meeting. She asked about motive, and it got me thinking . . . wondering . . . if Craig knew those men. Were they there because of a deal gone sour?"

"And?" Jana asked.

"And . . . I just don't know. I've spent hours looking through Craig's things, reading e-mails and phone messages, searching through records and files. It's a never-ending task." Faith sighed. "I also talked to someone at the missing children's organization. They said Lara and Hudson fall under the critically missing due to the circumstances surrounding their abduction. They assured me they're working closely with law enforcement."

"Yes," Jana said. "They were part of the search and rescue that set out to scour the area while you were in recovery."

"They offer group support, too," Faith said, "but I'm not ready for that." There was a pause before she added, "They'll contact me if they receive any tips about my case."

"What about tips coming into the police department after you were on the local news? Have you heard anything?"

Faith shook her head. "Detective Yuhasz said the phones were ringing like crazy after that, but if they have anything substantial, they're not letting on. Agent Burnett mentioned policy and protecting the rights of people not yet charged."

It wasn't long before they pulled up the long, S-shaped driveway, past the weeping willows and mossy rocks. They drove around the pond half-lined with dense foliage and cattails before coming to a stop behind three other cars.

"Looks like everyone else is here."

Faith nodded. Her heart raced. She never should have come. She wasn't ready to deal with the entire family in one house. *Breathe,* Faith reminded herself. *Just breathe.* She hadn't been with the family all at once since the incident.

After collecting a covered dish from the trunk, Jana told Steve to go on ahead, then stopped at the half-open window and said, "Come in when you're ready. No hurry."

"Thanks."

After her sister disappeared inside the old house with its gabled windows and wraparound porch, Faith climbed out of the car and made her way to the pond. She took a seat at the severely scarred picnic table that had been there for as long as she could remember.

A bullfrog croaked from behind a batch of tulles. On the other side of the pond, two ducks waddled out of the water and onto the grassy slope. A light drizzle began at the same time a noise prompted her to look over her shoulder toward the house.

It was Dad.

Using a cane for support, he made his way across the driveway that separated the pond from the house. Seeing him with a cane didn't change a thing. He was bigger than life. Always had been. His eyes were a turquoise blue, his hair thick and silver. He was six foot three, and she used to tease him about what it must be like to have his feet on the ground and his head in the sky with the birds and the planes.

She got to her feet, met him halfway, and then walked with him back to the bench, where they both took a seat.

"You're a sight for this old man's sore eyes."

"How are you feeling, Dad?"

"Like a twenty-year-old man trapped inside a seventy-year-old body."

Smiling no longer came easily, but she managed. "I'm sorry I couldn't be there for you when you were in the hospital."

He patted her hand. "You were in no shape to worry about me. Besides, you know how they all like to make a big stink about everything around here."

She knew he was downplaying his stroke, but she admired his stubborn pride.

"The worst of it is having to avoid salty foods and alcohol."

"You never liked drinking much anyhow."

"You always want what you can't have," he said with a twinkle in his voice.

Dad always had a way of cheering her up. Although he was the strong, silent type, he was also the jokester and the wise man all rolled into one. After thirty years as a sergeant in the army, Russell Gray was also the definition of calm under fire. Despite his keen ability to lead men into war, it was Mom who had been left to dish out the discipline when it came to Faith, Jana, and Colton. Never Dad.

"I've heard through the grapevine that you're a lot like your old man," Dad said, cutting into the silence, "and you're losing patience." He waited until the bullfrog finished croaking before he added, "We can all sympathize with what you're going through, Faith, but not one of us can put ourselves in your shoes. God knows it can't be easy. Craig was an amazing man. Losing him was like losing a son."

Dad's eyes welled with tears.

She leaned close and rested her head against his shoulder. He wrapped his arm around her, and for a few quiet moments they just stared out at the water.

Faith swallowed the lump clogging her throat. "Dad," she choked out. "I don't know what to do. I've given the authorities time. I am well aware of the fact that I'm not the only one with a case to solve. But you know as well as I do that every day that passes is one day too many."

"Well, you know what George S. Patton Jr. once said."

She shook her head.

"Lead me, follow me, or get the hell out of my way."

"What are you saying, Dad? That I should do my own investigation?" She exhaled. That was it exactly. She needed to stop relying on the police and find the kids herself. "I think you're right. I've been looking through Craig's things, hoping to find a clue, anything that might tell me why those men were there, but mostly I've been depending on the police."

He used his cane to push himself to his feet. "Don't be too hard on yourself, Faith. You were in intensive care hanging on by a very thin rope. Now that you're getting better and your memories of that day are coming back, I'm just saying that I think it might be time to let the police do their thing while you do yours."

Faith inhaled.

"If you're going to go around asking questions," Dad said, "you need to be able to protect yourself. Tomorrow morning I'm taking you to the range." He angled his head toward the house. "First things first, though. Let's go inside and get some meat on your bones."

Walking side by side, they made their way to the house, where close to a dozen family members were waiting for them inside. The moment Faith and Dad walked through the door, voices hushed.

"Aunt Faith?"

She looked down at her brother's oldest daughter, Kimberly. She and Lara were only a few months apart in age. "Hi, Kimberly."

Kimberly wrapped her arms around her waist and squeezed. "All my friends are wondering when you're coming back to school?"

The question caught her off guard. For the past ten years she'd worked at Ridgeview Elementary as a fourth grade teacher. The school and her students had been such a big part of her life. She and Craig used to joke that she had more than two kids to take care of. And yet, in that moment, she couldn't remember the last time she'd spared one thought to the school or her students. She knelt down, wrapped her arms around her niece, and held her close. She was so small, so fragile, so young.

Faith felt a hand on her shoulder. It was her brother, Colton. He headed off to the dining room table, where family was now gathering. Faith looked at Kimberly and said, "Tell your friends I miss them, but that I don't know when I'm coming back." She straightened, patted Kimberly on the head, and made her way to the dinner table.

Her sister-in-law, Bri, followed close behind. "I think Kimberly asked a valid question. Have you thought about returning to class? I think it might do you a world of good."

"Thanks. I'll think about it." Everyone was well meaning, but she'd never felt so alone. She went to the kitchen. Mom stirred gravy over the stove. "I'm sorry about the other day. I didn't mean—" Mom stopped her from going on and gave her a knowing hug before handing her a bowl of stuffing. Faith carried the dish to the dining room and set it on the table, then took a seat between Dad and Colton. It was too soon to think about returning to school. In fact, it was too soon for her to be sitting at the table without Craig and the kids. She thought about asking Dad if she could borrow his truck so she could head home, but instead she sat quietly and tried to hold herself together.

Sitting across from her were Bri, Bri's daughters, and Jana and Steve. The pitiful looks being sent her way were almost too much to bear.

Once everyone was seated, Dad looked around the table at each of them. "Faith has decided not to have a memorial service for Craig until Lara and Hudson are back home where they belong. I agree, but I want to say how thankful I am that he was a part of our lives. The first time I met Craig was at Thanksgiving dinner. He loved dark meat, and he would playfully fight some of you for the best pieces. He was a clever man, too. Always rushing to play with the kids while the rest of us put away the dishes. Craig McMann was a good husband and a loving father. There will always be an undertone of sadness now that he's gone, but to honor his memory we must find a way to transform the grief and instead use it to strengthen our family unity and stand by Faith while she finds the strength needed to do everything in her power to find her kids, my grandchildren, your niece and nephew and cousins."

They all said amen. Jana stepped away from the table to blow her nose. Mom disappeared inside the kitchen for a moment. Dad cut the turkey while everyone else passed the rolls and butter, the stuffing, green beans, and cranberry sauce. Wine and sparkling cider was poured while quiet unease hovered over them like a dark cloud.

Last Thanksgiving the kids—Colton's two girls and Lara and Hudson—had all sat together at their own little table in the living room. Faith looked over her shoulder. Crayons and coloring books were scattered across the coffee table and living room floor. A doll hung upside down, its leg stuck between the cushions of a chair. Images of that horrible day came back to her in a flash. The first thing she'd seen when she entered the kitchen was disarray. For the past week she'd seen the killer's face in living color and yet she'd forgotten about the mess—the upturned furniture, opened kitchen drawers, and scattered papers. Those men had been looking for something—but what? Her heart slammed against her ribs. She took a breath, looked down at her plate, and closed her eyes.

"Faith," Jana said as she returned to her seat across from her, concern in her voice. "What's wrong?"

There it was—a bloodcurdling sneer. "Where is it?" he'd asked.

When she opened her eyes and looked up, Colton was staring at her. They all were.

"They were looking for something," she said. "They tore the house apart." She looked at Mom and then Jana. "Did you see the mess they made? There were papers and kitchen utensils scattered about, splinters of wood, broken objects. How could I have forgotten that?"

"Faith," her brother said, his voice firm. "It's OK. Take a breath."

"The house was trashed, Colton. The man who grabbed me in the garage as I tried to get away asked me where it was."

Bri's mouth tightened into a grim line as she gestured toward her daughters. "Maybe we shouldn't be talking about this at the table."

Kimberly's eyes widened. "Did bad men take Lara and Hudson?"

Faith nodded. As she looked at Kimberly she felt a change within, a shift in her way of thinking, almost as if Craig was right there beside her, whispering into her ear, telling her to do whatever she must to bring their kids safely home. "Don't you worry, sweetheart," she said to Kimberly, "Aunt Faith is going to find your cousins and bring them home."

Kimberly wiped her eyes. "Can we go find them right now?"

Her small, heart-shaped face and the way she angled her head reminded Faith so much of Lara. Seeing the hopeful look in her niece's eyes caused her heart to swell. "I think that's a very good idea."

Kimberly's little sister, Dacotah, whimpered.

"Faith. Please. Not in front of the children." Bri stood and ushered her daughters away from the table and out of the room, but not before shooting her husband a glare.

"What were the men looking for?" Jana asked.

"I don't know," Faith said, her body trembling as that moment in the garage came back to her in a rush. "I begged him to let the kids go, let us all go, but as soon as I saw the expression on his face, the cold ruthlessness in his eyes, I knew there was a good chance we might die whether he found what he was looking for or not. I tried to get free, but he slammed me to the ground and everything went black."

"This is all so crazy," Jana said. "I feel as if we're talking about a movie where the bad guys are looking for a tiny capsule filled with important information. What could they possibly have been looking for? It makes no sense. Had Craig been acting strange or different in the days before?"

Faith shook her head. "Whatever it was they were looking for, they didn't find it. So why did they take my kids?"

Colton looked over his shoulder toward the living room to make sure his wife and kids were out of earshot. "Mom's been keeping me updated, and I've also been doing some research of my own. My first thought was that these guys must have come to your house because they wanted something. And now you're telling me that's exactly right." He sighed. "If they came to your house looking for something of value and then didn't find whatever it was . . . then it's possible they took the kids because they were worth something to them. I've been reading up on trafficking, and it appears that younger children bring in ridiculous amounts of money."

Everyone at the table fell silent.

"Trafficking?" Faith asked, unable, perhaps even unwilling, to make sense of what that could mean for her children.

"Human trafficking," Colton said. "It's a billion-dollar business."

Dad set his fork down. "Faith," he said, his tone grim, "nobody's asked for ransom. If they were going to kill them, they would have done it right there at the house. Maybe you should give some thought to what Colton is saying."

Mom placed her napkin on the table, pushed her chair back, and left the room. She didn't appear to be angry, merely disturbed by it all.

"Please tell me what you know about trafficking," Faith told her brother. "If I'm going to find my kids, I need to know what I might be dealing with here."

"Colton could be on to something," Steve said. "I saw a documentary about this human trafficking business. They talked a lot about young children being a commodity. Traffickers are getting bolder these days, too. I read a story about two younger guys who met a girl in the mall, followed her home, and simply took her. These guys are fearless."

Colton nodded. "People think human trafficking is confined to places like Thailand and Malaysia, but Sacramento is ranked number two for sex trafficking in the United States. Being in the trucking business I see way too much of it." He used his fork to poke at the peas on his plate. "Most truckers think they're paying for sex, but they're paying for rape since pimps are the ones pocketing the money."

Jana paled. "I think I'm going to be sick."

Steve pushed his chair back and helped Jana to her feet.

Faith watched them leave the room. There was no possible way she could allow herself to imagine either one of her children being sold for sex. The notion of anything so horrible wouldn't compute. And yet she squeezed Colton's arm and said, "I need a place to start, someone I can talk to."

Colton rubbed the bridge of his nose. "No way. This isn't the sort of thing you should be poking your nose into. Talk to Detective Yuhasz about it and see what he has to say."

"Faith's done enough talking," Dad said. "It's time for her to take matters into her own hands."

Stunned, Colton looked from one to the other, shaking his head before he said, "I'll see what I can find out."

Dad, Colton, and Faith were the only people left at the table. Faith said, "Sorry about ruining Thanksgiving."

"You didn't ruin anything," Dad said. "We need to find Lara and Hudson. That's all that matters."

NINE

That same night, Faith stood outside her neighbor's door and rang the bell. The last time she'd stood at Beth Tanner's front door had been more than a year ago after Beth's Chihuahua had escaped through a broken slat of wood in the fence surrounding her backyard. Lara and Hudson had begged Faith to let them play with the dog before they returned the animal to its owner, but so much of parenting was saying no.

Beth opened the door a few inches. With her dark hair cropped below the ears, she looked the same. She wore a matching set of pink velour loungewear and gray slip-on shoes.

"It's me—your neighbor—Faith McMann. I was hoping we could talk."

"You do realize it's Thanksgiving?"

Although she hadn't seen any cars parked out front, Faith nodded. "I know. I'm sorry. If you're busy, I'll come back another time."

The expression on Beth's face was hard to read as she opened the door fully and allowed her inside. The house had a nice, homey feel to it. The smell of pumpkin pie drifted through the air. Shadowed lights from the television bounced off the mirrored wall in the family room. The dog was nowhere to be seen. "Where's Prince?"

"He passed away."

"I'm sorry."

"He was fifteen. He had a good life."

They stood there awkwardly.

"Can I get you some pie?"

"No, thanks."

Beth gestured toward Faith's throat. "It's healing nicely."

Faith brushed a fingertip over the scar and nodded, then followed Beth into the family room. Beth grabbed the remote and turned the television off before she took a seat and told Faith to do the same. "I was wondering when you would pay me a visit," Beth said. "I figured it was only a matter of time."

"You knew I would visit?"

"Besides coming to thank me for saving your life, yes. But I also figured you might have questions about what happened and what I saw that day."

"Thank you," Faith said, her voice quieter than she intended, "for saving my life."

"You're welcome."

"The doctors said you pinched an artery and that's what kept me alive."

Beth tipped her head in agreement. "Years ago, my only daughter was leaving a party when she was attacked. Multiple stab wounds. EMTs arrived in record time, but they were inexperienced and couldn't save her. It was all too much for my husband. We divorced. I went back to school. I've been an ER nurse ever since. All those grueling hours in the ER came in handy when I found you." She tapped her finger against the cushioned armchair. "I think that pie is calling my name." She stood. "Sure you don't want a piece?"

"No, thank you."

Faith thought about telling Beth how sorry she was about the loss of her daughter, but when Beth returned with pie in hand, something stopped her from saying anything at all. Words just didn't seem like enough. While Beth ate, Faith filled the silence by telling her neighbor everything she knew about the case thus far, which wasn't much.

After Faith stopped talking, Beth put her plate to the side. Once again she pushed herself from her chair and left the room. This time when she returned, she handed Faith a large envelope. Inside were images of men she'd cut out from various magazines. There were also two sheets of paper, each with glossy cutouts glued to the paper. One was labeled "Suspect #1" and the other was labeled "Suspect #2." The number one suspect was Caucasian. He had a square face framed by curly brown hair. Green eyes. Sharp nose. Thin lips. Number two suspect was olive-skinned. Dark hair cut close to his skull and even darker eyes set beneath thick bushy brows.

Images of the dark-eyed man came to her. *Kill them both. Make it quick.* Her fingers crumpled the edges of the envelope.

"Are you OK?"

She nodded.

Beth didn't look convinced, but she filled the silence with her story of what she'd seen that day. "I've been collecting pictures of males I thought resembled the men I saw driving your husband's car that day. I made the suspect sheets while it was all fresh in my mind, figuring you or the police might need more information."

Faith was impressed and thankful. "Did you see my husband return home from work that day?"

"No. I had only been home for five minutes before I saw you and the kids arrive home. I had let Prince out and I was watering the plants out front when you drove by."

"I remember."

"Minutes after I turned off the water I heard your screams for help. I put the dog back in the house and went to grab my cell phone, but it took some time. Before I made it to the road, I saw your husband's SUV speeding off. If they hadn't been forced to slow down to make the sharp turn out of your driveway, I wouldn't have seen their faces at all."

"Did you see—"

"No. I didn't see either of the kids. But the windows were tinted, and my eyesight isn't what it used to be. Since you're here, I'm assuming neither of them have been found."

"No. Not yet." Faith's fingers brushed over the scar on her neck once again. "There were three men."

"I only saw two," Beth said.

"Do you think they saw you when they were leaving?"

She shrugged. "If they did, I'm not worried. I have a fondness for guns, and I keep a loaded pistol close at hand."

The woman was full of surprises. Faith held up the envelope. "Mind if I keep this?"

"It's all yours."

They both stood. When they got to the door, Faith said, "There aren't too many people who would or could have done what you did that day. If there's ever anything I can do for you, please don't hesitate to ask."

"You've got plenty enough to worry about. Just take care of yourself."

"You, too," Faith said.

"For what it's worth," Beth added, "I'll be keeping a close eye on things around here."

Faith thanked her, then gave her a well-meaning but awkward hug before heading for home. The door clicked shut behind her. Up ahead, two beams of sunlight squeezed their way between bloated gray clouds. Faith crossed the road and walked slowly down her driveway toward her house. She went to the area where she'd seen Craig's GMC parked that day. She could still see exactly where the tires had broken a sprinkler head and destroyed the lawn. There was absolutely no way Craig would have driven onto the grass unless something had been wrong. Had he been trying to leave her a sign? Trying to let her know things were not right inside the McMann household?

A twinkle of metal caught her attention. The grass around the tire tracks had grown tall, but there was something there. She got down on her knees. Between blades of grass, half-buried in the soil, was a button. She picked it up, examined it. She couldn't make out the design. It was dirty and tarnished. As she came to her feet, a thought struck her. *Why us? Why Lara and Hudson?*

The question wasn't a pitiful cry to heaven above, but merely speculation of what might have happened that day. The thought repeated itself. *Why would they take the kids?* If human traffickers were involved, where would she start? Who could she talk to?

It was too soon to rule any one thing or person out of the equation. Was Jana on to something? Had Craig been acting strange in the days leading up to the attack? He and his partner had started their own investment company, H&M Investments, eight years ago. Craig was an investment adviser. If anything he'd always run on the prudish side of things. Nothing made sense.

She looked at the broken sprinkler. Nobody had seen another car in the area.

Could those men have been in the car with Craig from the beginning? If so—why? He never would have brought them to the house if he'd thought there was any chance they might hurt his family. But what if they held a gun to his head? What then?

No sooner had the thought struck her than she felt a chill creep slowly up the back of her neck.

Somebody was watching her.

She stood perfectly still. A light breeze caused the branches of a giant oak to sway. The only sounds were the wind and the squawk of a bird in the distance.

Mr. Hawkins, the baker, lived in the house to her right. She couldn't see anyone looking out the windows. The neighbors down the road were too far away to see her unless they stood at the edge of the road. Behind her house was an empty lot—twenty acres of dead grass and trees.

She slipped the button she'd found inside her pants pocket and turned slowly, looking out over the high weeds. She then climbed through the slats in the fence and made her way to Mr. Hawkins's house. What if traffickers hadn't taken the kids? What if Lara and Hudson were locked in a closet inside her neighbor's house?

After knocking on the door and ringing the doorbell, Faith made her way around the side of the house and peeked inside the garage window. Mr. Hawkins's car wasn't there. Back at the front door, she lifted potted plants and examined every rock and decorative item looking for a key. A sheen of sweat covered her brow. As an after-thought, she lifted the rubber mat. There it was—the key—shiny and new. She picked it up and slid it into the keyhole. The door creaked open. "Anyone home?"

Something sounded in the other room, a light thump.

"Lara! Hudson!" She hurried down the hallway and found herself in the master bedroom in time to see a cat scramble under the bed. She got down on her hands and knees and looked under the bed.

It was just a cat.

Her heart pounded as she walked into the bathroom next and searched through tall cupboards and removed dirty clothes from a hamper until she could see all the way to the bottom of the wicker basket. She called out her kids' names as she looked around.

She yanked open the shower curtain.

Empty.

Adrenaline soaring, she made her way through every room in the house. She opened cupboards and closet doors, even looked inside the washer and dryer. Standing in the center of the main living area, hands on hips, heart pumping fast, she looked around. And that's when it hit her. She'd broken into Mr. Hawkins's house. Was Mom right? Did she need help? Had she completely lost her mind?

The sound of a car door being shut got her moving again. She rushed to the sliding glass door leading to the backyard. Her fingers fumbled with the lock. It took her too long to realize a piece of wood had been used to prevent the door from opening.

Through the curtain over the front window, she saw Mr. Hawkins's silhouette as he approached the entrance to his house.

She removed the wood. The door slid open at the same moment a key rattled at the front of the house. She took off and sprinted through the backyard, weaving around decorative bushes and fruit trees. At the fence, she squeezed her way back through the wood slats, then dropped to her knees when she saw Mr. Hawkins walk through the open slider. Crawling on all fours, she made her way across the field to the fence bordering her own property. Covered in mud and out of the breath, she made it back home.

TEN

Miranda was almost done braiding Jean's long, blonde hair.

She stopped for a moment and listened to the pitter-patter of rain on the rooftop. She thought of her room back home, the only room she'd ever known before she and her mom had been kicked out of the apartment, and how the droplets used to sound like the tiny feet scurrying around inside the apartment walls. For the first time in a long while she saw a flash of her mom's face in her mind's eye. She squeezed her eyes shut and forced away the memories.

"What's wrong?" Jean asked.

"Nothing. I thought I heard something—that's all."

Cow bells sounded, and she hurriedly finished with Jean's braid. "Come on," Miranda said. "Time to go. Mother wants us."

"I hate her," Jean said, her voice eerily calm for a ten-year-old.

Miranda's eyes rounded and her arm jerked outward, ready to slap Jean across the face, knock some sense into the little girl, but she stopped midair. She refused to let these monsters turn her into one of them.

Jean flinched.

"I'm sorry." Miranda's heart lurched. "I'll never hit you—I promise."

"I want to go home," Jean said, tearful now. "I want to see my mom and dad."

"Don't ever say that." She grabbed hold of Jean's small shoulders and then dropped to one knee so they were eye to eye. "Listen to me, Jean, and listen closely. I'm going to find a way to get you out of here. Do you hear me?"

Jean's body shook. "When can we leave?"

"Soon. But we need to be smart. I know this isn't easy for you. It's not easy for any of us. But you need to keep quiet. Don't ever talk about going home again."

"I don't want to stay here anymore."

Miranda sighed. "If you tell Mother you want to go home, she will beat you, Jean. She won't just send you to your room. She'll drag you to the barn and make one of the boys use a whip or a belt to hit you until you stop talking about home. You have to do what she says until I can find a way out of here. Do you understand?"

Finally the girl nodded.

Thank God. Miranda wiped Jean's tears away. She wanted to tell Jean that if she was ever taken to a man's house and asked to do things she didn't want to do, to fight him with everything she had and then run as fast as she could, but instead she wrapped her arms around her and held her close. "I'm going to get you out of here," she whispered. "I promise."

Together they walked into the main room.

As instructed, Jean sat on the couch with the younger girls and Miranda took a seat next to Felicity. She saw Adele across the way, sitting quietly with her hands folded in her lap, her eyes downcast, her shoulders drawn inward. Goose bumps sprouted on Miranda's arms as she took it all in. Adele's eyes were shadowed in darkness, her arms covered with bruises. She looked as if she were on the brink of death, and it frightened her.

Miranda pulled her gaze from Adele and looked at Mother, who had taken some time to do her hair and makeup. Her faded brown strands had been swept to the back of her head, then rolled and pinned. Lots of stray flyaway hairs stuck out every which way, but no one dared point that out or look at her for too long. With her hair pulled back away from her face, it was plain to see that Mother might have been considered pretty in her younger days. Nobody knew how old she was. Jasper once guessed her age to be thirty-five, but there was no way—forty-five minimum, Miranda figured. She did have high cheekbones, and every once in a while, like now, there was a brightness to her light-colored eyes that made her look younger. She'd exchanged her tattered blue jeans and faded gray T-shirt for a flowery print dress and a blue sweater with sleeves that stopped just above her elbows. If she'd resisted applying the powder-blue eye shadow and false lashes, she might look less like the street hookers Miranda used to see hanging out on Watt Avenue and more like one of the school moms at the market.

"I've got a surprise," Mother said, her gaze sweeping over each and every one of them. "We have a very important guest today. He's driven a long way, so I need you all to be on your best behavior. Mr. Smith has only a few minutes to make a decision before he leaves for San Francisco. A week from now, the girl who is chosen will get to spend time with Mr. Smith at a luxury hotel in San Francisco. You will be treated like a princess. Pampered and served whatever your heart desires. But . . . if you misbehave, even so much as frown, there will be consequences. Severe consequences. Do you understand?"

Every girl nodded in unison.

Mother forced a grin as she pointed at both sides of her mouth. "See this smile on my face?"

Again they all nodded.

"I want you to smile exactly like this." She swept a hand toward the twelve and under girls. "You girls go to your room and be quiet until I call you for dinner."

They all did as she said. Except for Jean. Jean looked at Miranda and waited for her to tell her what to do. Miranda didn't want Mother to see Jean hesitate, so she flashed her eyes and gestured with her chin for the girl to move on, letting Jean know she needed to do what Mother told her and make it fast.

Jean must have understood because she turned and followed the other girls up the stairs.

Mother lectured those who remained for another five minutes before Mr. Smith was escorted into the room. He wore jeans and cowboy boots, the kinds with pointed spurs. The buckle on his belt was a shiny silver skull. He was tall and broad-shouldered with a slender waist. He looked nothing like the other men who came to visit. He was so much older and scarier-looking. He never blinked. Folds of skin hung beneath his eyes, brought down by gravity and depravity. When he took off his cowboy hat, his greasy thin hair stuck in clumps to one side of his head. His nostrils were permanently flared, and it took everything Miranda had to force herself to smile at him. *Pick me, pick me* ran through her mind when he finally looked at her. She kept the smile plastered on her face and gave a very subtle nod of her head in greeting. His eyes seemed to look right through her. The idea of actually being picked by the hideous man made her sick to her stomach, but she couldn't allow herself to forget that this monster might be her only chance of escape.

When he finished looking each of the girls over, he exited the room without the slightest glance back. It took all she had not to let her shoulders slump forward in disappointment. She'd wanted this chance to leave this place so badly. The idea of staying here for another minute was too much to bear. Mother followed him out and didn't return for a full ten minutes. The room remained quiet.

Nobody dared say one word while she was gone. They had been trained well—whipped, kicked, and threatened into submission.

When Mother returned she stood in the center of the room, her mouth grim as she rubbed her hands together, something she often did before she grabbed the whip. Miranda's heart sank. Nobody had been selected. It had happened before, and the punishment had been ongoing—days of starvation, sleep deprivation, threats, and endless beatings.

But then a smile came to Mother's lips, and she pointed a finger directly at Miranda. It took a full minute for her to realize what Mother was saying.

She was the chosen one.

The idea that she might soon be allowed to leave the house for more than a few hours was too much to comprehend. Excitement rolled up her spine. For the first time in months she was going to have another chance to get away. The saddest part about what she was feeling, the thing she couldn't deny, was knowing she'd been picked above all the rest, especially above perfect Trudi, and how it made her feel somehow special.

A painful cramp formed a knot in her gut as she remembered the last time she'd felt this way—special, worthy. It was when Caroline had approached her after school and told her how smart she was and that she was a shoo-in for the job, which was supposed to have been homeschooling young girls. If she wanted the job, Caroline said, there was no time to talk to her mother. Now or never. She should have picked never.

The week after Miranda was chosen passed quickly. Mother kept close by her side at all times, instructing her on how to sit, eat, walk, and what to say—a long list of instructions considering she was supposed to keep to herself during her stay. The best part of being selected so far was getting out of doing chores. And she certainly didn't mind the long hot soaks in the tub even if that meant listening to more lectures about what she could and could not do while she was away. No giggling. No laughing. No talking or looking any of Mr. Smith's staff in the eyes. She was to keep her head down. She could say *hello, sir, goodbye, sir, good morning, sir,* and *good night, sir.* More than once, Miranda had to stop herself from rolling her eyes at the ridiculous list of rules.

Late the night before she was to leave for San Francisco, as she lay in bed staring at the ceiling, Miranda overheard two of the girls talking in hushed voices, confirming what she'd already come to terms with.

"Trudi told me we should be glad we weren't chosen and that it's not a vacation at all."

"What is it then?" Felicity questioned.

"Miranda will be forced to do the same thing we all do week after week, but instead of cockroaches, bedbugs, and the smell of body odor, she might get a feel for silk sheets and a taste of champagne."

"Why does Trudi keep changing her story?" Felicity asked. "When she returned from Las Vegas she told us she got to sit by the pool and eat steak and rich chocolates, but now suddenly when Miranda gets chosen, it's all doom and gloom."

"We all know how she likes to exaggerate."

"Maybe Trudi is jealous because she wasn't picked by the ugly man."

"She probably had visions of that ogre proposing to her like in that movie *Pretty Woman.*"

They both giggled, and Miranda spent the rest of the night planning her escape.

ELEVEN

Across the pond near the rose garden, a bride and groom, surrounded by family, were saying their vows. Faith, Craig, Lara, and Hudson were sitting on a blanket and eating fruit and turkey sandwiches from a cooler.

"Will you marry me?" Hudson asked Faith out of the blue.

Craig jumped to his feet and said, "Who wants to play Frisbee?" He and Lara ran off, leaving Faith to answer Hudson's question.

The look in her three-year-old son's eyes was sincere and heartfelt just like his proposal.

"I met your daddy first," she began.

"Daddy won't mind."

"I'm much too old for you, Hudson. Someday you'll meet a beautiful girl who will be just the right age for you."

"But I want to marry you, Mommy."

"Mommies and sons cannot marry each other, Hudson, but I want you to know that my love for you is forever and ever and that will never end."

He pondered that for a moment before he said, "Will you push me on the swings?"

She hurried to pack the food away. "You betcha!"

The memories faded as Faith looked away from the park across the street, the old-school kind with animals on steel springs, tetherball, and monkey bars, and headed for the entrance to police headquarters. Hope and a touch of excitement ping-ponged against Faith's ribs. She held a manila file close to her chest. She had spent the rest of the holiday weekend looking through every nook and cranny in her house, searching for clues of what those men might have been looking for. She'd also started gathering information about some of the people Craig had done business with. She'd sifted through files and taken names from his Rolodex, listened to old recorded phone messages and examined texts, then made a list of possibilities.

She was eating better, too, and Dad had already gone over firearm basics with her, including terminology—the difference between a handgun and a pistol, assault rifle versus assault weapon, clip versus magazine.

Walking at a hurried pace, she made her way to Detective Yuhasz's office. The door was open. The expression on his face when he saw her didn't appear to be one of annoyance, more a look of subtle defeat that took some of the wind out of her. Despite his odd behavior, she set her file on his desk in front of him. "I made a list of people I think you and your men might want to interview."

"Wonderful."

"And it might interest you to know there have been a few new developments in the case."

He sighed.

"Go ahead," she said. "Open it."

He opened the file and proceeded to skim over the list she'd made. When he was finished, he looked at her with pity in his eyes. She didn't understand his apathy, but she figured he must be tired. "Look at this." She pulled up the pictures she'd taken on her cell phone of the grass where Craig had parked his car and passed her phone to him. "Craig would never have parked in the grass, let alone ruin a sprinkler head, unless he was under duress. He always went out of his way to make sure UPS trucks didn't damage the lawn lining our driveway." She raised her eyebrows and asked, "Do you know what this means?"

He merely sighed.

"The fact that my husband drove onto the lawn and broke a sprinkler head could very well be an indication that someone was in the car with him," Faith continued. "Maybe Craig had a gun pointed at his head."

He glanced at the images and then handed her cell phone back to her.

"And that's not all," she said, excitement lining her voice. "I've been talking with my brother, and I was wondering if you and your men have considered that my children might have been sold to human traffickers."

"We're looking at that as a possibility."

Her eyes lit up. "Well, that's good news because it's come to my attention that Sacramento is a hub for sex trafficking. Did you know that?"

Without giving him a chance to answer, she tapped her finger on the file she'd set in front of him. "You need to take another look at my notes. Not only have I been researching human trafficking, I got a call from Corrie Perelman. Remember her? Her daughter, Samantha Perelman, was taken from the grocery store while her mom shopped in the next aisle." Faith kept talking, couldn't stop herself if she wanted to. For the first time in weeks, she had something to go on. Maybe they could find a connection between one of these cases and hers. "Upon searching the Internet," she went on, "I noticed another case that happened only a few short months ago in Stockton. A young girl was taken from the parking lot as her mother loaded the trunk of her car with groceries."

The detective raised a hand to stop her and said, "I need you to calm down."

"Calm down?" Flummoxed, she looked over her shoulder and noticed a couple of officers looking her way. "I've never been calmer, Detective. For the first time in weeks, my mind is clear. This is enthusiasm you're hearing in my tone." She pointed at the folder in front of him. "These men were at our house for a reason. They were looking for something. And when they didn't find anything, they took my kids instead."

Yuhasz leaned back in his chair. "And what were they looking for exactly?"

Ignoring the flippancy in his voice, she took a seat in one of two chairs in front of his desk, then leaned close and said, "The man who killed Craig asked me where 'it' was, but he never said what exactly he was looking for."

"And you're only now thinking to tell me this bit of news?"

"It didn't come to me until I was having dinner at my parent's house. As my mom mentioned to you once before, the doctor said this could happen . . . trauma to the head can cause memories to come and go when you least expect them." She raised a brow. "The good news is that I remembered."

He ran all ten fingers over his short spiky hair.

"The fact that they were looking for something," Faith continued, "could very well crack the case wide open."

"Watching a few too many detective shows, I see."

She angled her head to one side. "What?"

"*Crack the case wide open?* Do you have any idea how you sound?"

Insulted, she pushed herself to her feet. "I don't know . . . maybe like a mother desperate to find her children?"

"Sit down, Mrs. McMann. Otherwise I'm going to have to escort you out of here. You need to turn it down a notch."

She stared at the man as he shook his head in disappointment, and that's when she realized he'd shut her out from the start. He wasn't interested in what she had to say.

He'd merely been placating her.

In the time it takes to flick a switch, excitement turned to anger. "You're not the least bit interested to hear what I have to say, are you?"

Someone across the way called Yuhasz's name, said he had a call on line two, said it was important. She looked out the door toward the men at their desks. A couple of them caught her gaze and quickly turned their attention on something else. Every time she came to the station, she suddenly realized, Detective Yuhasz was conveniently called away.

"I'm going to take this call." He gestured toward the front of the building. "I want you to go have a seat in the lobby or walk outside and get some air. I'll come get you when I'm finished. And then we'll talk about finding Lisa and Hudson."

Lisa? Heat rose from her toes and clawed its way upward to her chest and neck. Anger and indignation turned to outrage, crackling like electricity in her veins. "You don't even know my daughter's name."

He looked confused, as if he had no idea what he'd done to cause such wrath.

Her hands shook. Her nostrils flared.

The fury she'd been trying to tamp down for days now rose within, churning and gurgling, threatening to erupt. Stepping around his desk, she reached for his computer keyboard and swung it at his head.

She hit hard.

Plastic cracked and keys flew off.

She struck again from the other direction. An explosion of plastic rained down upon them, but all she saw was red. Blood spurted from his nose.

People were shouting. Footsteps sounded. A sharp pain shot through her shoulder as both arms were yanked back behind her. She kicked as hard she could, turned her head, and bit into flesh. Curse words she'd never uttered in her life flew from her mouth.

Metal cuffs clanked shut over her wrists, biting into her skin as she was dragged across the room, through a metal door, and down a long, narrow hallway, where she was thrown into a holding cell.

TWELVE

Within hours of being arrested, Faith was transported to an adult correction facility in Roseville. Another four hours passed before she was allowed to talk to a family member. No longer cuffed, she was escorted to a room where inmates could talk to visitors.

Frustration continued to gnaw on Faith's insides. Although she knew she'd made a mistake, she ultimately blamed Detective Yuhasz for treating her case as if it wasn't important. Finding her children seemed to be low on his list of priorities.

Jana sat on the other side of the glass window. Her face was pinched. She picked up the phone. The moment Faith took a seat across from her and did the same, she said, "What were you thinking?"

Just like that, Faith's temper flared. "That man couldn't remember Lara's name!"

"So you bashed him over the head with a computer?"

"It wasn't a laptop. It was a keyboard. Yuhasz is not as tough as he looks."

Jana sighed. "You hit him more than once! You broke his nose."

"I admit. I lost control, but that man pushed me to the brink. For the first time in weeks, I was filled with optimism and hope, and all he had to offer was indifference."

Jana sighed.

"Yuhasz and his men are buried in paperwork," Faith said. "Finding my children is so far down their priority list it's pathetic."

"Oh, Faith."

"You have to listen to me." Faith leaned closer to the glass. "The day Craig was murdered, he parked his car on the lawn. He broke a sprinkler head. You, of all people, know how anal Craig was about anyone parking on the grass. He was trying to tell me something."

"Like what?"

"It was a warning. Those men must have been inside the car with him. I think they forced him to drive home and wait for me and the kids."

"I thought you said they were looking for something."

"Whatever it was they were looking for isn't at the house. We've all searched the place . . . me, the police, and the FBI. There's nothing there. You heard Colton. Trafficking is big business around these parts. They must have taken the kids as an afterthought."

"If taking Lara and Hudson wasn't part of the plan, though, why would they have bothered to wait for you and the kids?"

"I don't know—I'm speculating. For all I know those men just happened to be there when the kids and I walked in on them. Or maybe they thought threatening us would make Craig talk." Faith frowned. "I just don't know."

There was a long pause before Faith said, "The only thing I do know is that I need to get out of here. I need answers." Faith leaned forward and let her forehead fall softly against the glass. She was an idiot. If only she'd sucked it up and walked away when Yuhasz told her to. She wouldn't be in this mess.

Jana placed both hands over her growing belly. Her tone softened when she said, "Dad's doing all he can to get you out of here, but it's not looking good, Faith."

"How's he holding up?"

"He's the same as always, handling the situation in the same calm manner in which he handles everything life throws at him. He knows the judge in charge of your case. He might be able to work a deal. You're lucky to have him on your side."

"I'm lucky to have all of you," Faith said. Her sister was right. Faith had made a colossal mistake letting her frustrations take hold of her in such a way. She'd never harmed anyone in her life. Never thrown an object in anger. Never shouted at a stranger, let alone cursed in public. "What in the world have I done?"

Inmates were allowed to use a computer for no longer than thirty minutes a day, but it was on a first come, first serve basis. There were only six computers inside a small, windowless room.

Faith waited more than an hour, and when it was her turn, it took her a moment to get comfortable with the computer. She'd spent most of the night creating a checklist in her head. Check out the NCMEC website, scour websites for missing children, see if she could find chat groups, not for emotional support, but hopefully a place where other parents of missing children were proactive in looking for their children. The problem was she had the computer for only thirty minutes.

"I've read about you."

Ignoring whoever was talking to her, Faith typed her children's names into the search area on the computer screen to see if the media was keeping her story alive. A dozen articles popped up. She clicked on the write-up in the *Sacramento Bee*. The reporter had interviewed coworkers at the school where she taught. Apparently a rumor had made its way around Granite Bay. People were saying that the angry parents of one of Faith's students were to blame for her children's disappearance. It was an idiotic story with no basis whatsoever.

"So many conspiracy theories," the woman said over her shoulder.

Irritated, Faith turned around. "Excuse me?"

The woman hovering over her shoulder had a peacock feather tattooed on her right arm, a hummingbird in flight on the other. Her dark hair was cut short around her ears. "Take it easy," she said. "I'm just sayin' there seems to be a lot of theories going around as to what happened to your kids."

"What do you know about it?"

"Everyone in the area knows about your case, and everyone has their own ideas about what happened. You've been the talk of the town. Painting on your walls and then attacking law enforcement." She made a tsking noise. "That's one way to keep your story in the limelight. My mom and I think it's quite brilliant, actually."

Faith blew out a deep, laborious breath. "So what do you think happened?"

"Well, I do know of a girl who lived in Sacramento who was taken from her bedroom in the middle of the night."

Faith raised a curious brow and waited for her to go on.

"The police were called. Amber Alerts were broadcasted. Posters were hung. Local newspapers, radio, and television were contacted. Search parties were formed. You get the idea. The girl's mom did everything she could to find her daughter. And she never gave up."

"Did she ever find her?"

She nodded. "Fifteen years later, her mom got the call she'd been waiting for . . . her daughter had been found. By then the poor girl was a hooker and a junkie, but she was alive."

The idea that this could be Lara in fifteen years made her shiver. "Go on."

"Modern-day slavery," the young woman said as she pulled up a chair.

"You aren't the first person to mention it," Faith said.

"Traffickers are no longer just pimps who prey on runaways and prostitutes. Not anymore."

"So where was this girl who was taken all those years?"

"Not more than fifteen miles from her childhood home. They had changed her name, of course. They got her hooked on drugs, beat her daily, and spent every moment convincing her that her mother didn't want her. She believed them, too."

"Hey," someone shouted from the line of people waiting at the door. "If you're not using that computer, get out of the way and make room for someone else."

Faith looked at the clock. "I have twenty minutes left." She returned her attention to the woman sitting next to her. "So how did she finally get away?"

"Social media. It was 2010 when a friend suggested her mom use Twitter and Facebook and any other online social networking available to find her daughter."

"And?" Faith prodded.

"And so that's what she did. She found someone to make a website, and then she asked the public for help with finding her daughter."

"So the girl saw her mother online?"

"No. Her daughter was on the streets by then. But someone she knew recognized her and told her what was going on. It all happened pretty quickly after that. Mother and daughter were reunited, and the rest is history. For two years now, Mom and I have been working with public defenders and the courts to make it easier for juveniles to find a safe place to go."

She was talking about herself, Faith realized.

"More than half the girls we try to help return to their pimps. You know why?"

Faith shook her head.

"Because it's all they know."

"What's your name?"

"Emily Carver."

Faith turned back to the computer and typed her name into the search bar. There she was in full color, Emily and her mom standing next to the governor of California. The caption read: ANTITRAFFICKING ADVOCACY ON THE RISE. "So why are you in here, Emily?"

"Because the drugs got a hold on me . . . and they won't let go. Every time a pimp gets put away, I feel a sense of victory. But no matter how many hours I work, I still can't get all those johns' faces out of my mind. Disgusting, pig-faced johns who thought I wanted nothing more than to suck their dicks. Married men with families who feel no shame paying an underage girl to do to them what their own wives won't do. The pimps round us up and used to beat us good if we didn't make them enough money, but if you ask me, it's the johns who keep them driving around in those luxury sedans and living the good life in their big gated houses."

Faith felt sick. "These traffickers are taking kids from their homes?"

Emily nodded. "The younger, the better. Malls, restaurants, grocery stores." She sighed. "Basically you just need to keep doing what you're doing. Keep your story at the forefront of people's minds. Don't let them forget. Never let them forget."

Thirteen

Miranda sat in the front seat of Jasper's car. Once again Mother had blindfolded her, and for the first five minutes she could feel the tires rolling over a bumpy road and hear the loud whirring of more than one motorcycle in the distance.

The car came to a stop.

Jasper rolled down his window and talked to someone. She heard the squeaking of metal as a gate was opened, something she'd never heard when she was taken to visit a client. Was the farmhouse being guarded?

After they merged onto the main road, Jasper told her she could remove the band from around her eyes. She pulled it off, then immediately rolled down the window and let the wind blow through her hair. Her heart cried out, and freedom whispered in her ear.

Last night, while she'd lain awake, a plan had come to mind. *Jasper.* He would help her. She was certain. The idea of a future without rape and torture was a vision she couldn't let go of. She leaned forward, her chest pressed against the dashboard as she looked up to see the whole expanse of blue sky above.

If and when she escaped, she would never take her freedom for granted again. Gathering her wits, she turned toward Jasper. "Let's not go to San Francisco."

He chuckled.

"I'm serious." She grabbed his arm.

"Hey," he said, his voice firm. "Careful. I'm driving."

His expression was hard to read, his voice lined with annoyance. She released her grip. "Sorry. I was just thinking that this is our chance."

"Chance for what?" he asked without taking his gaze from the road.

"To run off together. You and me."

"Girl, you must be tripping. Haven't you learned anything?"

She frowned. "The last time we were together you said you cared about me."

"How much money do you have?" he asked.

"I don't have any money. I only have the things Mother packed for me, but you already know that."

"And she gave me enough money to buy gas to get to San Francisco and back."

Her spine stiffened. "So it's true."

"I don't know what you're talking about."

"Sex with me is your payment for working around the farm, milking the cows, feeding the chickens. I mean absolutely nothing to you."

"You're fifteen years old—"

"I'll be sixteen soon."

"Sixteen then. I couldn't run off with you if I wanted to."

"Why not?"

"You're underage, for one thing. And for another, Diane would find me . . . she would find us . . . and there's no telling what she would do to us."

Was that Mother's name? she wondered. *Diane?* She let it go for now. "Two against one," Miranda said.

He laughed. "Yeah, two against one and an army of hundreds behind her."

"We could hide out somewhere, find a way to make it work. We would have to stay on the run for a while, but we could manage somehow."

He snorted. "You have absolutely no idea what sort of people we're dealing with here. You're such a child . . . so naive."

She didn't like him talking down to her. She could read, and she was good at math. She was smart. If she'd never met Caroline, she would have made something of herself. If she could get away, she could still find a way to make a life for herself. "Can't you just pull over and let me go? Tell Mother I ran off."

He didn't respond, his gaze straight ahead, his jaw set.

How could he do this to her? She swallowed the knot lodged in her throat. After a while she asked, "How long until we're there?"

"Soon."

She'd been wrong about Jasper. He wouldn't help her after all. Her fingers rested on the door handle. The thought of being forced to spend time with Mr. Smith was too much to bear. She thought about opening the car door and tumbling out onto the highway. There was a lot of traffic, a good chance she would get run over.

It would all be finished.

She would be free.

She curled her fingers around the metal handle. One quick flick of her wrist . . . that's all it would take. It was suddenly difficult to breathe, felt as if a block of cement were pressing on her chest and suffocating her.

"Do you know how much money it costs to feed all of you and keep a roof over your heads?"

She glanced at him. Jasper looked unexpectedly anguished.

"I didn't ask to be brought to the farmhouse," she told him.

"I know that," he shot back. "Your mom sold you and I'm sorry about that, but we all know life isn't fair. Over time you'll adjust and things will get better."

"You're a liar." How could he say such a despicable thing about her mom? She'd never felt such hatred for anyone.

"You didn't know?"

"My mom never would have sold me. She loved me more than anything in the world."

"I'm sure she did. Maybe they convinced her you would be better off—a warm bed and food to eat."

"Shut up! Stop it! I hate you."

He sighed. "I shouldn't have said anything."

She turned toward the window, watched the cars swoosh by in a blur, everyone with someplace to go. She didn't need Jasper's or anyone else's help. She would find a way back home even if it killed her.

FOURTEEN

"Mom?"

Faith looked away from the pile of papers she was correcting and found Lara looking at her with big, sad eyes. "Do you think Pee Wee will ever come back home?"

It took Faith a moment to remember that Pee Wee was the bunny that Aunt Jana had given Lara for Easter. A year had passed since Pee Wee had squeezed his way through his wire cage and ran off. "Do you remember all the posters and signs we put everywhere asking people to call us if they found Pee Wee?"

Lara nodded. "We sent a picture to the newspaper asking for help. But why didn't they find him?"

"I don't know, but your daddy drove around the neighborhood every day looking for him. I'm sorry, honey. That was a long time ago. What made you think of Pee Wee?"

"I see him at night when I go to sleep. I try to pet him, but then he runs away. I think he's lost."

Faith looked over her daughter's head at her husband, who had over-heard the conversation. He grimaced and shrugged his shoulders, letting her know he wasn't going to be much help.

"The truth is," Faith told her daughter, "I don't know where Pee Wee is or what happened to him. I like to imagine that a nice family found him and is playing with him right now."

"I think we should make some more posters and keep looking for him."

Faith looked into Lara's eyes, unable to take away the hope she saw there. "OK, go get your crayons and I'll grab some paper."

Faith picked up the phone and held it close to her ear. Through the glass, she held Dad's gaze and saw the determination in his eyes. He hadn't given up on her.

For the first time since she'd knocked Detective Yuhasz over the head with his keyboard, she felt the full weight of her shame. "Hi."

"How are you holding up?"

She shrugged. "I screwed up. How am I supposed to help my kids if I can't even help myself? I feel like a fool."

He frowned. "I need you to hang in there for a few more days."

Her shoulders fell. How in the world had she made such a mess of things?

"Judge Lowell has agreed to hold a preliminary hearing on Thursday," Dad went on. "I brought you some clothes. I need you to dress up for your assigned court date and tell him how deeply sorry you are. I hired a lawyer. Michael Bennett will meet with you tomorrow."

"What do you think my chances are?"

"Assaulting an officer is serious business. I explained to the judge, in private, the stress you've been under. I think he'll take that into consideration, but I don't know, Faith. You're going to need to get a grip on your emotions."

She couldn't stand seeing him look so defeated. "I'm sorry. I never meant for it to come to this."

"No need to apologize to me. But if you're serious about finding your kids, it's time for you to stop and think before you act. Let's get you out of here, and then we'll talk."

———

The security guard stood behind Faith as she signed a form and collected her belongings at the window: purse, wallet, and the suit she'd worn at the hearing. The guard's footfalls fell heavily against the concrete as they walked toward the exit.

He followed her outside.

The chill in the air felt cool against her face.

The nameless guard unclipped his key ring from his waistband, unlocked the gate, and held it open. As Faith walked away, the metal bars clinked shut behind her. She headed toward Dad's truck parked at the curb. Dad had talked to Judge Lowell, and Yuhasz had agreed to drop charges, but only upon Faith's agreement to attend weekly anger management classes and remain under her parents' supervision for the next ninety days. Faith was just thankful to be out of lockdown.

Jana climbed out of the passenger seat and waddled toward her with arms extended and a wide smile plastered across her face. Her sister's stomach had grown to the size of a watermelon, big enough to make for an awkward embrace.

"Thank God you're out of that place," Jana told her.

"Amen to that," Faith said.

Dad took a little longer to climb out of the truck, but there was no cane in sight as he headed their way. He kissed her forehead and said, "You did good. Let's go home."

They stopped at Faith's house so she could gather mail, files, clothes, and anything else she might need while she was living with her parents. She didn't like the idea of being away from home, but that was the price she had to pay. As she walked around the house, a shell of its former self, barren and cold, she resolved to get a hold of her emotions and turn things around.

Thirty minutes later, Mom greeted the three of them at the front door of her parents' house, wrapped her arms around Faith, and didn't want to let go.

Her old childhood bedroom had been set up with a TV and a desk. Other than those two things, the room looked the same as it had growing up. Periwinkle walls, lacy curtains, and a bright patchwork quilt on the bed. Lara and Hudson used to love spending the night at Grandma's and sleeping in Faith's old room. She put her files on the desk and then began to put away her clothes.

Jana entered the room, took a seat on the edge of the bed, and watched her unpack. "Mom wants to know if you prefer roast beef and potatoes for dinner or grilled salmon."

"Either one is fine," Faith said. "Why don't you go home and spend time with your family?"

"Are you trying to get rid of me?"

"No. I just don't need everyone making a fuss."

"Roast beef or salmon?" Jana asked again.

"Either is fine."

"I'll tell her salmon."

Faith put her T-shirts in the middle drawer and her pants in the drawer beneath that one.

"Colton has to make a delivery in Bakersfield, which is why he couldn't join us for dinner tonight. Of course, Bri is busy with the kids."

The normalcy her sister was trying to project was too much. Faith gritted her teeth and hoped the annoyance she felt would pass quickly. She definitely wasn't herself.

"It's weird being in your old room. It brings back so many memories."

Faith nodded.

"I thought maybe we could go to the mall tomorrow."

"I'm not sure if that's allowed," Faith said, trying her best to keep focused on the task at hand.

"As long as you're with someone, you can go almost anywhere. Dad mentioned that you have a curfew and have to be home by ten every night. The only place you're allowed to drive all by yourself, though, is the anger management classes twice a week. I'll be happy to go with you, if you want."

"I'll be fine on my own. Thanks."

"I guess Dacotah has to go to a speech therapist. With Colton working such long hours, I don't know how Bri is possibly going to manage it all."

Faith rolled her empty suitcase into the closet and shut the door.

"Did you hear what I said?"

Faith nodded, then sat in the chair in front of the desk and turned on the computer.

"You don't care about what's going on with the rest of us, do you?"

Faith swiveled around in her chair, finally setting her gaze on her sister. "What do you want from me? I'm sorry for upsetting your neat, perfect little life. I've told everyone, including you, thank you for everything you've done for me." She raised her arms in frustration. "But I can't do this."

"Do what?"

"Pretend that everything is hunky-dory. Make you all happy by walking around with a smile on my face. *Salmon or roast beef?* Who the fuck cares?"

Jana was on her feet. "Who are you?"

Faith stood, too, her steely, unblinking gaze on her sister as she marched forward until they were nose to nose. "I'm your sister. The same sister who stared into her husband's eyes as his throat was slit wide open. I watched Craig choke and die on his own blood. You don't want to know what that sounds like. My kids are gone, and I have no idea where they are." She inhaled a shaky breath. "Did you know that Lara chose you as her favorite person in the entire world to talk about in the classroom that Friday in school?" Faith nodded.

"She did a report on Auntie Jana. And that same morning Hudson found out that he made the A-team in soccer. He's the fastest runner in his age group, just as you were at that age."

Jana's eyes were wide, shocked, her face pale.

"Those men took Lara and Hudson. Think about that for a moment. Visualize it, and then ask me again whether or not I want salmon or roast beef or if I want to go to the fucking mall."

Jana's eyes welled with tears.

"I lie awake at night wondering if my children are crying and hungry. I have no idea what those people have done with them. Do my kids wonder why Mom and Dad haven't found them yet? But you expect me to flick a switch and turn it all off so I don't make you uncomfortable. Let's go shopping and forget it ever happened. Sometimes I feel like I'm the only one around here who cares about what happened to them!"

"You're right." Jana put a hand to her forehead. "I'm sorry. I was only trying to help."

Faith's head fell forward, her chin nearly hitting her chest. "It's OK. None of this is your fault, but I need some time alone to sort things out."

FIFTEEN

It wasn't the old man from the farmhouse who greeted Miranda and Jasper at the front of the hotel where luggage was being transported from limousines and people from all walks of life were coming and going. The man who greeted them wore a fitted suit and dark shades over his eyes. It was so easy for these creeps to blend into society. All it took was a haircut and nice clothes. Nobody had a clue what she'd been through. Nobody cared. People had their own lives, their own problems.

She thought about screaming and running, but she wouldn't get far in her new heels. Besides, Jasper would probably grab her and haul her into the car before she could get more than a few feet away. *And then what?* She'd have Mother to contend with. The thought of being whipped and then spending days locked in a dark, windowless room without food or water was not the only reason she smiled at the stranger. She smiled at him because she needed to make everyone believe that everything was OK and she was happy to be there.

She watched the sea of faces, wondered if the elderly couple might come to her aid if she grabbed the lady's frail arm and pleaded with her to help.

Jasper retrieved her bag from the backseat. When he handed it to her she said in a low voice, "I'm scared. I don't want to do this."

He refused to look her in the eye.

Hands full, she watched the man in the suit reach into the inside pocket of his jacket. He was carrying a gun. She could see it clear as day tucked into his waistband. Why did he need a gun? Was he going to shoot Jasper?

Instead of reaching for his weapon, he retrieved a thick envelope from an inside pocket and handed it to Jasper. No words were exchanged. An envelope for the girl and the transaction was done.

Clean, simple, quiet.

Her knees wobbled; her hands shook. Jasper's gaze met hers, and she saw a flash of—pity? Regret? She wasn't sure. Was he thinking what she was thinking? That they could have used that money in the envelope to run off? Before she could say goodbye, he merged with oncoming traffic and sped off without another glance her way.

Her heart sank.

For a brief moment she'd dared to think that maybe, just maybe, she had misread him after all and he really did care enough to help her. But as she watched the dented bumper disappear around the next street corner, reality set in and she realized she was truly alone and maybe she always would be.

Sixteen

"We're going to have to cancel the trip to Hawaii," Craig said after the kids ran off to play in their rooms.

"But why?" Faith asked. "We've all been looking forward to this trip for months. We have airline tickets, and I already bought the kids bathing suits. You can't be serious?"

"We're close to signing off on our biggest deal yet. I need to be here. I'm sorry."

"Why can't you let Joe handle it?"

"He's going through a divorce. He hasn't been himself lately. Please, Faith, trust me on this one. Let me get through this deal, and then we'll reschedule."

But it never happened. They never did make that trip to Hawaii. And then at the end of the school year, pink slips were handed out and Faith had been so worried about losing her job, she hadn't given Hawaii another thought.

Until now.

She welcomed the memories. They were all she had. And yet if she could go back in time and question him further, would she have asked him what was wrong? It wasn't merely canceling the trip that bothered him that day. He had appeared unusually strained, as if there was something he wasn't telling her. But always too busy with grading papers and taking care of the kids, it seemed, Faith had let it go.

It was ten minutes before six o'clock. Faith sat in her car, her fingers clutched tightly around the steering wheel. The engine was off. Something creaked. Her head snapped up, and she looked around.

Naked tree branches swayed.

Nobody was out there.

Every once in a while, like now, an eerie, niggling feeling washed over her, telling her she was being watched.

In the distance, she saw movement, shadows between two buildings. A few cars dotted the mostly empty lots across the street. Her eyes narrowed as she tried to see inside the vehicles. It was no use. If someone was watching her, they could be anywhere: sitting at a desk in the top floor of the closest building, perched in the tree, or sitting low inside one of the cars.

She redirected her gaze to the building straight ahead where her anger management class was being held. Most of the people standing around outside had filed into the building a while ago. Apparently there were plenty of pissed off people in Placer County. This would be her first session at anger management. The judge had given her a list of rules. The first of which was arrive on time.

She had five minutes to get inside.

She glanced at the manila folder sitting on the passenger seat. Finding her kids was more important than spending time with a bunch of angry people. She wasn't violent. Not usually. What she did to Detective Yuhasz would never happen again. She wasn't a threat to society. She only wanted—needed—to find her kids.

A knock sounded on her window.

Startled, she plunked a hand on her chest, then opened the door a crack.

"Didn't mean to give you a fright." The woman standing there wore beige slacks and a button-up shirt tucked in and held in place by a tightly cinched belt. "Are you enrolled in this class?"

Faith wondered how she knew, but she nodded just the same.

"My name is Captain. I'm one of the instructors. You're going to be late."

Captain must be her nickname. Everyone was asked to use a nickname because a make-believe name was supposed to make it easier for everyone to talk about his or her problems in front of complete strangers.

The woman looked at her watch.

Faith grimaced. If she didn't get out of the car and go inside, she would be reported. And being reported meant facing Judge Lowell again, and then how would she find her kids?

Captain waited patiently for her to step out of the car.

Faith grabbed her backpack, shut the door, and followed Captain across the parking lot and into the building. The instructor sat in front of the room. His name tag read, ZZ Top, which she assumed had something to do with his long, silvery-gray beard. "Have you picked out a name yet?"

"No," Faith said. "I haven't."

"Why not?"

"I don't know. I couldn't think of anything that seemed fitting."

"Rules are rules," ZZ Top said, "and we prefer it if you don't use your real name. Why don't we go around the circle and some of the others here will tell you their nicknames and why they chose them?"

A large woman in her early thirties stood. She called herself Butterfinger because she came from a family of perfect people who had a bad habit of commenting on her weight, which only made her want to eat more. The man sitting next to Butterfinger called himself Mufasa, he explained to the room, because he tended to roar instead of talk normally. He'd grown up with eight siblings and said shouting was the only way to get anyone's attention.

There were many more stories told as they went around the circle. Some sad, some humorous, but all heartfelt.

The last person to speak was a young woman in her midtwenties who called herself Rage. Her head had been shaved except for a Mohawk, a quarter-inch high, down the middle. She wore little makeup, and her grayish-blue eyes had a haunted look to them.

"My name is Rage," she said, "and everything makes me angry. My mother was a schizo—an honest-to-God crazy woman. One minute she would press my hand against a burner, and in the next minute she would hold me close and sing me a lullaby. Dad couldn't handle coming home to a crazy lady, so he left us both. At fourteen or fifteen, it's all a blur, I ran away with a guy twice my age." She sighed. "My chance for a fresh new start. Only it turned out he had major trust issues, so he locked me in a dog cage all day to make sure I didn't stray while he was at work."

People murmured.

"I think that's enough sharing for tonight." She sat down.

ZZ Top thanked everyone for telling their stories and then focused his attention back on Faith. "So, does that help?"

Blindly, Faith traced the scar running across her neck. For the first time since she'd been released from the correction facility, she understood why she was being forced to attend anger management. She was still, despite being thrown in jail, beyond frustrated and angry. Not too long ago, her days had been filled with children's laughter on the playground and watching a child's face when they had an aha moment and something clicked in the classroom. She loved working with parents who appreciated what she did for the kids and enjoyed it when older children who used to be in her class came back to visit and say hello. She'd been blessed with a wonderful husband and beautiful children, only to have it all taken away in the blink of an eye. Her family had been violated in the worst way. Strange, nameless men thought they could barge into her house and kill her husband, leave her for dead, and then take her kids.

Those men would not get away with it.

She would find them and she would make them pay.

Blood curdled in her veins.

She stood tall, facing the group. "Three men came into my house uninvited," she said through gritted teeth. "They slit my husband's throat. My hands were tied behind my back and my mouth was covered with tape. I couldn't comfort him or tell him I loved him as I watched him die. I felt the serrated teeth of the knife's blade as it cut through my flesh, and I heard the whimpering cries of my children as they were swept from the only home they've ever known. The bastards took my children." She took a breath. "I'm going to find my kids and bring them home." Her hands curled into fists and her voice shook as she said, "You can call me *Furious*."

SEVENTEEN

Miranda was surprised when she was ushered to the hotel salon instead of being taken directly to a hotel room. Crystal chandeliers hung from the ceiling. Gold-toned walls and creamy, plush furniture filled the waiting area. She stood next to her escort, no longer smiling. Exhaustion had set in. Her eyes were tired, and her jaw hurt from all that beaming. Too many sleepless nights, the long drive with Jasper, and now she was finally away from the farmhouse and there was nothing she could do but stand there and wait and see what happened next.

A tall, stone-faced female approached. Her name was Cecelia, and she would be her new charge. A quiet nod was exchanged between the two strangers, and once again Miranda was handed off. Cecelia walked a few steps ahead, her strides long, taking her through a frosted glass door and then down a wide hallway. The woman stopped at the first door on the right and gestured for Miranda to go inside and change into the robe that was neatly folded on the table inside.

Looking at the woman with pleading eyes, Miranda grabbed hold of her forearm and said, "I need help. Please help me."

Cecelia gently removed her hand as she looked down her nose at her.

Miranda immediately saw the truth in her eyes—Cecelia knew exactly what was going on.

"Would you like me to call the manager?"

"No," Miranda answered softly. "I'm just tired after a long ride. I'll be fine." She stepped inside the room. When two women in white lab coats entered a few minutes later, Miranda didn't argue when she was told to strip and lay flat on the table. A water hose hung from the ceiling and for the next hour she was scrubbed thoroughly from head to toe. Afterward, warm oils were rubbed into every bit of her skin. A manicure and pedicure came next. And then hair and makeup before she was dressed in a royal-blue gown with a low neckline. The black dress she'd worn earlier paled in comparison.

It was Cecelia who led her into a private elevator and rode with her to the top floor. Miranda hardly recognized her reflection in the mirrored wall. The girl staring back at her looked like a grown woman from one of those expensive glossy magazines. Thick curls hung about her shoulders. Her lips had never looked so plump and red.

She followed Cecelia dutifully out of the elevator and to a suite at the very end of a long hallway. Cecelia used a keycard to gain access and then waited for Miranda to enter before shutting the door behind them.

The room was incredible: padded silk wall coverings, golden silk draperies, velvet fabrics, and beautiful wood furniture. Nothing like any living space she'd ever seen in her lifetime, not even in magazines or on TV. Miranda walked across plush carpet to the floor-to-ceiling window and looked out at the sweeping views of the city. It was getting dark out, and the city lights twinkled back at her.

Cecelia went to the built-in bar and returned with a glass of champagne that she handed to Miranda. She never once made eye contact. "Enjoy your stay." As soon as she left, Miranda set the fluted crystal glass on the coffee table, rushed across the room, and picked up the phone. An automated voice asked for a four-digit password.

She hung up and tried again. She hit zero, hoping an operator would answer. Nothing worked. She went to the door, jiggled the knob, her every movement frantic. Next she ran around the suite, opening drawers, looking for a key or the four-digit code needed to make a phone call. There had to be a way out of there!

She pummeled her fists against the bedroom wall, hoping someone in a room close by would call downstairs or come and open the door, but it was no use. Exhausted, she went back to the living room and plopped down on the couch, where she watched the tiny bubbles floating upward in the champagne glass. She took a taste. The bubbles tickled her tongue. She drank the rest in two gulps, nearly choked, then crossed the room and refilled her glass.

The door to the terrace was unlocked. She stepped outside and looked over the railing. The hundreds of people below, exploring the city, looked like tiny dots. They were all so far away. She wondered what it would be like to climb over the railing and jump off, end it all right now. *Splat!* Would it hurt? Or would it be over so quickly she wouldn't feel any pain at all? She didn't want to die, but neither did she want to live like this—trapped, scared, lonely.

She thought of her mom and what Jasper had said. Mom loved her. She never would have sold her only daughter for money. Her body suddenly felt oddly substantial, much too heavy for her legs. She stumbled back inside, using the wall for support. The glass dropped from her hand and rolled across the carpet, spilling its contents as it went. How many beatings would she get for that? She made her way back to the couch and dropped down onto velvet fabric. The room was spinning. She'd been drugged, she realized as her head fell back on the cushions before she drifted off.

EIGHTEEN

Faith heard the creak of the wood floors outside her bedroom door. There was a knock before the door opened. Russell Gray's broad frame filled the doorway, the glow of the yellow bulb in the hallway casting an eerie brightness over him. "Can't sleep?" he asked.

She shook her head, then turned back to the computer, intent on learning everything she could about setting up a website and offering a reward for any tip that led to finding Lara and Hudson.

Her father's footsteps were light as he entered and came to stand beside her. "Throw on some shoes and a sweater and come with me."

It was late. She had so much to do. Her shoulders drooped.

"It will only take a second. I want to show you something."

Dutifully, she followed him out of the room and down the stairs. She didn't question where they were going. But she was surprised when he took her through the kitchen, opened the back door, and led her across the grassy backyard to his barnlike workshop. As children, they weren't allowed to enter. It was Dad's private workplace. The last thing she expected to see when he opened the double doors was her mom, siblings, and brother-in-law, but there they were, sitting on folding chairs that surrounded a sturdy metal table in the center of the workshop.

Since she'd grown, of course she'd seen inside his workshop, but the room appeared much bigger than she remembered. There was a bathroom in the back corner. One of the walls was covered with a large map of California and Sacramento. There were also poster-size pictures of the men she'd painted on her living room walls back home. The other wall was covered by a giant whiteboard.

She raised a questioning brow.

Dad rested a hand on her shoulder. "We want to do everything in our power to help you find Lara and Hudson."

"You're not alone," Colton told her. He got up from his chair and walked to the map and explained the symbols. "The red X's designate known pedophiles in the area. Blue dots represent friends, neighbors, and teachers, anyone who knew Lara and Hudson person-ally. Yellow highlights indicate schools, grocery stores, dance classes, soccer fields . . . all designating locations where the kids have been before."

Jana came to her feet. She was wearing one of Steve's flannel shirts and sweatpants. Her hair was pulled back in a rubber band. It was first time in a very long time Faith could remember seeing her dressed in casual clothes and without makeup. "I wanted you to know that I've created a private hotline. Once you get your website up with the hot-line number, my job will be to screen the calls as they come in."

"Thank you," Faith said. "I appreciate it."

"Not a problem." Jana gestured toward Mom. "Mom's in charge of staying in touch with Detective Yuhasz, getting updates, and letting us know when and if there's anything new happening with the case."

"We're going to have to ask you to do everything you can to stay off the department's radar while we try to figure out where to start," Colton said. "It won't help matters if you get thrown back in jail."

Overwhelmed with gratitude, Faith had no words.

"We wanted you to know that we're all in this together," Dad said. "There are lots of people in the community who want to help. Mom has arranged for a candlelight vigil to be held Sunday night at Granite Bay High School."

"It will give you a chance to thank everyone who's been calling and offering support," Mom said.

Her voice wobbled; tears welled in her eyes. "Thank you."

"OK," Dad said. "You have electricity and Wi-Fi. If it gets too cold in here, there's a portable heater stored in the closet over there. This will be our command post. We'll meet here as often as we need to."

There was a list on the whiteboard:

WHO TOOK LARA AND HUDSON?

Pedophile

Neighbor

Random Kidnapping

Trafficking

H&M Investments

"After shooting practice in the morning, I'm going to talk to your neighbors," Dad said. "Get a brief statement from anyone who might have seen or heard anything, find out if there were any witnesses other than Beth Tanner."

"Once you have a website up and running," Steve said, "we can all help distribute flyers with the pictures of the men you drew along with information on how someone can contact us and remain anonymous."

"We also need to dig deep into Craig's life," Dad cut in. "Did he have any friends outside of home or work? What projects was he working on? Did he talk to anyone at the gym or have any romantic—" He stopped midsentence, looked suddenly uncomfortable as if he might have said too much.

"Go ahead," Faith said. "It's OK." Dad had spent years in the army until an injury to the head had forced him to retire a few years earlier than planned. He'd been a commander, leading the troops. Of course he would think this way. "Put it all out there," she told everyone in the room. "This is about finding the kids. Craig would understand."

"We need to ask the hard questions, including whether or not Craig had any romantic involvement with other women," Dad finished. "Did he use narcotics?"

"No way was he involved with other women," Jana said bluntly, and just those few words lifted Faith's spirits.

"I'd like to add Emily Carver's name to the list of people to talk to," Faith said. "She's the woman I met at the correctional facility. She and her mother have been antitrafficking advocates for years. I'm hoping her mother can shed some light on where we might look."

"I've got to get going," Colton said as he lifted himself from his chair. "I have a long day ahead of me tomorrow." He pointed to the other side of the room. "I put a list of truck stops on the cork board—the main stops where lot lizards hang out."

"Lot lizards?" Jana asked.

"That's what some of the drivers call the young boys and girls who approach them at the rest stops when they're sleeping inside their semitrailers. I think we should talk to some of the kids, see what we can find out."

"I'm going to fill the coffeepot," Mom said, heading for the exit. Colton said goodbye and followed her out.

Into the wee hours of the night, they all tossed out ideas for motives: theft, sex, narcotics, random acts of violence, a business deal gone sour. At one point, while Dad and Jana read articles on the national website for missing children, Steve pulled Faith outside under the pretense of getting some fresh air and said in a low voice, "I hate to be the bearer of bad news, but I'll be in and out of town on business over the next few weeks. Colton's trucking business is growing, and he doesn't have a lot of time. Your dad is still going to physical therapy, and Jana is seven months pregnant."

"And?"

"If you're serious about finding Lara and Hudson, it's my opinion that you're going to need to recruit more help."

Nineteen

Pain. Miranda felt pain. Her brain was fuzzy, muddled.

The discomfort between her legs was excruciating. She moved her head from one side to the other. Her eyelids were thick and heavy with sleep. She was back at the apartment where she'd grown up. She could hear the rats scurrying through the walls. Had her mother's boyfriend gotten into her room after all? She tried to scream, wanted him to stop, but no sound came forth.

Her lips were dry and cracked. She was so thirsty.

Finally she managed to open her eyes and focus enough to see gold painted walls in the foreground. It all came back to her then: the salon, the luxurious suite in San Francisco, the champagne. As her vision cleared, she noticed two young men, one on each side of the bed. They stood straight and tall, pale bodies with black leather strips wound around their hairless chests.

As the pain began to subside, the boy on her right slid a piece of leather between her teeth. And then it came again, an object, hard and unforgiving, being shoved between her legs, pushing through to the center of her being.

She clenched her teeth. Her body arched—the pain searing and hot, too much to bear. She was being ripped apart from the inside out.

Biting down on the piece of leather, her eyes bulging, she lifted her head and saw Mr. Smith sitting on a decorative chair at the end of the bed, facing her. He was naked, all shriveled white skin and saggy chest pulled down by gravity. Two young females, not much older than Miranda, stood by his side wearing black lace panties and matching bras. One ran both hands through his sparse silvery hair, dramatically, lovingly, her body moving gracefully as if she were turned on by the mere touch of him. The other woman leaned close and slid the tip of her long pink tongue over his shriveled chest. Grasped in his hands was an object she couldn't make out—the source of her pain.

His frail arms shook, and his forehead was covered with a light sheen of sweat as he looked at her, his expression cruel as if she'd personally done him wrong.

"Stop! Please!" she gritted out.

Her words merely spurred him onward, his eyes wild as he shoved the object inside her and then used his other hand to push the young woman's head lower into his lap, his eyes rolling to the back of his head as Miranda screamed her way into oblivion.

———

The next time Miranda awoke, the room was empty.

She had no sense of time. No idea how long she'd been lying on the bed unconscious. Nobody had bothered to throw a sheet over her naked body. There was blood smeared across her stomach and thighs. Her body was bruised and battered. Her head throbbed.

Seconds passed before she realized she was no longer bound. Scrambling off the bed, she fell to the thick, plush carpet, then clawed at the mattress and pulled herself to her feet. Every muscle screamed in pain. Her mouth felt swollen, her eyes, too. She stood still on wobbly legs and waited for the dizziness to pass before she went to the door.

Slowly, silently, she turned the knob, surprised when the door came open and relieved to see that the suite was empty.

Her heart hammered against her chest.

The blue gown she'd been wearing when she'd first entered the room lay in a heap on the floor near the couch. Before she had time to put the dress on, she heard a noise outside the main entry door. Frantically she looked around, grabbed a bronze statuette from a side table, and hid behind the door.

A maid walked in with an armful of clean towels.

Miranda swung hard and fast, making contact with the side of her head.

The maid crumpled to the floor.

Miranda grabbed the door before it could close, using the statuette to prop it open. Thinking fast, she stripped off the maid's uniform and put it on.

She saw the woman's chest rise and fall and was glad to know she hadn't killed her.

The shoes came off next. They were a size too big. In fact, the whole outfit was loose, but it would work. It had to.

There was no time for hesitation or making plans, she thought as she exited the hotel room, walking at a good clipped pace until she reached the elevators.

As she waited for the doors to open, she realized it was a bad idea.

The stairs. She would take the stairs.

Heading back the way she'd come, praying nobody would show up, she pushed through the door to the stairwell, didn't take a breath until the door clicked shut behind her. By the time she reached the nineteenth floor, her legs were shaking. But she couldn't stop now. She had to keep going.

Freedom called out for her.

If her legs gave out, she would crawl out of this place. Holding on to the iron rail, she took a step at a time.

The stairwell was empty.

She didn't pass anyone until she reached the tenth floor. It was a woman. She refused to make eye contact.

At the third floor was a sign for the pool. She needed to find a restroom and wash herself off before she attempted to make her way through the lobby and onto the street. Head bent forward, eyes downcast; she pushed through the door and followed a stone path.

The sun had decided to come out today, and there were people everywhere, sipping drinks in the heated pool or enjoying lunch overlooking the bustling city. She shouldn't have come this way. It was much too risky. She nearly tripped on uneven stone. A man grabbed for her elbow to help steady her. She pulled away, walking faster until she found a restroom. Somebody was taking a shower, while another lady touched up her makeup at the sink area. Miranda headed for the wall of lockers, nearly cried when she saw an open locker with clothes hanging inside. There was a floppy hat and a bathing suit cover. She grabbed cash and sunglasses from the purse inside. There was no way she could use the sink area now, so she hurried back the way she came. In the stairwell again, she changed into the bathing suit cover, rolled up the maid's uniform, and tossed it into the garbage on the way down. Sunglasses and the hat covered most of her bruises. She made her way to the bottom floor and stepped out into the parking garage. *Thank God.*

"Miss!" someone called as she walked across the concrete floor. "Can I help you?"

Following the exit signs, she kept walking, refused to slow. Whoever had called out didn't bother coming after her. Spine stiff, gaze straight ahead, she walked past the line of cars waiting to get out of the garage. She was ready to run if need be. But nobody took notice of her. Nobody cared, and this time she was thankful for it. The moment she stepped out into the crowded sidewalk she was just another person in a sea of hundreds. A cabdriver stood near the hood of his taxi. "Where's the nearest bus station?" she asked.

"Where are you going to?"

"Sacramento."

"You'll need to take a train. It'll cost you eighteen dollars to get you to the station on Market Street."

She counted the wad of money she'd shoved into her pocket. Sixty-three dollars. The hotel loomed over her, a sinister reminder that she was running out of time. She told the driver OK and then climbed into the backseat. A pedestrian stopped to ask the driver for directions. Up ahead she saw a man wearing a dark suit and aviators exit the hotel. He looked around, his movements frantic as he rushed from car to car, peering into windows, making his way to the cars parked at the curbside.

She leaned over the front seat and told the driver she was in a hurry. She held her breath until he finally climbed in behind the wheel. By the time he merged into traffic, the man in the suit was only a few feet away, peeking inside the window of a car just ahead. She felt his gaze on her as they drove by.

TWENTY

"Abuse is abuse," Captain said to the group as she paced the floor. "It comes in many forms: verbal, emotional, sexual, physical, and psychological." Her voice softened. "Having negative feelings is normal. When you're feeling angry, though, I want you to take a moment to recognize what your body is feeling. There are often physical reactions that precede your anger. Sweaty palms, the pounding of your heart. These are important clues that can help you. Try to figure out what caused your anger and whether there are triggers in your life—certain people or loud noises. It could be many things."

Faith felt all those things and more. She lay awake most nights wondering where her children were and how they were being treated. One minute she felt a surge of hope and in the next a crippling despair that threatened her sanity.

A woman nicknamed Jinx was talking now. She was five feet five with pale skin. Every once in a while she would scratch at her wrists, where it was plain to see she was a cutter. Thin, angry red lines crisscrossed over pale skin. "As some of you know, I work in retail. When my toes start to tingle that's when I know an outburst is coming. It happens every time a customer complains about something they bought. I can't handle it when they return their purchases. Why did they buy the purse if they didn't need it? It makes no sense."

"Impulse buys," someone suggested.

Rage, the angriest one in the group, sat in the chair across from Faith. A blue bandanna was wrapped around her closely shaved head. Arms crossed tightly over her chest, she tapped her foot against the ground and rubbed her temple as if she was in pain. Faith could see the storm coming from a mile away. The girl was a walking time bomb.

"That's life," Sunshine said matter-of-factly to Jinx. "Get over it."

As if on cue, Rage jumped from her chair. "If everything is so easy for you, Sunshine, then why are you here?"

"It's OK," Captain told Rage. "Sunshine was merely giving her opinion."

"No. It's not OK. Nobody can say anything around here without Sunshine putting her positive spin on everything . . . as if life is so damn easy."

Sunshine stood. She was as wide as she was tall with slits for eyes and a mop of tight curls on top of her head. She could easily take Rage in a wrestling match if it came to that. Faith's money was on Sunshine. Or was it? Rage had fire in her eyes. It would be close.

"Getting angry over having to do your job is pointless," Sunshine said, stepping closer to Rage. "And you want to know what's worse? Someone who can't keep his or her mouth shut for one damn minute. You need to learn to shut up and listen for a change."

Here we go, Faith thought as she readied to dodge a flying chair.

Before Rage had a chance to wipe that smile off Sunshine's face, a giant of a man nicknamed Beast came to his feet. He calmly situated himself between the two women, which wasn't easy considering his size and the fact that there wasn't much room in the center of their little circle to begin with. Faith wasn't sure exactly who Beast was protecting—Rage, Sunshine, or every person in attendance tonight.

Topping off at about six feet five, Beast possessed a thick neck and big, beefy hands. At the first meeting she'd learned that he was an ex-military man who had watched too many of his friends die in Afghanistan. Within months of returning home, his wife and child were killed in a car accident. He went to work with his dad in the bounty hunting business, and, like many of the people in attendance, it wasn't long before his anger got the best of him and he found himself having to choose between anger management classes or jail time.

Oblivious to the power struggle right in front of her, Jinx was determined to have her say. "You people don't understand," she wailed. "Customers are returning beautifully made handbags. They just bring the merchandise back and then walk out of the store without another thought." She began sobbing, unable to go on.

Faith's head started to throb. Attending these classes seemed so pointless at times like this.

The instructor asked everyone to take a seat, her expression one of surprise when they all complied. "Everyone in this room has their own personal triggers as to what sets them off," Captain explained. She looked at Jinx. "Mind if I share your story?"

Barely able to function, Jinx shook her head.

"Jinx was abandoned as a young girl. Her triggers are self-explanatory. Anytime a shopper returns an item, she feels the pain of her own abandonment."

Sunshine didn't look impressed. Nobody did.

"We aren't here to judge one another's pain or triggers. We're simply here to listen and help one another deal with the resentment, frustration, and anger we're dealing with. Any questions?"

The room was quiet.

Rage's knee began to bounce with nervous energy.

"You're all here," Captain went on, "so you can learn to effectively deal with your anger in a calm manner. Relaxation and daily exercise is helpful. When you feel angry, I want you to count to ten and try to think about something else." She pointed to the refreshments at the back of the room. "Help yourself to cookies and punch, and we'll see you all next week."

Faith didn't waste time getting out the door. She had managed to make a website using a free site, and she was eager to get home and see if there was any response to the reward she'd offered to anyone whose tip led to finding her children. Halfway across the parking lot, she realized she'd left her backpack inside. She made an abrupt about-face and knocked into Beast. She bounced off his rock-hard chest and would have fallen over if he hadn't reached out and grabbed hold of her. Up close and personal, he appeared larger than ever, like a giant oak with gnarly branches for arms.

Making sure she had her balance, he released his hold.

Rage walked up from behind Beast and stopped at his side. The top of Rage's head barely reached his elbow. She took a bite of a cookie, spit it out, and then used her sleeve to wipe her mouth. "Gross. Don't those people taste test their shit before using us as guinea pigs?"

For half a second they all stared at one another awkwardly until Rage said, "I saw your story on the news. Sorry about your kids."

This was the first time she'd heard Rage speak without anger. The sincerity in the girl's tone surprised her. "Oh . . . thanks." She wondered if she should offer sympathy for Rage's horrible childhood, et cetera. And then she wondered what the hell was wrong with her. Of course she should offer sympathy, just as she should have offered Beth Tanner and Corrie Perelman a few simple words of comfort for their losses, too.

Faith McMann was a compassionate, caring being.

But Furious was someone else altogether. No words would come forth. Her mom was right. She was messed up. She gestured toward the building and said, "I forgot my bag inside."

"I saw your website," Rage said next. "It needs some work. I mean . . . some serious work."

"That was my first attempt. I admittedly don't have the skill set for web technology. I've never been good at that sort of thing." Faith was about to start off again, but then she remembered what Steve had said about her needing additional help. "Do you know anything about web design? Or know of anyone who does?"

Rage looked at Beast, and Faith followed her gaze.

He shook his head as if Rage had asked him a question. Faith wondered what their connection was. She guessed his age to be close to forty, and Rage had to be somewhere around twenty-five. During the first meeting Faith attended, Rage had said she was an only child, so they couldn't be brother and sister.

Faith recalled Beast saying something about being a bounty hunter. Maybe he could help her. "The truth is," Faith said, "I'm desperate to find my children, and I can't do it alone." She strained her neck as she looked up at Beast. "You're a bounty hunter—isn't that right?"

He said nothing.

"I'm fully prepared to pay you to help me." She looked from Beast to Rage. "Bounty hunters look for criminals, don't they?"

"Pretty much," Rage answered. She nudged Beast with her elbow. "I think we should help Furious find her kids."

He rubbed the back of his neck. "Looking for idiots who dodged parole is a far cry from getting involved with organized crime."

His voice was deep, baritone, every word enunciated, making him sound like a cross between Vin Diesel and James Earl Jones.

"Organized crime?" Faith asked.

"Your husband was killed, and your kids were taken. I don't think that's something your average criminal would do."

"I understand," Faith said. Clearly he wasn't interested in taking the job. A part of her was relieved, mostly because of his intimidation factor. Somebody would help her, though. Maybe she would hire a private investigator. She anchored her hair behind her ear. "OK, well, I guess I'll see you both at the next meeting."

"See you then," Rage said.

As she headed back into the building for her backpack, she could hear them arguing. Beast said something about doctor appointments, and Rage cursed and went on about how he mothered her too much and needed to stop. By the time Faith returned to the parking lot with her backpack, they were gone.

TWENTY-ONE

To get to Sacramento, Miranda transferred trains at Richmond, which cost her another twenty-seven dollars. It was five o'clock when she stepped off the train. She'd fallen asleep and almost missed her stop, but she'd finally made it back home.

She was free.

For a moment, she merely stood frozen in place, unsure of what to do next. Thirsty, she found a bathroom and drank water from the sink faucet, drank until she was full and didn't pay any mind to the people standing in line staring at her.

She removed her floppy hat. Her hair was a tangled mess, matted with blood and semen. Using a wad of paper hand towels, she cleaned herself as best she could. She hadn't realized what bad shape her face was in until she removed the sunglasses. Her bottom lip had been split open. Her left eye was discolored and swollen, making it difficult to see how much money she had left.

A total of eight dollars.

She slid on the sunglasses and the hat and then headed back out to the area where passengers waited for the next train. She spotted a pay phone but didn't bother wasting a quarter. The only number she knew was the number to the apartment where she and her mom had lived before they were thrown out on the street.

Instead she walked up to the ticket lady and asked for directions to Watt Avenue. Her next stop was a concession stand, where she bought the cheapest snack food she could find. Starved, she ate the salty chips as she walked, didn't dare stop and rest since she wasn't sure she'd be able to get back up again. The thought of going to the police had crossed her mind, but the idea of spending hours trying to explain everything that had happened and then being thrown into foster care freaked her out. What good would that do her? Her freedom wasn't something she would ever risk again.

She kept on walking. No matter how sore, no matter how tired and bruised, with each step she took she felt an overwhelming sense of gratitude that she'd actually done it. She had escaped. The first thing she planned to do was find her mom. Then she needed to find a job. She would clean toilets for the rest of her life if she had to. She would work her fingers to the bone until she had enough money to get an apartment for her and her mom. She wasn't afraid to work hard. She'd learned her lesson. Nothing came easily.

Looking up at the blue sky dotted with clouds, she thought of Dorothy in *The Wizard of Oz* and how badly Dorothy had wanted to get home. Miranda felt the same way.

And then she saw him.

Jasper.

His hands were clenched at his sides, his back straight and his expression grim as he headed down the sidewalk toward her.

She swiveled on her feet and took off running. The floppy hat flew from her head.

When he called out her name, pleading with her to stop, she ran faster. He'd come to take her back to the farmhouse. How did he find her? She cut across the street, weaved through traffic. Horns sounded.

Tears stung her eyes. She would not ever go back to that place. Never! She would fight him to the death.

Strong fingers clamped over her shoulder. Whipping about, she kneed him in the groin, then spit and clawed at his face. He stumbled but managed to grab her before she could take off again. "Stop it!" he shouted. "I'm here to help you!"

"Liar!"

He had a strong grip on both wrists. People stopped at the light watched from their cars.

"Help me!" she cried.

"Please," Jasper begged, his breathing labored. "Walk with me. My car is back that way." He gestured behind him. "We'll drive around and find a coffee shop or a restaurant where we can talk. I swear I'm not here to take you back to the farmhouse. I haven't been able to stop thinking about you since I dropped you off in San Francisco. I never should have left you there. I'm sorry. You have to believe me."

The light turned green. The cars drove onward. A woman sitting behind the wheel of her car looked concerned, but somebody honked and she moved on. They were all busy people with important things to do. No time to save a girl with a fat lip and a bruised face. "How did you know where to find me?" she asked, all the while trying to twist her arms and make him release his hold.

"I couldn't sleep last night. I was helping Diane in the kitchen when she received a call from someone letting her know you had escaped. She was frantic—afraid you would go straight to the police. Did you call the police?"

She narrowed her eyes. "Maybe."

"I told Diane I would find you and bring you back."

She bristled, tried to get free. He held tight.

"You still didn't answer my question. How did you find me?"

"You're a smart girl. I figured you would find a way to get on the train and get back to Sacramento. And I was right." He let go of one of her arms so he could reach into his coat pocket and pull out an envelope. "I knew where Diane had put the envelope of money I gave her when I returned from San Francisco."

"You stole money from Mother?" She didn't believe him. Nobody in his or her right mind would steal money from Mother, especially Jasper. This had to be a trap. She looked at the tall buildings and at the cars parked nearby to see if anyone was watching them.

"Here," he said. "Take it." He released his hold on her.

She grabbed the envelope, held it tightly in her grasp. "If you want to eat with me," she told him as she stomped off, "you're going to have to follow me on foot. I will never get into your car again."

Exasperated, he followed her just the same. "Where are we going?"

"You'll know when we get there." She didn't trust him, would never trust him or anyone else again in this lifetime. If he was being truthful and he truly intended to help her, he would have to do things her way.

TWENTY-TWO

It was Sunday. The vigil was in full force at the local high school. Twinkling lights had been wrapped around multiple tree trunks. An enormous Christmas tree, decorated with cards and prayers for Lara and Hudson, shot up a good twenty feet in the middle of the main area outside where hundreds of people had gathered to show support for Faith and her family.

Pushed against the main building were long, rectangular tables loaded with stacks of pamphlets on how best to help in cases like this. Faith's family members were making the rounds, talking to people and thanking them for coming and mostly for caring. A high school teacher stood on a podium and talked about how the community needed to do everything they could to help keep Lara and Hudson in the forefront of their minds, reminding everyone to be vigilant and keep both eyes open. "Faith and her children are a part of our family, our community," she said. "And we need to show our support by doing everything we can to bring Lara and Hudson home."

Faith stood off to the side and talked to a long line of people who'd been waiting to have their say. Teachers and students, some stoic, some tearful, approached her and offered condolences. Amanda

Higgins from Lara's class told Faith she missed Lara and had been saving her allowance. She handed Faith a pink envelope before rushing back to where her parents stood nearby. The outpouring of love and support was uplifting and did her heart well.

Across the way, over a sea of people holding flickering candles, Faith was surprised to see Beast and Rage heading her way.

"Faith McMann?" someone called from behind.

Turning toward the voice, she found herself looking into the lens of a camera.

"Hi. I'm Tammi Clark with Channel 10 News."

Tammi Clark, tall and slender with fiery red hair and flawless skin, had been doing the local news for decades. "We've been looking all over for you," Tammi said as she reached out to shake Faith's hand. "Quite a crowd you have here. I was hoping you wouldn't mind answering a few questions."

"That would be fine," Faith said.

Tammi quickly gestured for the cameraman to start shooting. Lights flashed on. "This is Tammi Clark, live in Granite Bay. I'm here with Faith McMann, an elementary school teacher who survived a brutal home invasion that resulted in the kidnapping of her two children and the vicious murder of her beloved husband."

Faith squinted into the bright lights.

"I am sorry for your loss."

"Thank you."

"Members of the community want to know—how are you holding up?" Tammi asked.

"I'm OK. All of my focus has been on finding my children," Faith said. "That's why I'm here. That's why we're all here."

"And how is the investigation going?"

"My investigation or the police investigation?"

Tammi raised a brow. "Are they not one and the same?"

"The detectives have many more resources, but we're both working hard to keep the public aware and on the lookout for Lara and Hudson."

"Do I detect bitterness?"

"Not at all."

Faith's mom approached and said, "The Placer County Sheriff's Department is doing all they can. Everyone knows layoffs were avoided last year, but budget problems continue to hurt the department."

"Not everyone who loses a child has this much support, financial or otherwise," Tammi said. "What do you say to them?"

"I send my prayers to all families of missing children," Faith said. "I share their grief. I plan to do all I can to raise awareness and funds for the Missing and Exploited Children Foundation. I've also set up a website, and I'm offering a reward of twenty thousand dollars to anyone whose tip might lead to finding my children."

Jana held up a poster showing blown-up pictures of Faith's children. The camera zeroed in on their faces. "If you've heard or seen anything at all that you think might help us to find Lara and Hudson McMann," Jana said, "please call the number posted at www.FaithMcMann.com."

"We all sympathize, of course," Tammi said. "And yet I was wondering if you could explain your sudden violence against Detective Yuhasz, an officer of the law?"

Caught off guard by the question, Faith didn't know what to say.

"Many people found what you did to be inexcusable."

"I would have to agree," Faith said.

"It's my understanding you broke the detective's nose and then bit another officer as he tried to pull you away."

Rage appeared suddenly and stepped in front of Faith and jabbed her finger at the reporter. "Are you fucking kidding me?"

"Excuse me?"

"Look around you. All these people gathered here tonight are here to help Faith McMann find her kids. She had her throat slit and then was forced to watch her husband die as her small children were crying and dragged from their home. And yet you're here to talk about her outburst?" She turned and pointed to Faith's neck. "Look at the scar zigzagging across her face, lady! I think you would be angry, too, if everything you loved was taken from you in an instant."

Tammi's mouth fell open. She looked at the cameraman, who merely shrugged and kept on filming. Tammi, it appeared, was losing control of the interview and didn't like it one bit. Her face reddened as she stepped around Rage and shoved the microphone back toward Faith. "I wanted to give you a chance to apologize to the detective."

The reporter was obviously trying to bait her. Faith counted to three before she looked into the camera and said, "I would like to offer Detective Yuhasz my sincerest apology."

Disappointment flashed across Tammi's face. Clearly she'd hoped for something more explosive, something to give her ratings a boost. "I have one last question."

Rage crossed her arms.

"Go ahead," Faith said, refusing to let the woman get to her.

"It's come to my attention that you were pregnant and lost the baby during the attack. Did your husband know you were pregnant?"

Faith paled.

Rage took a hold of Faith's elbow and ushered her away. Faith could hear her sister giving the reporter hell. When she looked over her shoulder, she saw Mom, Dad, and Colton trying to get Jana to calm down.

Once they found a bit of privacy at the far side of the school, away from the media frenzy and out of the public eye, Faith doubled over, wrapping her arms around her middle.

"That woman is a bitch," Rage told Beast when he joined them.

"I need to get out of here," Faith said as she straightened.

"Are you OK to drive?"

Faith sighed as she remembered arriving at the school with her parents. "I don't have my car." She peeked around the corner of the building and saw Tammi Clark leaving the area as the cameraman rushed to put away his gear. Mom and Dad hadn't allowed the scene to disrupt what they were there to do. They continued to work the crowd, passing out flyers and pamphlets.

"We'll take you home," Beast offered.

"Are you sure?"

"Not a problem. Come on. My truck is parked on the street."

Faith used her cell phone to call Dad and let him know she was getting a ride home and would meet them there. The night air was brisk. She tightened the belt on her coat as they walked. Beast's truck was an old Ford F-100. Faith climbed into the backseat and gave him directions to her parents' house. The only noise was the rumble of the engine.

Faith felt restless. She wasn't ready to go back to her parents' home. She wanted to go to the house she shared with Craig and the children, had a strong desire to gather some of her children's things to bring home with her. She closed her eyes, tried to sense them, breathe them in. In her mind's eye, Lara reached out for her and Hudson smiled. They were alive. She had to believe they were alive. Leaning forward, Faith said to Beast, "Would you mind taking the next right on Barton instead? If you could drop me at my house I can grab my mail and check on a few things."

Rage looked over her shoulder at her. "I thought we *were* taking you home."

"I'm living with my parents—court ordered after hitting the detective over the head with a keyboard."

"I wish I could have been there for that," Rage said. "I'm sure he deserved it."

Beast took the next right without any questions, and for the next few minutes Faith simply breathed and felt a sense of camaraderie with Beast and Rage. It didn't matter that they had known one another for only a short time. They had all suffered through terrible tragedy and had the anger to show for it.

Faith gathered her mail at the box at the end of the street. "I can walk the rest of the way and then have Mom and Dad pick me up on their way home."

"We're good," Rage assured her. "We're not leaving you here alone."

Beast parked in front of the garage. They followed Faith down the front walkway and into the house. She turned on the lights. Beast stared at the painted wall. "So these are the guys, huh?"

"Yeah." She stood next to him and stared right along with him. She had memorized every feature. In fact, every time she saw someone with the same wide-set eyes or thin, straight nose, her palms would sweat and her heart would race.

A swoosh of water sprayed against the sliding door. They all turned that way.

Rage reached for her inside coat pocket.

"It's the pool cleaner," Faith said. "Sometimes it gets stuck and then sprays the house." She headed for the sliding glass door leading to the backyard. Beast and Rage followed behind in a single line. The moon was full and bright. Just as she'd thought, the pool cleaner had gotten stuck on the stairs inside the pool.

There was another sound too—a noise she didn't recognize—a swishing followed by a creak and a grind.

Faith unlatched the gate surrounding the pool and then made her way to the stairs leading into the shallow end of the pool. A toy basketball hoop, blown over by recent winds, was lodged underneath the diving board.

"Mom! Look at me!"

Lara jumped off the diving board, doing her best imitation of a swan dive.

Faith clapped.

Hudson liked to do everything his sister did. Craig and Faith watched him run to the diving board. Instead of his usual pencil dive, he went for it. His stomach hit the water with a smack.

Faith jumped up, ready to help him, but when his little head popped out of the water, he had a grin on his face as he dog-paddled to the edge of the pool, ready to try it again.

Faith's chest tightened as the image passed through her mind. She missed her family so much it hurt.

"What's that noise?" Rage asked, bringing Faith back to the present moment.

"It sounds like your pool filter," Beast said. "Mind if I go have a look?"

"Be my guest."

Faith untangled the cleaner while Beast walked back through the gate and disappeared around the corner of the house. It wasn't long before he called out for Faith to come have a look at something. She and Rage found him kneeling down next to the pool equipment. He had unclamped and removed the casing around the filter. From the looks of it, something had been crammed inside. "What is it?"

"It looks like a plastic bag, hard to tell. I wanted you to see this before I touched anything." He grabbed a handful of thick plastic and tugged until the bag came loose. Duct tape had been wrapped around the bag. He used his pocketknife to cut it open. The floodlight on the corner of the house made it easy to see what was inside—cash. Stacks of money bound by paper bands. Faith gasped at the sight of it.

"Holy shit!" Rage said.

Beast fingered through one of the stacks of hundred-dollar bills.

Rage moved around him and tapped on a rusty metal door. "What's this?"

"The heater," Faith told her.

Rage borrowed Beast's pocketknife and used it to pry open the rusty door to the heater. Another bag. Faith looked over her shoulder, peering past the pool into the dark field of tall grass. "If they're watching us, we're dead."

They both looked at her. "If who's watching us?" Rage asked.

"The men painted on her walls," Beast said.

Rage pulled the bag from the heater unit and carried it toward the house.

"What are you doing?" Faith wanted to know.

"We need to bring this inside and see what we're dealing with here."

Beast put the pool equipment back the way it should be. Faith grabbed the other bag, and they all headed inside. No sooner had Faith locked the sliding glass door and closed the curtains than a knock sounded on the front door. *They're here,* she thought. It was over. They were all dead.

Rage pulled something from her pocket as she headed for the door.

"Is that a gun?" Faith asked.

"Yes. But don't worry. I have a right to conceal permit." She snapped her fingers. "You should get one. All I had to do was prove that I was of good moral character."

"You're kidding, right?"

Rage looked at Beast, as if she wanted confirmation that it would be OK to punch Faith in the nose.

Beast shook his head.

"Why would I be kidding?"

"Nothing," Faith said. "Never mind."

Another knock sounded.

Rage looked through the peephole and said, "It's a woman. Stocky build with short, dark hair."

Faith looked through the peephole. "My neighbor. Beth Tanner." Faith opened the door.

A rifle pointed skyward was strapped to Beth's shoulder. She looked like a soldier making her nightly rounds. Everyone seemed to have a gun except Faith.

"Is everything OK?" Beth asked. "I was about to call nine-one-one." She slid her phone into her pocket. "I saw your outside lights go on, and I didn't recognize the truck in the driveway. Have you been away?"

"I'm staying with my parents for a while. I wanted to grab the mail and check on the house, so a couple of friends brought me by to take a look around. Sorry if we disturbed you."

Beth didn't move. She wasn't convinced, which made sense considering everything that had happened. "It's OK," Faith said again. "Would you feel better if I introduced you?"

"Yes, I would," Beth said flatly.

Faith opened the door wide enough so Beth could step inside and take a look around. Faith was relieved to see that Beast had slid the bags of money behind the couch. Gesturing at her friends, Faith thought about changing their names to something like Jane and Bob, but then she sighed and said, "Beth, this is Beast and Rage. We met in anger management class . . . sort of a long story, but there you have it. Beast, Rage," she went on, "this is my next-door neighbor, Beth."

Beth looked visibly relieved. "I just saw you and your young friend," she said, pointing at Rage, "on the news. Good job putting that silly reporter in her place."

That got a half smile out of Rage.

"I'll go now," Beth said, "and let you all finish with whatever you're doing." She stopped to look at the painting on the wall. "Nice work."

"Thanks for keeping an eye out," Faith said as she walked her out to the walkway leading to her door. "I appreciate it."

Beth was halfway down the walkway, the moonlight adding a silver shimmer to her hair, when she turned back around. "Oh, one more thing. On Thanksgiving Day when you paid me a visit . . . you didn't happen to see anyone walking around Mr. Hawkins's property, did you?"

Faith shook her head.

"Mr. Hawkins said he thought maybe someone had been inside his house when he returned home, but whoever it was ran out the back door."

"Did he call the police?"

"No. He was afraid he might have been the one to leave the door open in the first place and didn't want to look like an old fool." Even in the semidarkness Faith sensed that Beth Tanner knew exactly who had been inside Mr. Hawkins's house, but she said, "Oh, well. Thought I would ask. You take care."

Relieved by Beth's apparent willingness to let it go, Faith headed back inside and locked the door behind her. "I need to check on something." She walked down the hallway and went into the office, where she turned on the computer and waited for it to load.

Where did that money come from? she wondered. Panic fell over her in waves. The search bar flashed. She typed in her password and then logged into her bank account. There was close to $5,000 in the checking account.

Nothing unusual there.

She'd checked the accounts and paid a few bills right before she'd gone to the police station and ended up being thrown in jail. She scrolled through their accounts. Everything looked fine . . . except the fact that a payment from her husband's company, H&M Investments, should have been made on Friday. It was too late to give Joe Henderson, Craig's partner, a call, but she would visit him first thing in the morning.

Thinking back to her conversation with Joe after she'd returned from the hospital, it did seem as if he'd had acted a little strange. After offering his sympathies, telling her to let him know if there was anything she needed, she'd asked him whether the police had been by, and he'd scoffed at the notion. Too quickly, she realized now. He'd seemed a bit defensive as if there would be no reason for the police to talk to him. When she'd asked him about the possibility of H&M having any disgruntled clients, he'd said he had to go, but he would call again when he had more than a minute to talk. But she had yet to hear from him. She should have gone to visit him that first day she was back on her feet.

She shut everything down and made her way back into the family room.

"There's two million dollars here," Rage told her.

Faith walked over to where they stood over the bags of money. "I have no idea how this money got here," she said, "but I think it's time to call the police."

Beast grunted. "Are you sure you want to do that?"

"I can't keep it," she said, "if that's what you're thinking. Those men were looking for something, and now I think it's safe to say we all know what that something was." She pointed at the plastic bags. "Those men killed Craig for money . . . *that* money. It's blood money, and I don't want anything to do with it."

"But what if it could help you get your kids back?" Rage asked.

Faith raked a hand through her hair. "What are you suggesting?"

"You've already offered a twenty-thousand-dollar reward. I don't know anything about your finances, but you could use these assholes' money to buy advertisements in every magazine across the country. Hell, we could have a billboard made with this kind of cash."

"We?" Faith asked. "Does this mean you two are going to help me?"

Rage rolled her eyes. "What do you think we're doing here?"

"Thank you," Faith said.

"The way I see it," Rage went on, "either you trade the money for your kids, or we use the cash to find them. It's your call."

Offer the money in exchange for her children? It sounded so simple. But how? She couldn't think, didn't know what to do. She looked at Beast with his meaty fists and Rage with her badass attitude and wondered how it had come to this. The three of them now shared a secret, a secret that could very well be the key to getting her kids back.

They couldn't leave the money here, she decided. That much was clear. And if she handed the money over to the police, they might simply throw millions of dollars into an evidence room to collect dust. And what good would that do?

"If I'm keeping this money for now, I don't want anyone to know about it, including my family. If I go down, I'm going down alone."

Beast and Rage both nodded their agreement.

Faith walked to the sliding door and peeked through the curtains. From the start she'd thought she was being watched, but she'd swept the notion aside because she worried she was being paranoid. But the truth was she'd felt eyes watching her every time she and Mom climbed into the car and drove to the police station, and then again at the end of the driveway on Thanksgiving Day. And what about when she sat in the parking lot before anger management class?

"They've been watching me," she stated firmly. She leaned over and picked up the bags of money, which weighed about twenty pounds each. "I know where to hide it."

TWENTY-THREE

Miranda ordered a big juicy hamburger with a side of onion rings, French fries, and a chocolate milk shake. Unless Jasper pointed a gun at her and demanded she give the money back, she was keeping it—all of it. She could eat whatever she wanted. She'd never once before sat in a restaurant and ordered whatever she wanted from the menu. Not before or after being taken to the farmhouse. The truth was, she'd wanted every item on the menu: the pastrami sandwich, the roast beef dip, the stack of pancakes with a side of bacon. But for now, she would stick with the hamburger. She shoved an onion ring into her mouth while she dipped a French fry into the pile of ketchup on her plate.

Jasper had ordered a tuna sandwich. *Gross.* She would never eat tuna again. Mother had made a big deal out of it every time she served them tuna sandwiches at the farmhouse, acting as if she they were dining on steak and potatoes.

"I'm not giving you the money back," Miranda said between bites.

"I don't want it back."

"Hmph."

"I am sorry for leaving you there . . . at the hotel."

"You said that already."

"Because I am. And I'm glad you got away before anything happened."

Eyes downcast, she kept eating.

He angled his head as if to take a better look. "I'm not blind. I can see you took a beating, but the bruised eye and the split lip must have happened when you ran away, right?"

A bite of hamburger. Another onion ring followed by a greasy fry. *Delicious,* she thought, although she could hardly taste a thing. As she chewed and swallowed, she brought her gaze back to his. "It's none of your business," she finally answered. "You dropped me off and left me there. I begged you not to do it, but you did—just drove off without a word, and you can never take that back. What I experienced in that hotel room is something I will never talk about . . . ever . . . not to you or anyone else. So don't ever bring it up again. Do you hear me?"

"You seem different."

She was different. She was stronger and smarter, too. And she knew exactly how she needed to handle Jasper. For more than a year she'd watched him cower whenever Mother bossed him around. If Miranda wanted to stay in control—keep the upper hand—she would need to make him believe she was in charge. "From the moment I stepped off that train," she told him, "I felt free. In here," she said, touching her head. "And in here." She put a hand over her heart. "I will never again depend on anyone but myself."

"I hope that's not true," he said. "I hope that over time you'll learn to trust others, especially me because you were right . . . I do care about you."

His words made her feel absolutely nothing. Not a stirring of happiness or even a flicker of hope. If he'd said those same words forty-eight hours ago, she probably would have melted into a gooey pile of helpless girlishness.

He pushed his plate to the side. "We need to stick together because sooner or later they're going to come looking for me and you . . . for us."

She lifted her chin a notch. "I'm not afraid. If they ever do find me, whoever they are, I'll fight them to the end."

"That's what I'm worried about."

She wiped her mouth. "First I need to find my mom."

"It'll be dark soon. Why don't we find a place to rest, and then set out in the morning?"

She pulled out the envelope and flipped through the bills as she counted. There was a little more than $2,000. It was a lot of money, more money than she'd ever seen in her lifetime, but the idea of being sold to that man for $2,000 made her want to barf. For the first time since escaping, she thought about revenge, too. If she ever saw that ugly old man again, she would find a way to make him pay for what he did. "How much is a room?"

"We can probably get a cheap motel room for forty bucks."

"I don't want to spend seventy-eight dollars for two rooms."

"I'll sleep on the floor."

She shook her head. "You can sleep in your car."

TWENTY-FOUR

The next morning Faith was peering out the bedroom window at the backyard, looking for one particular tree, when she heard the door- bell and then Rage talking to Mom downstairs. Rage had insisted on picking her up in the morning so they could visit Joe Henderson at work.

There it was—the tree fort. She could barely make out the wood shingles on the roof of the fort in the distance. After Beast and Rage had dropped her off last night, with a bag of money in each arm, she'd hurried to the backyard, trudged through tall dead grass until she came to the enormous oak set on the back of the property. The crisscross of branches had made it difficult to see the tree fort last night, a place where Colton, Jana, and Faith had spent many hours when they were kids. As she'd done when she was small, she'd used the pieces of wood nailed to the trunk to make her way to the top, then used the rope as a pulley to get the money up the tree and into the fort. It had taken some muscle, but she'd gotten the job done and with time to spare before her parents returned home.

Turning away from the window, she grabbed her things and headed downstairs. She found Mom and Rage in the kitchen. "These eggs taste delicious," Rage told her mom. "What did you put in them?"

Mom beamed. She was in her element. "Eggs, a dash of milk, scallions, mozzarella, real bacon—not any of that fake stuff they try to pawn off on people these days, and a pinch of oregano."

Faith had never seen Rage look so relaxed . . . so normal. It was nice to see.

After eating, they decided to take Faith's car, since she had a full tank of gas.

Faith turned on the engine, and they buckled up.

"You're lucky to have such a warm, caring mom," Rage told her as Faith pulled out of the driveway and onto the main road.

"You're right," Faith said. "It's easy to take that sort of thing for granted. You know . . . since she's always been there for me. I'm sorry about your mom. Do you know if she ever got the help she needed?"

Rage shook her head. "I have no idea. I can't lie and say I haven't wondered, because I have. I don't think I can handle the truth. What if she asked me to come home—you know, told me she needed me. She used to be very persuasive. Despite everything my mom has done, I love her. But it has to end there."

Faith nodded.

The drive was short. As soon as Faith pulled into the parking lot and shut off the engine, she could see that something wasn't right.

"Is your husband's business still open?" Rage asked. "The place looks deserted."

Faith said nothing. She had no idea what was going on. One lone car was parked in front of the main entrance. They climbed out. Rage followed Faith inside.

Loretta Scott, Craig and Joe's longtime administrative assistant, stood in front of a row of file cabinets and transferred files to cardboard boxes. Usually dressed in slacks and silk blouse, today Loretta wore jeans and a T-shirt. Her hair was pulled back in a plastic clip. Loretta let out a long sigh as she greeted Faith with open arms. After they embraced, Faith introduced Loretta to Rage and then looked around the room and asked, "What's going on?"

"Didn't Joe tell you?"

"After I returned from the hospital," Faith said, "Joe called to see how I was doing and let me know all was well with the business."

"Don't know about that," Loretta said sourly. "As you can see, it's been nothing but chaos around here for the last few days. First it was the police and then the FBI."

"Joe told me the police never contacted him."

"Joe has lost his mind. The police and the FBI showed up within days of Craig's death."

"Why would Joe lie to me?" Baffled by what she was seeing and hearing, Faith looked around the office.

Rage pulled a paper cup from a dispenser next to the watercooler, filled it up, then took a seat at one of the empty desks.

"Where's Joe?" Faith asked.

"Joe is missing," Loretta said matter-of-factly. "He's been missing for three days now. It was obvious after the attack that he was having a difficult time coping. He was devastated when he learned about Craig's murder, we all were, but looking back, there was something very odd about Joe's demeanor—the way he paced his office all day, coming and going without telling anyone where he was going or when he would be back."

Faith fingered some of the files. "Craig told me that Joe's wife left him. Maybe that's why he was acting strange."

"It's true," Loretta said. "Joe's wife took the kids and moved back to Texas where her family lives, but that happened three or four months ago. If anything, Joe appeared relieved after she took the kids and left."

"I still don't understand. Where is everyone?" Faith asked. "Why does it look like the business has been shut down?"

"Because that's exactly what happened," Loretta said. "If you had come here a few days ago, this place was crawling with FBI agents. It reminded me of the internal audits that were done in the past, only on a much larger scale. I gave them everything they asked for—and the next thing you know, they told us to pack up and go home because they were shutting the place down. A few others stayed and helped me get the word out to our clients. I was told not to discuss the investigation with anyone." Loretta exhaled. "It's been a very stressful time."

"So what did they find?"

Loretta lifted her shoulders. "I don't know. They wouldn't tell me. They took most of the computers and files, too. I've been instructed to box everything else and have it put into storage. I wish someone would tell me what was going on. I know they are very interested in talking to Joe."

Loretta walked to her desk, then handed Faith a business card. "Matt Jensen. He was the agent in charge. Give him a call. Maybe he can tell you more."

Faith slipped the card into her bag. "Do you have any idea at all where Joe might be?"

Loretta shook her head. "If I knew, I would tell you. Hell, I would have told the FBI, too. Joe never should have left me alone to deal with this. I haven't been paid in weeks."

Guilt rolled through her in waves as she thought of the money she'd found. "Do you think Joe knew the FBI was here?"

"You bet I do. The very first day the FBI showed up flashing their badges, I swear I saw Joe drive by. I kept thinking eventually he would grow a pair and join me in the fun, but that never happened."

Faith was abruptly struck with the realization that not only had Joe lied to her, he'd lied to her for a reason. He knew something. That's why he disappeared. He must know about the money hidden in her pool equipment, too. Faith turned back to Loretta. "Exactly how long has it been since you received a paycheck?"

She thought about it for a moment. "I haven't been paid in at least six weeks."

"That means H&M Investments was having problems prior to the attack."

"Definitely. Joe took over accounts payable after giving me a long, convoluted story about an internal audit coming up. He's the boss—what was I supposed to do?"

Rage looked at Faith and asked, "Can we get our hands on a client list?"

Loretta lifted her arms. "They took everything, computers, spreadsheets, files—you name it. The only thing left is this file cabinet filled with eight years' worth of pamphlets and brochures."

"Do you remember Craig or Joe working with any notable clients?" Faith asked.

"What do you mean—like a celebrity?"

"Not exactly. More like a mafia type . . . extremely wealthy."

Loretta put the lid on a box, then picked it up with a grunt. "Most of their clients had money, enough to retire on." She frowned. "I'm sorry, but I've been here since they opened for business and nobody has ever stood out."

"Here, let me help you." Faith took the box out of her hand.

"I'm just taking these to the car. I'll store them in my garage until we get word from the FBI." Loretta grabbed her keys, and when she did so, her mouth fell open.

"What is it?" Faith asked.

Loretta jingled her keys. "Look at this. I forget all about the flash drive on my keychain. It has everything . . . spreadsheets with a list of our clients, payroll—you name it."

Faith's pulse accelerated. She had to stop herself from getting overly excited. No need to get her hopes up too soon . . . but still, it was something. "Can I borrow that?"

"Hell, you can have it. Just don't tell anyone you got it from me."

TWENTY-FIVE

Miranda was exhausted. She'd spent the entire day walking around downtown Sacramento looking for her mom, but it was as if she'd disappeared into thin air. Old friends, like Jane Paden, the waitress who used to give them leftovers and day-old bread every morning, said she hadn't seen her mom in months.

There had been something about the expression on Jane's face that made her think she might not be telling her everything . . . like maybe she knew something but didn't want to tell her. She sat on the bed staring at the television screen, but she wasn't watching or listening to whatever show was on. If something had happened to Mom, Jane would have told her, wouldn't she? Miranda had become so distrustful, she realized; she no longer trusted anyone. Strangers on the street . . . they all looked guilty and afraid, filled with secrets. Everyone was hiding something.

Out of the corner of her eye, she caught sight of the envelope on the nightstand. The money wouldn't last long. What would she do when it was gone? She could get a job, but spending her life looking over her shoulder, waiting for a pimp or her recruiter to find her wasn't how she wanted to live. Ultimately, she needed to find her mom and get out of town—and she needed to do it fast. She'd already checked out every homeless shelter in the area. She and Jasper had looked around McKinley Park and hung out for a long while at Loaves & Fishes, but Mom never showed up.

She slid off the bed, peeked through the curtain, and saw Jasper sitting on the trunk of his car facing the road, enjoying a smoke. For the past two nights he'd slept inside his car without a single complaint. Her conscience wouldn't allow him to spend another night out there.

After grabbing the coat she'd bought at Goodwill, she shoved the envelope of money inside the pocket and headed for the front office. She would buy cookies and a soda from the vending machine and then invite him to come in out of the cold and sleep in the room on a cot.

Nobody was at the check-in counter when she entered, but she could hear a television blaring in the back room. She counted out change and then inserted the correct amount. She hit the button and watched the soda drop with a thunk.

Pop. Pop.

Gunfire!

She dropped to the ground. Heart hammering against her chest, she crawled across the floor until she had a view of the parking lot.

No!

Jasper was sprawled across the back of his car, blood dripping from his head, his arm dangling over the side. A dark figure headed across the parking lot toward her room. He walked right in. Seconds later, he rushed back outside and looked around.

He was looking for her! She rushed to the back office. The manager, half-asleep in his recliner, looked up, surprised.

"Is there a back door?"

He pointed to the next room.

"Call nine-one-one," she said, and then she ran for her life.

TWENTY-SIX

The first thing Rage and Faith did after they left H&M Investments was drive to Joe's house—a large home sitting on a quiet cul-de-sac in Rocklin. From the looks of it, Joe had done some updating since she'd been here last. The driveway had been redone with stone, and a decorative water fountain had been installed.

Faith noticed newspapers piled near the entryway. There was something taped to the door. It was a bank repossession notice. She rang the bell, waited, then knocked. She looked in the kitchen window. There was no clutter. The place looked clean. She went around to the backyard and called his name. He didn't appear to be home.

"Where do you think he's hiding out?" Rage asked when she got back into the car.

"I have no idea. The man has obviously been skimming off the top, though. Did you see that place? There was a brand-new pool in the backyard." Faith sat quietly for a moment, staring straight ahead, her hands clamped around the wheel.

"What's wrong?"

"I should have gone to see Joe sooner." Faith turned in her seat so that she was facing Rage. "Even before we found the money . . . it makes sense, doesn't it, that there must be some sort of connection to my husband and his work?"

"Until two minutes ago, when you learned that your husband's partner lied to you, there was nothing to say flat out that that money you found last night was connected to your husband's work. Absolutely nothing. This is all guesswork. Besides, you're a school-teacher, not an investigator. Cut yourself a break."

Rage was right. At least they were making progress. She just needed to stay focused and take it all one day at a time.

"Should we go see what's on that flash drive?"

"I think that's a good idea." Faith gave Joe's sprawling house one last look before driving off, wondering where he might be. He used to talk to Craig about fishing every once in a while. She also recalled him mention hiking Mount Tallac, but other than that, her mind was a blank when it came to Joe Henderson.

Once they returned to the command post in Faith's parents' backyard, they got right to work going through the files on the flash drive. There were a total of eighty-two names. They Googled every name, looking for anything that might stand out: money, family, career.

Exhausted after a long day of running around followed by hours of Internet searches, Faith blew out enough air to push strands of hair out of her face. "I really don't know what the hell we're looking for, but from what I've seen so far, there's nothing out of the ordinary here. Nothing is standing out."

"Same here," Rage said as she stretched her arms above her head. "I haven't found anything unusual."

There was a knock on the door. Rage walked across the room and let Beast inside.

"Are you two ready to go?" he asked.

The plan was to talk to Teague Fowler, the local pedophile on record. Faith's eyes were beginning to cross from looking at the computer for so long. She pushed herself to her feet, anxious to question Fowler. It could be another dead end, but it was something she needed to see for herself.

On their way out, they ran into Jana, who had taken an early leave of absence from work so she could help Mom take Dad to his therapy sessions. After Faith introduced everyone, Jana told them about all the calls that had come in on the hotline number posted on Faith's website and flyers. "I'm still sorting out some of the tips," she said, "but twenty-five percent of the messages appear to be pranksters. The rest are mostly well-meaning people who probably call in every time they see a kid crying in the grocery store. One message looked promising."

Faith brightened. "Really? What did they say?"

"One of the callers was positive she'd seen Lara and Hudson at a local Walmart, so I forwarded it to the police." Jana shook her head and added, "Authorities checked security video, though, and it wasn't them." She sighed. "I'll give you a call if anything else comes up, OK?"

They headed for the truck. Rage sat in the passenger seat, and Faith climbed into the backseat.

"Were you able to talk to your husband's partner?" Beast asked as they drove off.

"Rage and I went to the office earlier," Faith told him. "It turns out Joe Henderson lied to me about the police never contacting him. He's been missing for three days, which tells me he might very well know the reason as to why those men came to the house."

"The feds shut down her husband's investment business," Rage added. "They sent all the employees home and confiscated computers and files."

"But we were lucky enough to get our hands on a flash drive with a list of client names," Faith said.

Rage made a face. "It's basically a dump of basic customer data that their administrative assistant kept in case the computer ever failed. You know, client name, when they signed up, beginning and ending account balance. That sort of thing."

"Find anything of interest?"

Rage grunted.

"Nobody stands out," Faith said. "I called Joe's ex-wife, but she has no idea where he could be. I think the police and FBI have a better chance of finding him. And when they do, I definitely need to have a talk with him."

"I think that's a good idea. Let the police handle Joe Henderson so we can stick with our plan. After we visit the pervert, we need to check out a few tattoo shops downtown, see if anyone recognizes the symbol you saw. Next we'll distribute flyers with the images of the men who attacked your family, get the word out that we're looking for the thugs who took your kids."

Faith exhaled, her thoughts still on the money and the idea that Craig could have been involved in any way. He never would have stolen money from a client or the company he helped build from the ground up. And if he were to hide money, he never would have hidden it in the pool filter. Just like he never would have driven his car onto the grass. There were certain things Craig never would have done . . . stealing was only one of them.

The light turned green, but the white Honda in front of them didn't move. Beast threw the gear into Park, then climbed out of the truck and made his way to the car in front of them. He reached inside the window, took the cell phone right out of the woman's hands, and broke it in two.

A honk sounded behind them.

"What's going on?" Faith asked.

"He broke her phone in half, and now the woman is being lectured about texting while driving."

"He's done this before?"

Rage snorted. "Oh, yeah."

A minute later Beast was behind the wheel and they were on the road again, the phone incident forgotten. "When we get to Fowler's house," Beast said, his voice gruffer than before, "Rage and I will stand back while you knock on the door. If he sees me standing on the other side, he'll never open it."

Faith nodded as she wondered what she'd gotten herself into.

The house was a one-story set back on an acre of land. Everything about the place seemed eerily deserted. Weeds had overtaken the front yard; dead vines choked the mailbox as if nobody had lived on the property for years.

Faith walked up to the door and knocked three times.

When there was no answer, she knocked again with much more force.

Footsteps sounded.

The door opened a few inches. It was dark inside, hard to see the man standing in the shadows. "Hello," Faith said. "Are you Teague Fowler?"

"Who wants to know?"

"I need a few minutes of your time to talk to you about—"

Before she could finish her sentence, Beast came out of hiding, stepped in front of her, and shouldered his way inside.

"What's going on?" Fowler asked as he stumbled backward. "What do you think you're doing?"

Now that Faith could see him better, she recognized the man from his picture on the pedophile website. His thick blond hair was swept neatly to one side. All in all, he was a regular-looking guy with green eyes and well-maintained facial hair. Throw him into a lineup and she never would have pegged him as a pedophile, a disturbing thought considering she knew better than to judge character based on looks.

"We're going to take a look around," Beast informed the man. "We want to make sure you've been behaving yourself."

Fowler pointed at Faith. "I saw you on TV. You're the one whose kids were taken."

"Are they here?" Rage asked as she opened a coat closet, shoved sweatshirts and coats aside, and took a good look inside.

"Who?" He snorted. "You think her kids are here?"

About to take a look around, Faith stopped and glanced over her shoulder, waiting to hear what Fowler had to say.

"I have no idea where her kids are. I want to see some ID. Never mind," he said. "I'm calling the police."

"Sit down!" Beast growled.

Red in the face, Fowler plopped down onto the sofa.

"Come on," Rage said as she headed past Faith. "Let's get this over with."

Something niggled deep within, something telling Faith that Beast and Rage had done this before.

"You can't just rifle through my things," Fowler shouted after them.

"Sit still and be quiet," Beast warned. "If they don't find anything, we'll walk out that door and it'll be as if we were never here."

Faith followed Rage into what she assumed to be the master bedroom. The entire house had a musty smell and was cluttered with knickknacks. The bed was unmade, and clothes littered the floor.

Rage disappeared inside a walk-in closet while Faith headed for the bathroom. *Disgusting.* The bathtub and toilet were covered in grime. She worked fast, opening drawers and cupboards, just as she had done at Mr. Hawkins's house, searching for any sign that her kids had been there. Her stomach roiled.

Rage stood in the doorway. "Nothing in the bedroom. Are you OK?"

"I'll be fine. Nothing in here, either."

They checked through two more bedrooms, the kitchen, and then the laundry room.

No children. No hints of any wrongdoing.

Rage disappeared inside the garage and returned with a shoe box. Walking past Faith, she went back to the main living area and turned the box upside down on the sofa next to Fowler. Pictures cascaded out of the box, sliding onto the floor into a pornographic puddle. "He's got a camera, an old mattress, and kids' toys in the garage," Rage said. "All kinds of sick goodies set up in there, where many of the pictures appear to have been taken."

Beast leaned over and picked up a glossy photo of a naked, scared young boy. As he looked at the photo, Faith saw his facial features transform. His skin tightened, and the muscles beneath his jaw slid from side to side as if he was grinding his teeth. His nostrils didn't instantly flare, but instead slowly worked their way open as he drew in a breath the way a dragon might before it released a stream of fire. His eyes grew dark and round, and she noticed an almost imperceptible twitch in the creases of his eyelids. It all happened in a flash, and yet ever since she'd watched Craig die, she'd been hyperaware of movements and sounds, as if certain events played out in slow motion.

Sensing disaster, Fowler scrambled from his seat. Tripping and falling, he eventually made it down the hallway to his bedroom. The door slammed shut behind him. She heard the lock click into place.

As Beast straightened, his massive shoulders appeared broader, the veins in his neck thicker. A scar Faith hadn't noticed before appeared like a thick white rope across the left side of his jaw. His hands rolled into fists; his knuckles were padded with scars.

Rage stepped out of his way.

He went to the kitchen and ripped the phone line from the wall, then made his way to the bedroom down the hall where Fowler had disappeared. Each angry footfall echoed off the walls. Before she could figure out how he planned to get inside the bedroom, his solid fist shot through the door like a battering ram. Wood cracked and splintered as he shoved his arm far enough inside so he could turn the knob and let himself in.

Fowler's high-pitched screams sent chills through Faith's body. She ran that way, but Rage caught up to her and stopped her. "Let Beast do his thing. He won't kill the man."

"How can you be sure?"

"Teague Fowler won't get any more, or any less, than he deserves. Come on. Let's go wait for him in the car."

TWENTY-SEVEN

Miranda brushed her newly dyed wet hair down over her eyes. Then she picked up the scissors and cut her bangs straight across her forehead, right above her eyebrows. She snipped the length next, cutting it an inch under her chin. Long pieces of moon-white hair fell to the floor and into the sink. She took her time getting all the stragglers, then set the scissors down. The next five minutes were spent carefully lining her eyes with the black kohl pencil she'd bought at the drugstore. Dark lipstick came next. Before exiting the bathroom, she took a good, long look at herself.

They would never recognize her. Nobody would.

After cleaning up, she went to the bed, picked up the remote, and shut off the TV. The motel she was staying in was better than the last one. At sixty-five dollars a night, she couldn't stay very long. But she'd needed a safe place where she could change her looks without worrying about some dude with a gun knocking down the door.

She put on the jeans she'd bought from a secondhand store. They felt soft against her skin. Long-sleeved cotton shirt, socks, boots, coat.

Last she slid the strap of a worn leather bag over her shoulder, then gathered garbage and any evidence of her ever being there.

One last sweep over the room and she was ready to go.

———

After leaving Fowler to lick his wounds, Beast, Rage, and Faith drove to the Red Ink Tattoo Parlor in West Sacramento. Not the best area, but the place was clean.

A tattoo artist, a thin man with long, brown hair, sat on a stool as he worked on a woman's back. Her skin was red and raw. He used a needle connected to a long tube and a foot pedal. The machine sounded like a dental drill. Another man, who supposedly worked at the parlor but who wasn't the least bit interested in customer service, used an elbow to support most of his weight on the glass counter as he flipped through a comic book. He didn't bother sparing them a glance until Rage walked up to him and showed him the picture of the tattoo Faith had painted.

"Where do you want it?"

"I don't. We were hoping you could tell us where the tattoo might have been done."

He smelled like chewing tobacco, and he had a cemetery tattooed on the side of his face, complete with little grave markers that read, "RIP." "Like looking for a needle in a haystack," he said. "But I'll tell you this—if that picture is at all accurate, it's amateurish work. Nothing more than a symbol or a fancy letter. My guess is that it could be the letter *A, H, K,* or *R.*"

They thanked him and moved on. From there, they took to the streets, hanging flyers and showing anyone who would take a look the pictures of Lara and Hudson along with a photograph of the two men Faith had painted on the wall. A few people appeared concerned and took a flyer, but most were uninterested, making it clear they had problems of their own. One girl with short white hair and too much kohl smeared around her eyes had looked frightened when Faith shoved the picture in her face, but she took the flyer anyhow and walked off in a hurry. There were also the exceptions—the people who pretended to know something in hopes they would be paid for information. Like the elderly woman who walked hunched over and who'd been following Faith around for the past thirty minutes, grabbing her arm and poking at her side with a crooked finger as she talked about her horrible life and asked for a handout.

Across the street, Faith saw Rage yelling at a man with long hair and a bushy mustache, ready to jump him before the guy wisely slunk off. A few feet away, Beast picked up a guy by the front of his shirt and pressed him against a graffiti-covered wall outside a liquor store, cursing him up and down while his girlfriend beat her fist against Beast's back.

Faith sighed. Clearly her new friends had picked their nicknames for a reason. At this rate, she could end up back in jail, and then how would she ever find her children? But then again, who else would be so willing to help her? It was simply time to call it a day. "Listen," Faith said, turning to face the woman who had yet to stop poking her. "I already gave you my last ten dollars. And you gave me nothing in return. I'm going to ask you one more time to please leave me alone."

"For someone who wants answers," the old woman muttered, "you're not a very good listener."

"Are you kidding me?" Faith's temper flared. "You've told me your whole life story. Your husband died of AIDS, and you haven't seen your kids in who knows how long because you chose the needle over your family. You had a shitty childhood and more than anything in the world, you need a hit of heroin or meth or whatever the hell your drug of choice is because you're getting all wobbly in the knees and your eyes look like they're ready to pop out of your head." Faith stopped, took a breath, pushed hair away from her face. What was she doing? Why was she yelling at this poor woman? She used to take her kids to visit an old folks' home because she wanted to teach them how their elders should be treated . . . with respect. "I'm sorry," she said. "Forgive me. It's been a rough day."

The woman continued to stare at her. There was no fear in her craggy old face. No emotion at all. It was true. The woman had made bad choices and lost everything along the way. She had nothing left but tattered memories and a craving for any chemical substance that might keep the pain at bay for one more day, maybe only an hour. Faith was about to walk off when the old woman reached out once more and said, "I also wanted to tell you I've seen that man before."

Faith's brow furrowed. "What man?"

"The one in your picture." She pointed a finger at the flyer in Faith's hand. "The one with the curly hair and pointy, birdlike nose."

Cheap perfume, stale smoke, and forgettable music filled the air at Dinah's Place, the seedy strip club where the hunchback woman had said she'd seen the curly-haired man a few short weeks ago. It was a sordid little place: dark and hungover. Although they didn't serve alcohol, there was a bar next door. Convenient.

They found a table close enough to the door where they could ask customers coming and going if they recognized the curly-haired man in the picture. It had been a long day. It was nearing midnight, and Faith's throat was sore from breathing in secondhand smoke. A young woman in the back of the room was giving lap dances to patrons. Her movements were robotic, her eyes a blank stare.

The man she was dancing for glanced Faith's way. He looked familiar. Picture in hand, she walked that way, taking a closer look at the customers as she went.

"Piss off," someone told her.

"Twenty dollars for a blow job," a man sitting at the bar offered.

At closer view, she realized she'd never set eyes on the man before.

She continued on, determined to check the place thoroughly, making double sure the curly-haired man they were looking for wasn't there before she left.

"Time for you and your friends to leave."

Faith turned around and found herself face-to-face with a slender male. His black hair was slicked back with gel. His mustache was a thin, dark line above his upper lip. She assumed he was the manager since she'd seen him ordering people around.

"I'm looking for someone," Faith explained as she showed him the picture she was carrying.

"Never seen him before. Unless you're buying a lap dance, sweetie, you need to make yourself scarce."

Ignoring him, she continued on her original path.

He grabbed her arm and squeezed so hard she felt his fingernails dig into her skin through her shirt.

"Ouch."

Beast appeared, his eyes dark and foreboding as he grabbed hold of the man's wrist. Faith swore she heard a bone crunch. The manager grimaced.

"We're going to take a look around," Beast explained. "I'm sure you don't mind."

Beast let go of the man's wrist and then proceeded to escort her to the back, watching over her as she checked the faces of every man and woman in the place. Beast explored the men's restroom while she checked inside the ladies' room.

All clear, nothing to see here, Faith thought as she exited the restroom.

Rage waited for them at the door, and together the three of them made their exit.

Instead of heading for his truck, Beast's attention was on a customer who had exited the bar next door and was now staggering across the street toward his car. His body swayed as he dug into his pocket for a key.

Beast crossed the street. Without a word said, he took the drunken man's keys from him and tossed them onto the roof of a nearby building. The guy bitched and complained, every word slurred as Beast pulled his phone from his pocket and made a call.

"He's calling the guy a cab," Rage said as if she'd seen it a hundred times before.

Faith recalled hearing Beast's story in anger management class . . . how he'd returned from war only to lose his family. "I know Beast lost his wife and daughter in an accident. Do you know what happened?"

Rage nodded. "The driver, an eighteen-year-old female, had been texting her boyfriend."

That explained his anger over the driver he'd caught texting, Faith thought.

"The girl survived," Rage went on, "and was charged with assault. Beast requested she travel to schools in the area to talk to students about texting while driving, but nope, she didn't want to do that. Instead she served six months in jail and paid a fine. A real pisser if you ask me."

Faith watched as Beast settled a beefy hand on the drunken man's bony shoulder and led him to the curb to take a seat while they waited for the cab.

"I should get home," Faith said.

"What about the curly-haired dude with the big nose?"

"I'll have to come back. It's past my curfew."

"Curfew? As in be home before a certain time?"

"It's part of the deal I made with the judge. I'm supposed to be home by ten o'clock every night."

Rage snorted. "We should probably all go. You're all set up on Instagram and Twitter, and I was able to link Amber Alerts to your Facebook page, but I still have some work to do on your website."

"I appreciate all you've done. Let me know what I owe you."

Rage waved off any talk of money. "If sex traffickers are involved," she said, "we might want to hang out on Watt one of these nights and talk to some of the girls who do business there—see if they know anything."

"Good idea," Faith said. "After class this week?"

"Sure. Miniskirt, tank top, and heels so we blend in."

"I'll try to put something together."

"Yeah, and do something with your hair. You know . . . no pony-tail. And maybe a little eyeliner."

Faith grimaced. "Anything else, boss?"

She gave her a once-over. "Hmm . . . maybe a push-up bra would help."

TWENTY-EIGHT

Through tinted windows, Richard Price saw more than one pedestrian running to catch the light rail around the corner. Across the street, a man he didn't recognize opened the door to Bill's Liquor Store off Del Paso Road and disappeared inside.

He had his brother to thank for dragging him into this godforsaken business. Growing up, he and Randy had never seen life through the same lens. While Randy got high with his friends and sold drugs on the street corner, Richard put himself through law school and became a public defender, fighting for the inalienable rights in the Constitution. Richard made sure the French-speaking murderer went free because the cops failed to read him his rights in his native tongue, and he stood by the beautiful young woman who'd robbed the old lady next door of her life's savings. Long hours in a cockroach-infested office finally took its toll, and when his brother, now living the life of luxury in a million-dollar condo with a view of downtown and the Capitol dome, suggested to Richard that he come over to the dark side, or should he say "darker" side, Richard jumped at the chance.

And so here he sat five years later in his brand-new Mercedes. He had it all—a flashy office, a big house, a beautiful girlfriend . . . so why the hell did he feel so damn helpless and depressed? Sadly he knew the answer. Because he'd become one of them . . . one of the guilty parties he used to defend. And he didn't like it one bit. He wanted out. This wasn't a Hollywood movie. He knew of other people who'd found creative ways to get out of the business. There had to be a way. He just needed time to come up with a plan.

He straightened and glanced at the clock. Time to go.

He wasn't looking forward to talking to Aster. But he'd put off this meeting long enough. Bells clanked as he pushed open the door. The young kid behind the cash register gave him a subtle nod of his chin as Richard made his way to the back of the store. The place smelled like cigars and Johnnie Walker Red. He had to shimmy his way through high stacks of boxes to get to the door to the back room.

He knocked twice, waited, then entered a smoke-filled room. He always thought it was strange that his boss conducted business in the back of a liquor store instead of a pricey high-rise or an office building closer to his home in El Dorado Hills, but who was he to question these things?

Aster sat at a massive library desk made of solid oak set squarely in the middle of the room. His work area was a mess, piled high with stacks of papers and overfilled ashtrays. The other guy, the one Richard had seen enter the store a few minutes ago, patted him down.

He didn't like being touched, especially by a simple thug in ratty clothes who was probably hired right off Craigslist. "Nobody dresses up anymore?" he asked.

Surprisingly, Aster pushed himself to his feet, came around his desk and met him halfway. He clapped him on the back and then introduced him to his friend Patrick.

Aster had gained a few pounds since he'd last seen him. The boss's face was getting jowly. Two necks had become three. He kept his gaze on Aster's eyes, which wasn't easy considering the caterpillars he had for eyebrows.

"Take a seat," Aster said as he walked back to his chair.

Richard smoothed out his tailored suit, pulled out a thick envelope from the inside coat pocket, and set it on Aster's desk. Then he took a seat on one of two spindle-backed chairs and tried to get comfortable before giving up.

"Have you found the money?" Aster wanted to know.

He shook his head.

"And what are you doing about it?"

"We're keeping an eye on the woman, but so far she hasn't been much help."

"What about her husband's partner? Have you talked to him?"

"He's vanished. We don't know where he is, but we're looking for him." He didn't have the heart or the balls to tell Aster that the feds were also looking for the guy.

"Bottom line," Aster said, "your men failed to deliver. For weeks, because I respect you and the work you do, I've looked the other way. But I can't ignore it any longer. Now that the McMann woman has recovered, she's becoming a nuisance. Isn't that right, Patrick?"

"It's true. She's everywhere."

Richard loosened his tie. "What do you mean *everywhere*?"

"Are you serious?" Aster looked at Patrick, who merely shrugged.

"The McMann woman invited reporters and cameraman right into her living room to look at a painting she did of your idiot men on her fucking wall! It might have served you well to tell the idiots to wear a fucking mask. To make matters worse, the crazy bitch picks up a computer keyboard and bashes it over a detective's head." Aster's face was red, and his jowls were flapping. "The woman knows how to stay in the news! But that's not good enough; she somehow befriends a fucking giant and another bitch crazier than her, and they all make a spectacle at that candlelight vigil thingy."

Aster had worked himself into a tizzy, spittle flying from his lips like hot oil. "That woman is determined to find her kids, and she's asking the whole damn world for help. She's gotten thousands of likes on that site where teenagers like to hang out."

"Facebook?"

"Yeah, and the others, too," Patrick said.

Aster waved his fat fingers through the air and sort of hunched over his desk as if he'd worn himself out. "All that social media crap is for the birds. Waste of time, but millions of people seem to like it just fine. And that's a problem."

Richard raised his eyebrows. "What's she going to find on Facebook?" He shook his head. "Is that why you called me here?"

Aster grimaced. "The point is, the McMann woman is making a fuss—a big fuss. She's making sure everyone sees the picture she painted of the two fucking idiots who killed her husband and took her kids."

"I've seen it," Richard said. "There's no likeness to my men whatsoever. Nobody would recognize them from one of those paintings."

"Patrick disagrees."

Was Aster married to Patrick? Who was this guy?

"If she locates one of the idiots you've got working for you, they could connect them to you, and then to me. Get the picture? That would mean trouble," Aster continued. "And if there's one thing I try to steer clear of, it's trouble."

"Listen," Richard explained calmly, despite his growing irritation. "They've been laying low for a while now. They're out of the public eye. No one is going to see them."

Aster shook his head, and his jowls followed suit. "Not good enough. I want them out of the country by next week."

"Can't do. They're two of my best."

Aster laughed. "Two of your best? Seriously? Those guys were your best?" Before Richard could answer, he pounded a fist on his desk. "I'm not asking you. I'm telling you." The lines in his face deepened. "Don't piss me off, Richard! This whole thing is fucked up. I can't do anything with these kids right now, not with their pictures all over the place. I don't need your guys anywhere in the city. In fact, I don't want them anywhere near the Sacramento airport, either. I want both your men driven to Arizona and flown out of the fucking country."

"For Christ's sakes, you've got to be kidding me."

"This is no joke."

"For how long?"

"Until I tell you otherwise."

Frustrated, Richard started to stand.

"That's not all," Aster said.

Teeth clenched, Richard forced himself back into the chair. It took everything he had within to remain seated.

"Patrick here is going to keep an eye on McMann and report back to me every few days."

"Jesus."

"If she's doing anything that makes me uncomfortable, you'll be the first to know."

"Sure. Fine. I'm not worried. How much trouble could one little schoolteacher cause anyhow?"

Twenty-Nine

Whenever Faith couldn't sleep, she got on the computer and immersed herself in the world of human trafficking. As she clicked through various websites, she found another victim's account of her experience. She read it slowly, looking for clues that might somehow help her find her kids.

> I was transported to Sacramento and immediately taken to a run-down house and locked in a small room. The windows were boarded up and I couldn't get out. When my boss returned a few days later, I was cold and hungry. He told me I would be working as a prostitute. I told him he had the wrong person and that I had only come to serve food and drinks at a restaurant. He said I owed him for transportation costs and I needed to work off my debt before I could leave. I fought him, and he beat me. Every day after I was physically and verbally

abused. There were other girls, too. The
guards abused us if we argued with them.
If we refused to be with a customer, we
were beaten. If we adamantly refused, they
brutally raped us, one after the other, to
teach us a lesson. We worked seven days
a week, twelve hours each day. Our bodies
were bruised and swollen. If anyone became
pregnant, we were forced to have abortions.
The cost of the abortion was added to our
never-ending debt. The torture continued for
six months; other women were enslaved for
much longer. The enslavement ended when
law enforcement raided the brothels and
rescued us. I don't understand the people
who do this to us—the recruiters, the pimps,
and worst of all the johns, businessmen who
come from all walks of life, monsters in suits
who keep the nightmare alive and well.

The next day as Faith sat in the passenger seat of her sister's car, she couldn't get the young girl's story out of her head. She always thought things like this happened somewhere else, somewhere far, far away. To think there were thousands of girls and boys trafficked in America every year boggled the mind.

After Jana dropped her off at Firestone, a restaurant in Midtown, Faith thanked her and then reminded her that Rage would be picking her up.

Inside, Faith found Marion Carver, an advocate for antitrafficking, sitting at a booth by the window. Faith introduced herself before sliding into the seat across from her.

"I've seen you on the news recently," Marion said. "I'm hoping for a speedy return of your children."

"Thank you."

"Why don't we order and then get started? I have to be back to work shortly." Marion called the waitress over. After they ordered, she said, "So, you've met my daughter?"

Faith nodded. "She's a smart young woman who's very proud of her mother."

"Thank you. Emily has a way to go, but I'm doing everything I can to get her the help she needs." She sipped her water. "What is it exactly you would like to know?"

"Emily told me the story about her abduction, and I was hoping you could shed some light on sex trafficking in the area."

"First off you should know it's rare that traffickers risk going into one's home to remove a child."

"But it happens."

"Yes, Emily is proof of that. Did Emily mention the young woman who befriended her at school?"

Faith shook her head.

"The woman was a recruiter—about twenty years of age although she did her best to appear much younger. She knew enough about Emily to know that my daughter was vulnerable. Her father and I were fighting back then. He'd moved out of the house at the time, and Emily wasn't happy with either one of us. When Emily failed to meet with the young woman as planned, she, along with a male friend, came to the house and took Emily right from her room."

Marion reached across the table for Faith's hand. "If your children were taken by human traffickers, it's my opinion that the people who took them had a personal vendetta against you or your husband."

The money, Faith thought. They had come for the money. "I must find my children. I'll do whatever it takes." Faith looked into Marion

Carver's eyes. "The truth is, I was hoping you might know the names of some of these pimps and the men they work for."

Marion rubbed the back of her neck. "I wish I could give you a list of names, but unfortunately the names and faces are constantly changing. We catch one and another pops up. These guys are always rotating, always moving. They stick together for the most part, and we have no idea who they're working for. That's why many of us focus on helping the victims."

The waitress brought their food. After she left, Carver said, "Sacramento has definitely become a hot spot for trafficking. It's convenient for traffickers to transport their victims along Interstates 80 and 50."

Faith nodded. "I've done some research. It seems to be out of control."

Marion wiped her mouth with her napkin. "It's become so lucrative that gangs are joining together in order to maximize profits made purely off selling young women."

"How do you stop these guys?"

"One recruiter and one pimp at a time. Prop Thirty-Five increased penalties for traffickers, and it's a good start, but it's not enough." She reached into her case and slid a list of statistics across the table toward Faith.

No longer hungry, Faith read it over while Marion ate. The United States was one of the top three destination points for trafficked victims; it was estimated that sixty thousand men and women were being held in underground brothels, which didn't take into account sweatshops or other domestic slavery positions; the average age of a trafficked woman was twelve to fourteen. The list was never ending.

Faith looked at Marion. "If there's even a slim chance that they have my kids, I need an idea of where they might be right now."

"They would be in lockdown," she said matter-of-factly. "Probably in a commercial establishment with security or an isolated location. The persons in charge usually operate under the guise of any number of establishments—massage parlors, escort services, restaurants, adult bookstores, bars, and strip clubs."

Faith's heart dropped to her stomach. At times like this it all felt so overwhelming, like searching for a lost ring on a long stretch of beach.

"Keep doing what you're doing. Talk to the media whenever you can. Keep the focus on your kids." Her cell phone buzzed. "Looks like my time's up," Marion said. She tried to pay the bill, but Faith wouldn't let her. Marion pushed herself out of the booth and said, "I'd like to talk to you further and offer additional resources. Maybe you can come to my office." She handed Faith a business card. "Whatever you do, don't ever lose hope."

———

Faith exited the restaurant. As planned, Rage sat in an old Jeep parked across the street waiting for her. She looked at her phone, hoping to see a return call from Joe Henderson. She'd called his house more than once and left a message with his mother-in-law and his brother, numbers she'd found on her computer contact list. She opened the passenger door, climbed in, and buckled her seatbelt.

"How did it go?"

"Marion Carver is an amazing woman."

"But?"

"But I have to wonder how they'll ever put a dent in trafficking, let alone put an end to it. One pimp at a time . . . it seems so damn imposs—"

"What is it?" Rage asked when Faith didn't continue.

As Rage pulled out of the parking space and into traffic, Faith noticed a dark sedan three cars back, the same car she'd spotted when she'd first exited the restaurant. "I think we're being followed."

"Where? Who?" The car weaved slightly when Rage tried to get a good look in the rearview mirror.

Faith's heart beat faster. "There's two men. I can't make out the license plate number, though. What if they're armed? What should we do?"

"We need to stay calm," Rage told her. "I've done ride-alongs with Beast and his dad. I have an idea. Get ready to take a picture using your phone. I'm going to pull over, and when they drive by, take a photo."

Faith rolled down her window, then reached inside her bag and fumbled around with the phone until she finally had it ready. "OK, I'm ready." Her heart was racing.

Rage pulled over to the side of the road.

The car sped past them. The driver looked their way.

Click. Click. Click.

"I think I got him."

Rage waited a few minutes before she merged back onto the road. Driving steadily, she got onto the highway and adjusted the rearview mirror.

"Do you see them?"

Rage peered into her rearview mirror. "I do. They must have pulled over and then followed us onto the freeway."

Faith leaned closer to the side mirror, trying to get a good look at the men.

"Do you recognize them?"

"No. They're too far away."

"Use your phone to get directions to the nearest police station."

"Good idea," Faith said. According to the app, the closest station was downtown. "You need to take the next exit. We're going to have to circle back the way we came."

Rage did as she said, and then, without warning, she made a sharp right. The wheel hit the curb, jolting them forward before she made a wide, yet efficient, U-turn into a car wash. She sped past the ticket stand, pulled into the semidarkness of the washing tunnel, and hit the brakes. An automated voice told her to back up, but Rage ignored it and stayed right where she was.

"There they are!" Rage said. "It's a green Chevrolet Impala. First three digits are 6MB!"

"S2," Faith added. "That's all I could see." Frustrated, she pulled a pen and a scrap of paper from her purse and quickly wrote down *6MBS2*. "We're missing two numbers."

They sat quietly for a moment. Faith looked at the pictures she'd taken. "Damn. The photos are blurry."

"Let's go visit Beast at home," Rage suggested.

Faith raised a questioning brow.

"He and his dad are bounty hunters—remember? They have connections."

"What about heading for the police station?"

"We've lost them. No reason to go there now. Beast and his dad will know what to do."

THIRTY

Miranda's legs felt as if they were on fire, every muscle and joint aching. She didn't know what else to do, where else to look. She'd spent most of the day walking along the bamboo, grasses, and oaks that lined the Sacramento River where she and her mom had lived on and off for months. Groups of homeless people, denizens of the riverfront, still huddled together here and there, but it was as if Mom had vanished.

"Rita . . . Rita Calloway, is that you?"

Stunned that anyone might recognize her after her makeover, she didn't dare turn around. She kept on walking, waiting to feel the sting of a bullet in the back of her head.

"Rita, it's me, Calvin!"

Calvin? When she and her mom had no choice but to live on the streets, it was the old man Calvin who had shown them the safest place to sleep and where they could find food.

Miranda whipped about. It was the first familiar face she'd seen in forever. Tears streamed down her face as she ran straight into his arms. He wrapped warm arms around her and held her close. "Where have you been?" he asked. "We've been looking for you."

"Calvin, my God, it's been a long time." She stepped back and used the sleeve of her jacket to wipe her eyes. "Where's Mom? She didn't sell me to those people, did she?"

"What people? What are you talking about?" He looked worried.

"A woman offered me a job and brought me to a farmhouse and wouldn't let me go. It's a long story," she said as she looked back toward the people huddled near the river. "I've been to hell, Calvin, but I escaped. And more than anything, I need to see Mom."

"Oh, dear child, I guess you haven't heard?"

"Heard what?"

"Your mom done passed away." He shook his head. "Two short weeks ago."

Her heart skipped a beat. "Passed away? How? What happened?"

"Come on," he said. "Let's walk. They'll be serving brown beans and sausages at the shelter today. I'll tell you everything I know."

Miranda and Calvin sat at one of many long, rectangular tables set up to feed the homeless. There was a cacophony of sounds: the honking of horns outside, pots and pans clanging together in the kitchen, people talking all at once, kids playing chase.

Calvin ate and talked while Miranda listened in a daze, pushing the beans around on her plate. She'd known her mom was sick—she'd been sick, it seemed, for as long as she could remember. But dead? It couldn't be true.

"I don't know what this is you heard about your mom selling you to the devil, but I can tell you it's not true. That woman was sick as can be, but that didn't stop her from going in search of you, every single day, morning till night, until her legs couldn't carry her another step."

Miranda wiped her eyes. Caroline, Mother, and even Jasper had robbed her of being with her mom in her final moments. She would never again have the chance to tell her mom that she loved her. She didn't even get to say goodbye. She felt dizzy with emotions.

How could she possibly move on with her life? *What now?*

She thought of Adele and Jean and all the other girls she'd left behind, then remembered the flyer. She retrieved it from her pocket and smoothed it out on the table.

"Are you gonna eat that?" Calvin asked, pointing to the food still left on her paper plate.

"No, you go ahead."

He put her plate on top of his empty one and dug in while she stared at the piece of paper in front of her.

MISSING: Lara and Hudson McMann.

The little boy had a mop of brown hair and freckles across his nose. She hadn't seen any small boys at the farmhouse, and there was nothing familiar about his face. Her gaze swept to the right-hand corner where a little girl with long, blonde hair stared back at her.

It was Jean.

Sitting quietly for a moment as Calvin ate, she realized she would have to push her grief aside if there was any hope of keeping her promise to Jean and helping her and the other girls escape. She needed to find a phone and make a call.

"I've got to go, Calvin." Leaning over, she wrapped her arms around him. "Thanks for being there for Mom when she needed a friendly face."

"One more thing," he said before she left.

"What is it?"

"There were people looking for you, asking about Rita Calloway. In fact, that's the reason I recognized you with that new hair of yours . . . because I was sort a keeping an eye out for you."

Her pulse accelerated. "Did you recognize them?"

"Not at all. They didn't belong here—I can tell you that. Nicely dressed, cologne, expensive watches."

"Did they give you a name or tell you where they could be reached?"

He shook his head. "Just asked a group of us if we'd seen a girl named Rita Calloway." He tapped a dirty fingernail against the table. "I was sittin' right here at this very spot."

Her gaze shifted, darted around the room. Her heart thumped against her chest. Nobody stood out. Whoever those men were, they could be anywhere, and most likely they were close by. Reaching into her pants pocket, she pulled out a twenty and slipped it into Calvin's palm. "I gotta go, Calvin. You take care of yourself."

THIRTY-ONE

Beast, his dad, and Rage all lived together in a tiny dilapidated house in old Roseville close to the train tracks. Rage parked the car, and Faith followed her across the street. They climbed three rickety wooden stairs and then hopped over a gaping hole in the middle of a weathered porch.

The door wasn't locked. Rage headed inside, said hello to a giant of a man standing in the kitchen, explained what they were doing, and then disappeared in a back room.

Faith shut the door.

"Come on in," the man said, waving a dented metal spatula at her. "You must be Furious."

Being called Furious by someone other than Beast, Rage, or one of the people in anger management took her by surprise, but she recovered quickly and said succinctly, "Yes, I am."

The man standing before her could be none other than Beast's dad. He was almost as large and just as intimidating, that is, if he wasn't so quick to smile. She shook his hand, felt the power of his grip. "Little Vinnie," he said, "father of the beast." He laughed, a deep baritone sound.

She smiled back at him.

"I'm cooking up some Hamburger Helper. I'll fix you a plate, too."

"No, thank you," she said. "I just ate." Little Vinnie was anything but little. If he jumped, the top of his head would go right through the popcorn ceiling. Like his son, he had a roundish head, a neck the size of a tree trunk, thick with tendons, and shoulders as wide as a large refrigerator.

Little Vinnie's demeanor suddenly changed, and he kept his eyes on dinner and said, "I'm sorry about what happened to you. Life is strange like that. It gives us more than we ever thought possible, and in the blink of an eye it reaches out and takes it away." He looked at her, his eyes moist. "I've never understood it, and I've given up trying."

Beast came through a back door, said hello, then headed straight for the living room couch. He opened the laptop sitting on the table and typed in his password. As he waited for the machine to fire up, he said, "You got a picture of the guy who was following you?"

Faith pulled up the pictures on her phone and handed it to him along with the partial license plate number. "6MBS2," Faith said. "We didn't catch the last two digits on the plate and the pictures of the men in the car are blurry."

"It was a green Chevy Impala," Rage said to Beast as she joined Little Vinnie in the kitchen. Little Vinnie said something to Rage that made her laugh.

Faith looked around at the bookshelves filled with mementos and pictures. Someone had picked a bushel of wild flowers and stuck them in a jar of water sitting on a side table beneath an old lamp. The room was filled with love.

"I meant to ask you earlier," Rage said. "How's the gun practice going?"

"Not too bad. Dad and I practice most mornings and I'm getting better, but I still have a lot to learn about firearms. Hitting a target isn't as easy as it looks." The truth was, she liked everything about holding a gun in her hands. Mostly, she liked feeling strong and in control. She never wanted to feel as vulnerable as she had during the home invasion.

"You should go to the shooting range with us. Don't you think, Beast?" Rage looked over at Beast. He grunted. Rage smiled and added, "We go most weekends."

"I'd like that," Faith said.

"OK," Little Vinnie said as he passed out bowls of beef and noodles. "Dinner is served." It looked like Faith would be eating after all.

By the time Rage drove Faith home, Beast had yet to learn who the Chevy Impala belonged to, but he had it narrowed down and seemed certain he would have a name in the next few days.

———

The next night, anger management class ended early. While Beast talked to the instructor, Faith waited by the door.

"Where's Rage?" she asked Beast when he approached.

"She's not feeling well."

"Oh, that's too bad." She pursed her lips. "I guess I'll have to go it alone then."

"Go what alone?"

"We were going to hang out with the ladies on Watt Avenue, see if we can learn anything, find out if there's anyone in the 'business' who might know something . . . a name . . . anything."

"You're not going to let up, are you?"

She looked long and hard at Beast. "No, not even for a minute."

"Come on, then. I'll take you."

"You don't need to do this, Beast. You've done enough."

"I agreed to help you. Let's do this."

"OK," she said, thankful to have him on her side.

As they walked toward the car, he said, "You'll never find your kids if you get yourself killed." He tapped a finger against the side of his head. "Be smart."

"OK. I'll keep that in mind."

"Are you carrying?"

"What do you mean—a gun?"

"Yeah, a gun." He gave her a sideways glance. "This isn't a game. You need to be able to protect yourself."

"You're absolutely right."

"I'll give you one of mine to carry."

She nodded.

"I'll be watching you closely," he told her, "but don't push these people too far. Most of the girls on the street have problems of their own and aren't going to give a rat's ass about your problems. When you're finished asking questions, I'll drive you back here to your car."

"I appreciate it. Um, Rage wouldn't let me pay her, but maybe you'll let me help," she said as they reached his truck.

Once they climbed in and buckled up, he said, "Listen. I don't mean to offend you, but we don't want your money."

"Why not? Why are you helping me then?"

"I'm doing it for Rage." He shook his head. "That didn't come out right. I also want to help you find your kids. It's the right thing to do." He rubbed his sausagelike fingers over his jaw. "She doesn't like to talk about it, but I think you should know that when I say she's not feeling well, that's an understatement."

Faith recalled the deep-set eyes framed by dark circles. Rage always wore hats and bandannas, but it was her badass attitude that had thrown Faith off track. She'd been too preoccupied with her own problems to realize something was seriously wrong. Her heart dropped to her stomach. "How sick is she?"

"Brain tumor."

"Benign?"

He shook his head.

"What stage?"

"Stage four astrocytoma. Inoperable."

Her gut twisted. "I should have known something was wrong."

"You've had a lot on your mind. Besides, she prefers people not to notice. She doesn't like to talk about it."

"Oh, no. How long does she have?"

"Six months . . . a year at the most."

Faith turned away, unable to fully process the idea that Rage could truly be dying.

How could that be? It didn't make sense.

Life was unfair. She got that. But Rage never had a chance to be embraced by a loving family. She was much too young. "That's not enough time," she said, her eyes welling with tears.

"It's not, but it is what it is. Rage doesn't want anyone crying over her. She prefers people get past thinking about her dying because other than that, nothing has changed."

"But why would she want to help me?"

"She gave her baby up for adoption. Christopher would be two now. Since she won't ever see her son again, it's important to her that she helps you find yours."

He started the engine. They were quiet for the rest of the ride.

———

Faith climbed into the backseat of Beast's truck and slipped on a denim skirt that she'd cut at least an inch too short. Blue eye shadow, her sister's stilettos, and red lipstick completed the look.

They had been driving around for more than an hour. So far not one person would talk to her, let alone give her a name or tell her if they recognized either man when she showed them a copy of the picture she'd painted.

Once they arrived at their final destination for the night, she slid out of the truck, then waited at the crosswalk for the light to change colors.

Walking the streets was much more terrifying than she'd imagined. Her heart beat triple time as she headed across the street, trying to look braver than she felt. It was cold out and the pavement was slick from a light rain. A couple of hoots and hollers from passing cars didn't do much to calm her nerves. She glanced over her shoulder, relieved to see Beast standing in the shadows.

"This is my street corner," a woman told Faith the moment she stepped onto the curb. Black boots rode up high around her thigh. She was tall and thin with silver eye shadow that glittered under the moonlight. "You need to go find your own corner."

"What about those girls over there?" Faith used her chin to gesture at the group huddled close to the graffiti-covered wall.

"They know to stay out of my way."

Faith rubbed her arms and tried to keep her teeth from chattering. "Do you work for yourself?" Faith asked, undeterred.

The woman snorted. "Not a good idea. Not unless you're suicidal."

Faith slipped a hundred-dollar bill in her hand. "Just answer a few questions, and I'll leave you alone."

About to stuff the money into her bra, the woman paused. "Are you with the police?"

"No."

She didn't look convinced, but that didn't stop her from taking the money.

"What's your name?" Faith asked.

"You can call me Tina."

"How old are you?"

"Old enough."

Faith pulled a folded flyer from the tiny purse strapped around her shoulder and showed it to the woman.

"Those your kids?"

Faith nodded. "Can you help me?"

Tina looked around nervously. "You shouldn't be out here. Those kids are young. If you're saying that someone around these parts might have them, it's not gonna be one of the two-bit pimps hangin' around here."

"What do you mean?"

"They keep a close eye on the young ones—that's all I'm sayin'."

"Who are *they*?"

Tina's gaze shifted from left to right. "The boss—the big boss—one of the mucky-mucks tucked away in some fancy estate with ten bathrooms." She flicked a finger toward the flyer Faith had put away. "They probably live right around the corner from you."

"What about these men?" Faith asked as she pulled out another sheet of paper. "Ever seen either of these guys before?"

It happened fast, but Faith saw it—the flash of recognition before she blinked.

"They look familiar," Tina said, "but do you know how many men I see a week?" Her laugh was a cross between a bark and a snort. "Too many to count."

A car pulled up to the curb.

As Tina strutted that way, the windows came down and a bunch of teenage boys crowded in the backseat threw insults along with trash and empty beer cans at her. Tina cursed at them as they drove off, tires screeching. The other girls joined in, whooping and hollering and thumping their fists in the air.

Faith was shocked by what happened. "You're bleeding."

Tina pulled a Kleenex from her waistband and wiped the blood above her eye. "Stupid kids."

"Who were those boys?"

"Them? That was nothing. Happens all the time. They either throw eggs and cans or shoot at us with their BB guns. But that's life. Either come here and make some money, or go home and get whopped."

"Where's your pimp right now?"

Tina peered out into the night. A car honked as it drove by. She held up her middle finger. "I'm sure he's around here somewhere. Never around when I need him, though."

"Do you get to keep most of the money?"

"You don't know much about this business, do you?" Tina didn't wait for an answer before she added, "He takes it all and then buys me a ten-dollar outfit and pays for me to keep my nails done up nice, but that's about it." There was a short pause before she said, "Most pimps make a lot of promises, but they're really just selling dreams to girls like me. 'Gonna get you a nice house and a nice car,' but in the end, they just want your money. All the rest . . . it's just a big ol' lie."

Another car pulled up—a sleek black Mercedes. The window rolled slowly down, revealing a white man with a fine straight nose and a strong jaw. "Which one of you ladies is going to take care of me tonight?"

Tina looked at Faith as if to say goodbye.

"Please," Faith said, desperation in her voice as she shoved another forty dollars in the palm of her hand. "You recognized those men in the picture. I saw it in your eyes. I need a name."

"The guy on the right," Tina said, "is definitely in the business. He uses violence to control his hoes. He used to be in charge of kiddie strolls."

Faith raised a questioning brow.

Tina plunked a hand on her hip. "Shit, girl, you don't know anything, do you? Kiddie strolls are runway shows for johns who prefer children."

Faith felt sick to her stomach.

Tina looked around. "Listen, honey, that's all I got for you. I gotta go."

Faith scribbled out her number on the flyer and handed it to her. "If something else comes to you, anything at all, give me a call."

"I don't have all night, ladies!"

The muscle in Faith's jaw hardened. Knowing these men were out roaming the streets looking for sex was one thing, but seeing their dickless arrogance up close and personal was too much. She knew she was being naive, but she couldn't hold her tongue. "I think you should tell the asshole to move along. You don't need to do this."

"And then what?" Tina asked. "Are you gonna take me home with you?"

"You got five seconds," the man said.

"Calm down, honey," Tina shot back as she walked toward his car, hips swaying. "Looks like me and you are gonna spend some quality time together."

THIRTY-TWO

Faith took off her shoes before she turned the key and pushed the door to her parents' house slowly open. After locking the door behind her, she tiptoed across the entryway. No sooner had her foot hit the first stair than she heard a click and the lights came on.

"Faith, where have you been?"

She whipped around.

Mom stood close by in a nightgown and robe. Her short gray hair was a mess, flattened on one side of her head. She gave Faith the once-over. "You look like a streetwalker."

"That was the idea," Faith said. "I had questions, and I needed to talk to a few working girls."

Mom stepped closer and took hold of her hand. "You're so cold. I'm worried about you. You hardly sleep these days, and you're still not eating enough. I don't like seeing you like this."

Faith wrapped her arms around her mom and squeezed her tight. "I'm sorry." She pulled away and put her hands on her mom's shoulders. "I have to keep looking, Mom, but I could talk to the judge about moving back home. I don't like worrying you and Dad, and my being here could very well be putting you both in danger."

"Don't even think about moving back to that house of yours all alone. And of course you have to keep looking for Lara and Hudson. Stay right here. I have something for you."

Faith waited until Mom returned a minute later with a box. "Here you go. This is for you. It's a Taser X26c. I watched a demonstration on YouTube. This model has the highest takedown power available. There's a training manual inside."

"Thanks, Mom. Where's Dad?"

"He's asleep."

"Agent Burnett with the FBI left a message on my cell. She wants to meet with Dad and me first thing in the morning."

"I'll let Dad know," Mom said. "Another interview?"

Faith shook her head. "I want to talk to them about Craig's business and also get an update on the case."

"Any luck with finding Joe?"

She sighed. "Dead ends all around me."

Mom pulled her robe tighter around her waist and said matter-of-factly, "Lara and Hudson are coming home. It won't be long now. You just keep plugging away."

———

Faith and her dad were led down a wide corridor to a conference room with minimal decor. The female who escorted them to the room asked them to take a seat. She told them Agent Burnett and Jensen would be with them shortly. No sooner had she shut the door than it opened again and the two agents appeared. Introductions were made, and they all shook hands.

Agent Elaine Burnett, whom Faith had previously met at the police station, took a seat across from her. Agent Matt Jensen, a short and stocky man with a bad case of adult acne, sat next to Agent Burnett.

"Faith and I met previously," Agent Burnett began, "but I'd like to tell your dad how sorry we are for your family's loss. We also appreciate your call," she said to Faith, "along with your willingness to come see us on such short notice."

"Thank you," Dad said. "We are curious to know what's going on. We realize you reached out while Faith was recuperating, but I was bothered to hear about H&M Investments being shut down before my daughter was contacted."

"Technically we are only obligated to inform the owners of a business before it's shut down. According to the articles of incorporation, Faith McMann is not listed as a shareholder."

Dad grumbled under his breath, but he remained silent.

"We would like to know," Agent Jensen said to Faith, "if your husband ever talked to you about running the business?"

"We were married, so yes, of course."

"So you discussed the ins and outs of the business on a regular basis?" he asked.

She thought about it for a moment and realized she couldn't remember the last time she and Craig had actually discussed his work. It was usually the employees they talked about since it was a small business and they were all very close—who was getting married or divorced. Who was pregnant or what college their child had gotten into. "In the beginning, when Craig and Joe were first starting out," Faith said, "we talked about good business practices and how many employees might be needed . . . things like that. But once they were up and running, we tended to talk more about the lives of his employees and less about the actual running of the business."

"What about the financial aspects?" Burnett asked. "Did you discuss that?"

Again Faith took a second to think about it. "Rarely," she said. "Only if we were budgeting for something. For instance, when Lara wanted to take dance lessons."

"In your opinion, were you and your husband living a good life?"

"We were living a wonderful life," Faith said. "Now, if you're talking in terms of money, we were doing OK with two incomes, but certainly not living a life of luxury."

"Here's the thing," Jensen said. "Joe Henderson has a house in Rocklin that has been recently renovated. Six months ago, he bought another house in San Diego—three bedrooms, lots of decks so you could see the ocean from every room. He has two cars. Both new. Lots of nice things in the past year or so."

"I never heard anything about a second house, but I know Kristen, his wife, came from money. Her parents used to take them on extravagant vacations and buy their kids whatever they needed."

"How about clientele?" Jensen prodded. "Did your husband ever mention concern about what he thought might be a shady deal?"

"No. Never."

"Do you know his clients?"

"Personally? No. I could name names, though, if I were pressed to do so." Faith angled her head. "Could you please tell me what's going on? Employees have been sent home, the business has been shut down, and yet I have no idea why."

"After the attack," Agent Burnett answered, "we went to see Joe Henderson to find out if there was anyone, employees or clients, who might have wished your husband harm."

Faith raised an eyebrow. "And?"

"Joe had a bad habit of putting us off," Agent Jensen said, "which raised a red flag and led us to begin an investigation into his personal affairs."

"Leading us to his recent purchases of high-priced items," Agent Burnett added. "We talked to his wife, and she has no knowledge of where he might have gotten hold of such large sums of money. In fact, she knew nothing about the home in San Diego."

Faith sighed. "And then he disappeared."

Agent Burnett nodded. "And we took over from there."

"So where's all that money coming from?" Dad asked.

"So far, there is no money trail."

Dad was not convinced. "Come on. You have access to everything in that place. You must have some idea."

"Nothing we can share with you at this time."

Faith sat back and tried to take it all in. Had Craig been involved? Was that why $2 million had been hidden away inside their pool filter? She felt the blood rush from her face.

"It stands to reason," Agent Jensen said, "that if Joe Henderson had access to large sums of cash that perhaps your husband did, too."

Dad's face turned a bright shade of red. "I don't appreciate the accusatory tone you're using with my daughter."

Burnett rubbed his chin. "We're not accusing Faith or her husband of any wrongdoing." Agent Burnett leaned over the table, directing her attention on Faith. "Do you have any idea where Joe Henderson might be hiding out?"

"No."

"Do you or did you ever have any reason to believe your husband was hiding anything from you?"

"No. Never."

"Did your husband ever buy you an extravagant gift or take you on a surprise vacation?"

Faith shook her head. "We hadn't taken time off since Hudson was born, and we stopped buying each other gifts years ago."

"Do you have any objection to our having a look around the house you shared with your husband?"

"While Faith lay in the hospital," Dad said, his voice raised, "there were at least a dozen FBI agents at her house, scouring the grounds. Nothing was left untouched. We cooperated fully because we wanted nothing more than to find the people who killed my son-in-law and took our grandchildren, but I don't like what you people are insinuating. My daughter is a victim, not a criminal. Tell me exactly what it is you're looking for, and I'll take you there personally."

Agent Burnett released a ponderous sigh. "Mr. Gray. I'm sorry you're upset, but you need to understand that our investigation of Craig McMann and Joe Henderson's business practices has taken us down another path, a path that needs to be fully explored. We're doing all we can to find Lara and Hudson, and that's exactly why we need to conduct another search of the house where your son-in-law resided. The first time we were there, we were looking for forensic evidence. This time we'll be searching for any clues Craig McMann might have left behind concerning H&M Investments." She paused and then added, "The house will be searched with or without your permission."

Frustration lined Dad's face. He was about to argue further when Faith stopped him. "I have no objection to you looking around, but if you have a suspect, I need the name of the client involved."

"Why?"

"Because whoever it is could be the link to finding my kids."

"We're sharing information with the police," Agent Jensen said.

Agent Burnett nodded. "It's an ongoing investigation. I'm afraid you're going to have to be patient."

THIRTY-THREE

Beast climbed out of his truck, grabbed the bouquet of sunflowers he'd brought, then shut the door and took a moment to collect himself. Determined to put on a happy face before heading inside the hospital, he worked the muscles in his jaw and lifted the corners of his mouth.

As he walked across the parking lot, he thought of Rage. At the ripe old age of twenty-seven she'd already endured more hardship than most. Few people knew the whole story—that she'd only left the abusive boyfriend after she discovered she was pregnant. Knowing he would never willingly let her go, Rage snuck out while he was sleeping and hitchhiked from New York to California. Homeless, but resilient, she found a job, and nine months later Christopher was born. Since she couldn't afford a roof over her head, let alone day care, she knew deep down that it would be best if she gave Christopher a chance at a decent life by giving him up for adoption. But after handing him over to social services, the aching sadness wouldn't go away. Drugs helped with the pain, but pain-numbing substances weren't cheap, and pretty soon she was working the streets to pay for her habit, anything to forget. It wasn't long before she learned the hard way that pimps didn't like strong-minded women who thought they could work without a middleman.

And that's where Beast came into the picture.

He had found Rage, left for dead, on the side of the road. He'd brought her to the old Victorian in Roseville that he shared with his dad. For weeks, Rage bitched and complained about living with two ugly giants who didn't know how to cook or clean up after themselves.

His dad killed her with kindness.

Beast ignored her.

But despite the endless complaints, she stuck around. And she grew on both of them. Strangely enough, she gave Beast's life purpose again. She got a job at the coffee shop around the corner from where they lived, and for a short time she seemed content . . . until three months ago when cancer came knocking on her door.

The news changed her. Made her mean, or should he say meaner. She wasn't angry at life, God, or the unfairness of it all. No, she was angry with herself. It made no sense to Beast, but there it was. She blamed herself for her mother's mental illness and her father's inability to cope. She blamed herself for running away with an abusive and obsessive man. Mostly, though, she blamed herself for giving up Christopher. Karma was a bitch, she liked to say, figuring she had absolutely deserved to get a malignant brain tumor. In her mind, it all made perfect sense.

Beast walked through the hospital lobby and onto the elevator. He exited on the fifth floor and made his way down the wide corridor to the nurses' station. "Hey, Barbara. How's she doing?"

"Stubborn as ever. Nothing has changed in that regard. The doctor is with her now—third room on the right."

Beast caught the doctor as he was leaving and pulled him aside. "Has she agreed to surgery?"

He shook his head. "Because of the infiltrative nature of this tumor, complete removal is impossible."

"But you did say that if you remove most of it and then hit the tumor with chemotherapy or radiation, she could live another year or two—isn't that right?"

"Studies show that there's no benefit from chemotherapy. Although the tumor cells are resistant to conventional therapies, radiation could double her life expectancy."

"If she refuses treatment, what can we expect?"

"Headaches will worsen, vomiting, nausea. If and when she starts having seizures, she could suffer personality changes and verbal, cognitive, and motor loss."

After Beast finished talking with the doctor, he headed into the room where Rage was sitting in a wheelchair waiting for him. "They won't let me walk out of here. I have to ride in this thing, so let's go."

"Good morning to you, too."

She snorted, then crossed her arms, letting him know she was out of patience.

"I talked to the doctor. He said you've dismissed all forms of treatment."

"The tumor is inoperable."

"Radiation could double your life expectancy."

"By a few months at most. The side effects would not be fun, and for what? It would not save my life. No matter what, Beast, I'm going to die. If I agreed to treatment, my hair would be burned off and my scalp would be left with third-degree burns. Palliative treatment could change my personality completely." She pointed a finger at his raised eyebrow. "Don't get funny with me."

"What? I didn't say a word."

"I know what you're thinking. Maybe I'll stop bitching and start living in the moment."

He grunted. "The thought never crossed my mind. I like you just the way you are."

"I don't want to spend these last good months unable to talk or walk. I prefer to live even while I'm dying."

She was on a roll now, talking fast, and he could see that these decisions had not been easy for her to make. He kneeled down so that they were face-to-face, his hands on both sides of the wheelchair. "It's your decision, and I respect that."

"Sometimes you scare me."

"Why is that?"

"I named you as my health care agent in the event a doctor wants to resuscitate and I am no longer able to communicate. Sometimes I wonder if I made a mistake in naming you."

"Because I care about what happens to you?"

"Because you care too much."

"I would never let you suffer."

She rubbed the back of her neck. "I appreciate everything you've done for me. You know that, right?"

He nodded.

There was a long pause before she said, "Today is Christopher's birthday—two years old." Her voice hitched.

When Rage was upset she tended to talk quickly, randomly changing course without notice, sort of like she was doing now. All he could do was hang on tight and listen as best he could.

"A year ago," she was saying, "I wondered if he'd taken his first steps. I remember at that time pondering whether Christopher eats with his fingers or a spoon. Does he know how to turn the page of a storybook? I think I can, I think I can . . . what was the name of that book?" She snapped her fingers. "*The Little Engine That Could.* My father used to read it to me when I was little. Do you think they ever read that book to Christopher?"

"I'm sure his parents read it to him every night before he's tucked into bed."

She smiled in that special way of hers, letting him know that she was on to him and knew he was merely appeasing her, but also that she appreciated his answer. She sighed, then added, "Two years old, can you believe it?"

He shook his head, wishing he could take away all her troubles and fears, all her pain.

"I wonder if he talks in whole sentences? Do you think he's already sleeping in a big bed? No, it would be too soon for that."

Before Beast could respond in any meaningful way, she said, "I've been having dreams about Faith's children." She looked at him with wide, thoughtful eyes. "We have to find them, Beast."

"We're doing all we can."

"No," she said, her voice a whisper. "I don't think we are, and I'm afraid I'm running out of time."

Back at the house on Rolling Greens Way, Agent Burnett suggested Faith and her dad find a place to sit and make themselves comfortable, preferably somewhere out of the way.

Since it wasn't raining, they chose to sit at the table near the pool.

There were four vehicles and one van parked in the driveway. Two agents were searching through the office, while Agent Burnett and Agent Jensen walked the grounds, taking photographs and notes. Every time one of them walked by the pool filter at the corner of the house, Faith tensed.

"If they leave even the tiniest sign of fingerprint dust, your mother will have their heads."

"Thanks for coming with me, Dad."

"I don't know what they're looking for, but we both know Craig was a good man. I used to warn your husband about Joe Henderson, but he wouldn't listen."

Faith frowned. "You didn't trust Joe?"

"Craig never told you what I said?"

"No. And neither did you. I always thought Joe was a perfectly nice man."

Dad leaned closer and said sternly, "It's time for you to take off the rose-colored glasses and see people for who they are."

Rarely did she see her father look so serious.

"Joe Henderson was a salesman," Dad said matter-of-factly, "a fake, someone who says only what they think you want to hear."

From where she sat, Faith caught sight of Special Agent Burnett stooped down next to the pool equipment. She called Agent Jensen over to look at something on the ground.

Faith stiffened.

Dad must have noticed because he looked over his shoulder at Burnett and Jensen, then turned back to Faith. "What's going on?"

She looked at her father long and hard. "I'm going to tell you something that might make you angry, but no matter what you think of me, I need you to know that the reason I haven't told you or the rest of the family is because I was trying to protect you."

Her dad paled. "Out with it, Faith. What did you do?"

She kept her voice low. "I found two million dollars in the pool equipment over there and hid it in the tree fort in your backyard."

He didn't flinch. In fact, it was hard to tell if he was breathing.

"If I called the police," Faith went on, her voice low enough that they couldn't be overheard but loud enough that the agents wouldn't be suspicious, "I figured they would throw it in an evidence room and forget all about it. I kept the money because I'm determined to find those men and offer them a deal."

Dad said nothing.

"It could give me the leverage I need to get my kids back. But if you tell me right now to walk over there and tell them what I just told you, then that's what I'll do."

The silence between them stretched on for nearly a minute before Dad finally spoke. "If I thought giving the money back would help us get my grandkids back sooner rather than later, then I would have you march over there and tell them. But as I see it, I think you did the right thing. We keep it for now. We also keep this between the two of us."

"Four of us. Beast and Rage were both here with me when we found it."

He sighed.

"The question now is do I spend my time and energy trying to find Joe Henderson, who seems to have disappeared off the face of the earth, or do I let the FBI search for him and put my efforts into finding out more about who the players are in the area?"

"Players?"

"Human traffickers." She leaned closer to Dad. "Think about it. Lara and Hudson weren't killed. They were taken. No ransom has been demanded. And Sacramento happens to be one of the biggest hubs for trafficking. It could be a shot in the dark, but to me it makes sense." She paused before adding, "Someone recognized one of the men I painted on the wall and believes him to be involved in prostitution. I think my time is better spent going after those men. What do you think?"

"I think you have good instincts and that you should follow them."

THIRTY-FOUR

It was Saturday, and Faith got a whiff of newly cut grass through the open window. Craig was outside with the kids while Faith took a rare moment to play a song from Phantom of the Opera *on an old upright piano passed down from generation to generation. Some of the keys were missing ivory, but she'd kept the piano tuned and the sound was decent. She'd taken piano lessons for a few years at a young age, but mostly she was self-taught. Even as she played, out of the corner of her eye, she saw Lara straining to open the sliding glass door. At six years old, it took every bit of muscle for her little arms to open the slider, but she didn't like anyone helping her, so Faith kept right on playing and pretended not to notice.*

"Mom!" Lara said the moment she squeezed through the door. She ran toward her, tears in her eyes.

Faith stopped playing. "Is your brother all right?"

"He's with Dad," she said, big droplets rolling down both sides of her face.

"What is it then?" Faith looked her over. "Are you hurt?"

"I don't want you and Dad to die."

"What?"

"Dad said everyone dies someday. I don't want you to die."

Faith was an elementary school teacher. She had an answer for everything, but in that moment she stuttered a bit before she remembered a beautiful book she'd read about life and death and how it was really all about living. "Look at me, Lara."

Her daughter did as she said, and Faith wiped her tears away. "I'm here now, aren't I?"

Lara nodded and sniffled.

"And your Dad is outside playing with your brother—isn't that right?"

She nodded again.

"I will never lie to you, Lara. It's true that everyone will die someday, but the important thing for you to know is that someone will always be here to take care of you. You have Mommy and Daddy, Grandma and Grandpa, Aunt Jana and Uncle Colton. You will never be alone. OK?"

That seemed to appease her. Lara nodded, and Faith held her close. She felt a few last shudders leave Lara's body. Faith breathed her in, wondering where the years had gone. It seemed like yesterday that she and Craig had brought their baby daughter home from the hospital.

"Faith. Earth to Faith."

She blinked and found her brother, Colton, waving a hand in front of her face. "The truck is ready," he said. "And I need to explain a few things."

Rage, Beast, and Colton were standing next to a semitractor in the parking lot of Colton's trucking business. It was seven thirty at night, and the sky was already pitch-black. If not for the floodlights, they wouldn't be able to see one another. Tonight the plan was to talk to the teenagers who hung out at rest stops and offered their services to truck drivers.

"OK, here's how this is going to go down," Colton told them. "You three will be inside the trailer while I sit in the cab and wait for someone to approach. Depending on whether it rains or not, it could turn into a waiting game. If I'm approached, I'll do some negotiating and then bring her to the back of the truck where you three will be waiting. You're going to have five to ten minutes to talk and find out what you can."

"Why such a short time?"

"Because her pimp will be watching. If she takes too long, he'll come after her."

"Why don't you two drive with Colton?" Beast said. "I'll take my truck and watch from across the street."

Rage frowned. "You're going to follow the pimp home, aren't you?"

His expression remained the same, grim and unreadable.

Rage crossed her arms and then directed her attention back at Colton. "It sounds like you've had a lot of experience with this sort of thing."

"Unfortunately I have. I was a trucker for ten years." He put a hand on the cab. "I lived and breathed the trucking business well before I started my own company. Prostituting . . . trafficking . . . it's always been part of the landscape."

Faith shook her head with disgust.

"Just so we're clear, I've never approached one of these girls, but I've seen it happen plenty of times."

This dark world she was suddenly inhabiting made her realize how out of touch she'd been her entire life. Talk about living in a bubble. "We should get going," Faith said.

Colton waved a hand toward the office building. "I've got to lock up shop first. I'll only be a minute."

Faith kept finding her attention going back to Rage. This was the first time she'd seen her since she'd learned from Beast that she was sick. Her skin was pale, and yet her big eyes looked brighter than usual.

Every time Rage caught Faith looking at her, she looked away. Except for this time. This time she narrowed her eyes at Faith and then turned her head and fixed her gaze on Beast. "You told her, didn't you?"

"You weren't at class," Beast said. "She asked me about you."

"Furious asked about me?"

Faith raised her hands in question. "I'm right here, guys. And why is that so surprising that I would ask about you?"

Rage pointed a finger at her. "That look on your face right now? Get rid of it."

"Why?" Faith asked. "What am I doing?"

"I'm serious. Don't ever give me that look again."

Faith looked at Beast. "What did I do?"

"It's the same look the nurses and doctors give me every time I go in for more tests. It's that look-at-the-poor-sick-girl look—pitiful and woeful—it makes me want to scream."

Faith moaned.

"What was that?"

"A moan," Faith said with a laugh, hoping to distract Rage since it was obvious she didn't want to be pitied and for a brief second that's exactly what Faith had done. "I can't moan?"

"What's so funny?"

"You are."

"Fuck you, old lady."

"Up yours."

Rage's eyes widened before she burst out laughing. "Nobody says 'up yours' anymore."

"Well, I do."

"OK," Beast said with a sigh, leaving them to argue. "I'm going to wait in my truck till we're ready to go."

———

Faith and Rage sat in the back of the trailer where goods were usually stored. The trailer was huge—thirteen feet high, eight and a half feet wide, and forty-eight feet long. It was also damp, dark, and dusty.

They had been at this for hours, already talked to one sixteen-year-old boy and three girls between the ages of eighteen and twenty-three, if they were to be believed. The boy actually gave them a name, but when Beast ran it through his database, the person didn't exist. The girls, on the other hand, were closed-mouthed and refused to talk. This was their second rest stop of the night. It had been forty-five minutes since the last girl left the back of the truck with a hundred dollars in her pocket.

"I'm sorry about earlier," Rage said out of the blue. "Sometimes I just wish Beast would keep things to himself."

"I'm sorry if I was staring at you. I wasn't feeling pity," Faith lied. "I was just wishing there was something I could do."

"Nothing anyone can do," Rage said. "Just the luck of the draw. And if you don't mind, I prefer not to ever talk about this again."

The back door to the truck rolled open. Faith straightened. They both did.

Colton jumped up into the trailer and then helped the girl inside. He rolled the door down and turned his flashlight toward the back where Rage and Faith were sitting. "This is Angel."

Dark-skinned with hair that hung to her shoulders in perfect curls, she couldn't be much older than sixteen. She visibly tensed when she saw the two of them waiting at the back of the truck and then turned to leave. "I don't want no part of this," she said.

Colton stopped her. "We just want to ask you a few questions."

"Look, mister! If I'm not out of here in the next five minutes with a hundred-dollar bill in my hand, things are going to get ugly. And my ass ain't the only one that's going to get kicked, if you catch my drift."

Faith quickly pulled a hundred-dollar bill from her pocket and handed it to the girl. "Here you go."

Angel took the cash, then flipped her curls to the side and said, "What kind of questions you want to ask anyhow?"

"We need your boss's name," Faith said.

"You trippin'? No fucking way. You people are crazy." She looked at her cell phone, appeared to be reading messages, the glow of light hitting her face just so. One thing was clear—she was scared.

"Please," Faith said as she handed the girl a flyer and asked Colton to shine the flashlight on it. "Those are my kids, nine and ten." She thought of Hudson turning nine without her at his side. "We think they may have been taken by traffickers, and I need your help."

"I'm sorry, lady, but you have no idea who you're dealing with. They don't take shit from nobody. If they knew what you were doing in here, asking me questions, they would shoot you and leave you in some dark alleyway to die."

Rage pushed herself to her feet and stepped closer to the girl so that they were face-to-face. "I'm not going to go away, Angel. I really don't want to make problems for you, but we need to find these kids sooner rather than later. We're running out of options. And just so we're straight with each other, those dudes you work for aren't the only ones who carry a gun. I need a name. And I need it now."

Angel's mouth tightened in a straight line before she said, "Shit. Those kids could be anywhere, but hand me another hundred and I'll give you two names." She pointed a finger at Rage. "But you have to promise me you'll never come back here again."

Rage looked at Faith, who nodded and handed the girl another hundred.

"OK, then. There's a guy named Fin," she said in a low voice. "He works at a tattoo shop. I don't know which one, but I overheard him bragging once about branding a ten-year-old girl with blonde hair."

"Branding?"

"Yeah, some of these people get a little crazy. They like to tattoo their name or a symbol onto the young ones, make sure everyone knows which family they belong to."

"What's Fin's real name?"

"Hell if I know."

"We're running out of time," Colton reminded them.

"Gracie's Salon on Stockton Boulevard," Angel spit out before heading for the end of the truck, where Colton stood by the roll-up door ready to let her out. "They keep the younger girls in the back rooms where they can keep a close watch on them."

"Do you ever talk to the girls?"

"What planet are you from, lady?" Angel snorted and then crossed her skinny arms. "I don't talk to no one, and I sure as hell shouldn't be talkin' to you. You didn't hear none of this from me," she said. "Now open this door!"

———

Long after Colton's semitrailer left the parking lot, Beast stayed low in his truck, keeping an eye on things. There were three girls working the parking lot. It was well past midnight when one of them left the back of a semitrailer and signaled with a quick sweep of her hand in the air above her head.

A silver Nissan pulled up next to her, and she climbed inside.

Beast followed the Nissan, taking note of the plate number and the direction they were headed. Before merging onto the freeway, the Nissan slowed and pulled over to the side of the road.

Beast did the same. He left the engine running and the headlights on. A light drizzle hit his windshield.

Minutes passed before the driver's door of the Nissan opened and the driver climbed out. Broad-shouldered, he wore a dark leather jacket. He had a swagger to his step—slow and steady, his upper body swaying left to right, his chest puffed.

Window down, Beast waited patiently for his arrival.

The man in the leather jacket came right up to Beast's window and put a gun to his head. "Motherfucker, you following me?"

The guy reeked of tequila. "Yeah, as a matter of fact, I am." Beast grabbed hold of his gun and twisted it out of his hand, then jabbed his right elbow into the guy's throat. The man stumbled backward, both hands around his neck as he struggled for a breath. Beast climbed out of his truck, kneed him in the groin, and held the muzzle of the gun against his skull. "You have two seconds to tell me who you work for."

"Shit."

"Wrong answer." Beast cocked the gun.

"OK, OK! A guy named Patrick pays me when I bring him new girls, but that's all I know!"

Beast pointed at his thigh and fired a shot.

Screaming, the man grabbed his leg and rolled to his side.

Up ahead, the car door opened and the girl started to climb out of the Nissan.

"Get back in the car!" Beast told her. "Last chance," Beast said, redirecting the gun at the man's head again.

"Del Paso Road . . . Bill's Liquor Store. That's where you'll find him." He grimaced as he held his leg.

Beast unloaded the cartridge from the firearm, used his shirt to wipe off any prints from the piece, then tossed it on the ground and left.

THIRTY-FIVE

Mom had taken Dad to his therapy appointment and Faith was fixing a cup of coffee when the doorbell rang.

Her heart skipped a beat.

Mom hadn't said anything about expecting a visitor, and Rage wouldn't be coming for another few hours.

She ran to the sliding glass door and looked through the curtain to the backyard. It was raining so hard that it was difficult to see beyond the workshop. She turned around and ran upstairs to grab the pistol Beast had loaned her. By the time she hit the last step, somebody was knocking.

She walked slowly to the door.

Her hands were shaking.

She stood off to the side. "Who is it?"

"It's Corrie Perelman. I need to speak with Faith McMann."

Faith peered through the peephole. It was indeed Corrie Perelman. Slippered feet stuck out of a long raincoat. Water dripped from an umbrella at her side. Faith opened the door, surprised by the women's perseverance.

"I'm so glad I found you. I've been desperate to talk to you."

"Why don't you come inside," Faith said with a sigh, "and I'll fix you a cup of coffee. Do you drink coffee?"

"Yes, that would be nice."

Corrie shook the water from her umbrella and left it on the welcome mat; then she stepped in and pulled the wet hood away from her face. As she followed Faith across the hallway and into the kitchen, she let out a ponderous breath and said, "My husband didn't want me to come, but I had to see you."

Faith gestured for her to have a seat on a stool at the kitchen counter. She set a mug of coffee along with cream and sugar in front of Corrie. Feeling a bit of guilt after the way she'd talked to her the last time on the phone, Faith reached over and placed a hand on hers. She'd done a little research about Corrie, and it wasn't all good. Ever since her daughter had disappeared, people referred to her as Crazy Corrie. It wasn't nice, and it wasn't fair.

"I saw my daughter in my dreams again last night," Corrie blurted. "I often see her when I dream, of course, but this felt different somehow. Have you ever had a dream like that? One that felt so real that you woke up and had a hard time convincing yourself it didn't really happen?"

Faith's heart tightened, and she found herself nodding. "I've been dreaming a lot myself."

Corrie's face brightened. "The thing is . . . the reason I came, is because last night I saw Lara, too."

Faith wasn't sure what to say. Corrie's husband was right. She shouldn't have come, but she was here and clearly she was in pain. "Oh, Corrie," was all Faith managed.

"I'm sure you must think I'm crazy for paying you a visit like this, unannounced and all, just to tell you about a silly dream."

"It's OK," Faith said. "I don't think you're crazy at all. I think you're just trying to find a way to keep going."

The woman lost it then.

A few kind words appeared to be the key to unlocking the wall Corrie Perelman had obviously been building for a very long time. In that moment, Corrie stopped trying so hard to be strong and simply wilted instead. Her shoulders and head slumped forward, and her body quivered.

Faith went to her, wrapped both arms around Corrie, a woman with whom Faith shared nothing and yet everything at the same time, and offered a comforting embrace, the only thing she had left to give.

———

Faith and Rage spent the morning visiting tattoo shops. Nobody they had talked to so far had ever heard of anyone who went by the name Fin. Afterward they drove to Stockton Boulevard, parked across the street from Gracie's Salon, and kept surveillance on the place to see if there might be any truth to what Angel had told them last night.

"So you think that woman who visited you this morning is truly crazy?"

Faith realized she never should have told Rage about Corrie Perelman's visit. She shook her head. "No. I don't think she's crazy at all. I think she's still trying to find a way to live with what happened and is having a difficult time moving on."

"It scared you, though, didn't it?"

"What?"

"That if you don't find your kids, that could be you?"

"Yeah," Faith said. "It scared me."

"Look," Rage said, pointing at the man entering the salon.

It was two o'clock in the afternoon and so far two older men, two teenage girls, and one woman in her midforties had entered the shop. Faith sighed. "That's two men in the past thirty minutes having a pedicure?"

"I've never been to one of these places," Rage said. "I wouldn't know."

When Faith looked at Rage's haunted eyes and pale coloring, her motherly instincts kicked in, filling her with the urge to wrap her arms around her and let her know she wasn't alone—that she could talk, about anything, and she would listen. But instead, recalling what Rage had told her about never talking about her illness again, Faith kept her hands to herself, looked across the street, and said, "Lara could be in there."

"Then what are we waiting for?"

"I don't want to endanger her or anyone else. We can't let them know why we're here."

"So, what do you want to do?"

"We need to go inside, act natural . . . just two friends in need of a manicure. If they can fit us in, we take a seat and stay calm, but we'll be taking notes, paying close attention to who's coming and going. If I see anything suspicious, I'll take a picture or maybe use the video on my phone."

"You have my number," Rage said. "Text me if you see something."

"Good idea." Faith lifted an eyebrow. "Ready?"

"Always."

A bell chimed when they entered the salon.

"You have appointment?" one of the ladies asked in broken English.

"No," Faith said. "We were driving by and thought we'd stop in and see if you had time for us."

"OK. Not busy yet." She wagged her finger at the display case. "Pick a color. Pedi? Mani?"

"Pedicure," Faith said.

"Manicure for me," Rage said.

Faith chose the first red polish she saw while Rage grabbed black. Rage used her elbow to nudge Faith in the ribs and then

gestured toward a humongous cockroach skittering across the lino-
leum floor.

"Nice."

The woman who'd greeted them led Faith to a worn leather chair
in the back, while another woman seated Rage at a table closer to
the door. The first thing Faith noticed was that the two men and the
teenagers she'd watched enter the salon were nowhere to be seen.
The middle-aged woman was seated in a leather chair across from
Faith. Her feet were soaking in a tub of water, and she was reading a
magazine. Two other salon ladies sat at their stations, checking their
phones and talking to each other in Vietnamese. At the very back of
the salon was a sink area and two doors. The strong smell of chemicals
and the fact that there was no ventilation made it difficult to breathe.
She glanced at Rage, who appeared to be preoccupied with something
straight ahead in her line of vision.

Time held still as Faith watched, waited, listened. Between the
constant chattering and the jerky movements of the woman working
on her toes, overall the salon ladies seemed nervous, skittish. The
woman working on Rage's nails had a sunken-in face, malnourished
and lined with fatigue. Her clothes were wrinkled, and she had a
stain on one of her sleeves. The floors were unwashed. The place gave
her the creeps. Faith wasn't sure how much longer she could sit still.

She looked at the backpack clutched in her lap and slowly went
over the steps needed to work the Taser her mom had given her. She'd
registered the stun gun and activated the code. It was fully charged
and ready to go. All she needed to do was put the cartridge in place,
slide a lever, and then pull the trigger. If she could stay calm and not
let her nerves get the best of her, it would be child's play.

The salon worker scrubbed the bottom of her feet using a stone.
She rubbed hard. Faith winced. When she was finished with that
she began to massage Faith's calves. "No massage," Faith said, feeling
antsy. "Just polish."

The woman frowned but did as she asked.

One of the doors at the back of the salon opened. A man in blue jeans and a collared shirt exited the back room, smoothing his hair as he walked through the salon and out the main door to the sidewalk lining the street.

Rage looked over at her, concern in her eyes.

Faith reached inside her backpack for her phone. She'd never been great at texting, but it was time to give it a shot. She found Rage's name and number under her contacts, hit the message button, and typed:

```
Need distraction when I go to the bathroom.
```

Before she could blink, there was a beep and a reply:

```
Got it.
```

As soon as the cotton was pulled out from between Faith's toes, Faith told the woman she needed to use the restroom. When she stood, she made eye contact with Rage and then headed for the bathroom. Being barefoot was the least of her problems. The woman who had painted her toes stayed at her side, leading her to the door to make sure Faith didn't stray . . . a red flag that something was up. Faith swallowed the lump in her throat as her fingers settled around the doorknob to the bathroom, hoping Rage would create a scene before she went inside.

A loud crash and a high-pitched screech answered her prayer.

The woman left her side and ran to the front of the salon. Without hesitating, Faith rushed through the door the man had exited moments ago and clicked it shut behind her. She found herself looking down a narrow hallway. It was much colder back there than inside the main area. The walls were painted black, but the dim lighting couldn't hide the water stains and mold on the ceiling. There were two doors on the left and two on the right.

Her heart raced, and her hands trembled. Knowing she had to work fast, she stepped up her pace and opened the first door on her left. No one was inside. No windows or closets, only a thin dirty mattress and a flimsy blanket. A nightstand was pushed against the wall.

She rushed to the next room on the right. The two teenage girls she'd seen enter the salon earlier were inside, sitting on the edge of a mattress clicking away at their phones. They looked up at the same time, eyes wide. One of them jumped to her feet. Faith put a finger over her mouth and said, "Shhh."

Somebody in a room farther back cried out.

"Stay where you are," Faith whispered to the girls before making her way back into the hallway and shutting the door behind her. The whimpering was coming from the next room to the right. Images of her kids bound and gagged on the couch flooded her mind. Her blood curdled. She pulled the Taser from her bag, clipped on the cartridge, set the timer, and then released the safety latch. Quietly she continued down the hallway, slowly turned the knob, and opened the door.

It was difficult to register what she was seeing.

A scrawny naked man, bony and pale with dull-brown hair circling a bald spot at the crown of his head, wriggled like a newly caught fish on top of a young girl in her teens. He'd used thick twine to tie her wrists to a nightstand on each side of the bed. Wooden legs scraped against the floor as he bucked and writhed with no care for the girl lying beneath him. The girl's mouth was bound with cloth that had come loose, and her eyes were filled with a wild look of fear as she pulled on the ropes and struggled to get free. The moment she saw Faith, her eyes grew round and she struggled harder.

The man on top of her looked over his shoulder, saw Faith, and tried to scramble away from the girl. Faith Tasered him in the buttocks. His body shook. She held the trigger until it stopped automatically. Little yelps was all he managed before he fell to his side and rolled off the mattress. Tempted to place the Taser over his heart and pull the trigger, she positioned the prongs on his stomach instead and sent electricity directly into every muscle fiber, making them contract uncontrollably. She'd done her research, and she knew that she was taking control of his central nervous system. By the time she hit him with a third jolt, she heard the sound of a door opening and closing. In the distance, she heard frantic shouting.

Faith put away the Taser, grabbed her phone, and dialed 911. She gave the operator the name and address of the salon and told them young girls were being held captive and raped. They were still asking questions when she shut the phone and shoved it into her bag. She rushed to the other side of the bed and removed the binding from the girl's mouth, then worked on removing the twine from around her wrists. The knots were tight. Her skin was raw. She was crying uncontrollably.

Rage arrived first. She knelt down by the man on the floor and felt for a pulse. "He's alive."

Grimacing, Faith struggled with the knots, determined to set the girl free, adrenaline coursing through her veins. "He deserves to die," she said. This girl could have been her daughter. Who were these men who paid to have sex with young girls? They knew exactly what they were doing. "Fucking assholes," Faith said. "Raping young girls. What kind of asshole does this sort of thing?"

"Here, let me help." Rage pulled out a pocketknife, flipped it open, and easily cut through the twine. The girl fell into Faith's arms. She held her close as she stared at the man on the ground and wished she had killed him.

At the police station, the FBI questioned both Faith and Rage for more than an hour. It was now Detective Yuhasz's turn. He'd called Faith inside his office for a private talk, leaving Rage to wait in another room and fill out a report. The last time Faith had seen Detective Yuhasz was when she'd hit him over the head with his keyboard.

"So," he said. "I see you've been keeping out of trouble."

His sarcasm was hard to miss. "We were having our nails done."

"All the way over in West Sacramento?"

She stayed calm as she reminded herself she needed to play nice and do whatever she must to keep him from throwing her in jail again. As far as she knew, she hadn't broken the law, but these days there seemed to be a fine line between right and wrong. "I've been meaning to tell you in person that I'm sorry for losing my temper. I don't know what came over me." She lifted her chin. "You might be glad to know that I have yet to miss an anger management class."

"From what I witnessed in the salon, I can see it's working."

She snorted.

"You do realize that you might be pissing some people off? And I'm not talking about me or the FBI."

"Please don't suggest I sit at home and do nothing."

"I'm only saying that by stirring the pot you could end up jeopardizing your children's lives."

She thought about it for a moment. "I can't think that way." She shook her head. "I just can't. I don't see how doing nothing puts my kids in less danger than they're already in. What's that saying about shaking the hornet's next?"

He shrugged. "I don't know."

"Neither do I," she said. "But I do know that bears endure stings to get to the prized honey. In other words, I can't worry about the bees or shaking the hornet's nest and pissing off a bunch of scumbags with guns. Sitting at home fretting hasn't exactly helped Corrie Perelman, now has it?"

"Just do me a favor and try to stay inside the law as you sniff around."

"I'll do my best."

There was a long pause before he scratched his chin and said, "The truth is, I would also like to apologize."

"For what?"

"For upsetting you and making you feel as if your children were merely a case number. I have two children of my own and grandkids the same age as Lara and Hudson." He fidgeted in his chair as if talking about his private life made him uncomfortable. "My ex-wife used to accuse me of being coldhearted." He rearranged a stack of papers on his desk. "What I'm saying is I understand your frustration . . . as well as any outsider might. I've been in this business a long time. Long enough to know that you don't have to look very hard or very far to find the scum of the earth lurking around almost every corner, which brings me to human trafficking. It's an epidemic. I know it. The FBI knows it, and something tells me you know it."

His gaze was on hers. He was letting her know she was on the right track and yet for whatever reason he couldn't say it outright.

"I was born and raised in Chicago," he went on, breaking eye contact. "We lived in a rough neighborhood, which is why I decided to become a police officer. I wanted to make a difference. I thought I was ready for anything. I felt invincible. But there was a problem. I felt too much empathy . . . for everybody. Every homicide, rape, robbery, and aggravated assault leaves a victim in its wake, and there wasn't a day where I didn't feel his or her pain. I would go home after every shift and lie awake in bed thinking of that victim. How would she support herself now that her husband was gone? Would that nice couple ever be the same after losing their only son to gang violence?"

He scratched the side of his head. "Empathy wasn't helping me. I had to find a way to get enough sleep so I could do my job properly."

She said nothing, just watched him stare into open space while he collected his thoughts and then finally continued.

"I taught myself to disconnect from it all. Callousness and hard-heartedness can be learned until it becomes habit."

What he was saying made sense, and she couldn't imagine doing his job, dealing with criminals and trying to help the victims of horrible crimes day in and day out. When it was clear he was finished she said, "I appreciate you sharing."

He nodded.

"What will happen to those girls from the salon?"

"They'll be taken to child services, where hopefully they'll get the help they need to move on."

Realizing the desperation of it all, Faith sighed. "I should get back to my friend. Are we finished here?"

"We're done," he said. "But I want you to know that not a day goes by that I don't think of your kids. I'm doing everything I can to stop them from slipping through the cracks."

Everyone had their own personal demons to deal with it, she thought. For the first time since meeting him, she wondered if perhaps he really was on her side. Faith stood. A knot in her throat stopped her from telling him she appreciated all his hard work. They shook hands. She swallowed before managing a heartfelt, "Thank you."

"I realize we got off to a bad start," he said, "but don't be afraid to share information with me. We do have resources available."

She nodded and then walked out the door.

Thirty-Six

Diane usually left the chores to the little whores, but at the moment everyone was in major lockdown, thanks to Jasper and Miranda. She'd even locked Phoenix in the barn. She didn't trust anyone.

She scrubbed harder, needing to get out her frustrations. She put her entire upper body into washing another pan as she looked through the kitchen window and out at the wide-open fields. Ever since Miranda and Jasper had disappeared, the girls at the farmhouse seemed on edge, everyone afraid they might be next to disappear. Even precious Trudi had been walking around the house with suspicious eyes as if she thought an assassin might jump out of the kitchen pantry at any moment.

Rumor had it that Miranda and Jasper were both dead, but Diane knew otherwise. Aster wasn't the only one with eyes and ears on the streets of Sacramento and its surrounding areas. No cash had been found on Jasper's body.

That really pissed her off.

Miranda could live for months on that kind of money.

She needed to find the girl before anyone else did. If Miranda talked to authorities, Jasper wouldn't be the only one to pay for his mistakes with a bullet to the head.

As she scrubbed, she noticed how her hands had aged. Before her hair had grown limp and the lines around her eyes deepened, Diane had been Aster's number one mistress. She used to wear beautiful clothes and nice jewelry. Now she was nothing more than a babysitter to a bunch of little sluts—sluts like sweet, innocent Jean. Soon after Miranda had left the farmhouse, the youngest girl, Jean, had become closer to some of the other girls. She usually spent most of her time alone, staring out at nothing or reading whatever book she could get her hands on. But lately she had a defiant look to her and more than once, Diane had caught her talking to Adele. Unlike most of the girls in the house, Adele had been taken from a grocery store while her mother shopped. The girl refused to obey the rules. It had taken months to convince her that her mother, Corrie Perelman, had given up looking for her. Runaways were much easier to train. If she didn't know better, she would say Adele was up to her old tricks. She and Jean had bonded and the two of them appeared to be conspiring ways to escape.

Diane didn't like it one bit, so back into the closet Adele went. Jean was ten years old, for God's sake, but you would think she was much younger. Grow up! By that age Diane had been forcibly subjected to every act of indecency imaginable. The thought pissed her off—so much so she left the pan and frantically looked around the kitchen, her heart beating rapidly against her chest as she grabbed a knife from the counter. Gripping the handle tightly, she marched through the house, keys jangling around her wrist as she unlocked one bedroom door after another until she found the room where beautiful little Jean was sitting on the floor with Trudi and Victoria.

"Oh, isn't this nice," Diane said. "Playing cards with your friends, I see."

"Is someone here to see us, Mother?" Victoria asked.

"Is someone here to see us, Mother?" Diane repeated in the same sickly sweet, kiss-ass tone of hers.

"What's wrong?" Trudi wanted to know.

Diane waved the knife in Jean's direction. "That's what's wrong."

The girl simply stared at her with those big blue eyes. She never blinked. The little bitch had been treated like a princess since the day she arrived. Aster called every week to check on the girl as if she were some sort of national treasure. "Hold her down," she told the girls.

"What?"

"You heard me! I said hold her down!"

"Who?" Trudi asked.

"Jean. I don't like the way she's looking at me."

Jean didn't move. Nobody did. Diane sucked in a mouthful of musty, manure-filled air and tried to calm herself.

Trudi had always done what she said, never had to be asked twice before now.

"My," Diane said, "how the tables have turned." The tension hovering between them was thick and nasty. Ever since discovering that Jasper had stolen her money and ran off with Miranda, she'd let her guard down around here . . . stopped paying attention to what the little whores were up to.

"Do it now!" Diane shouted. She stabbed the knife in the air in front of Victoria and felt the blood rush to her head. "You hold her arms to the floor and you," she said, pointing at Trudi, "hold her legs."

This time they did as she said.

Jean didn't cry, didn't squirm, didn't even let out a whimper as the girls held her flat to the ground. Her god-awful stare was wide and unblinking like a porcelain doll's.

Diane got down on her knees. "Did you know that your mom doesn't love you anymore?"

"That's a lie," Jean stated calmly. "You're a liar."

Trudi exchanged a worried look with Victoria.

"We're your family now," Diane told Jean. "Trudi, Victoria, and all the other girls here at the house are your sisters. I don't know how much the girls have told you, Jean, but pretty soon you're going to have to earn your keep around here."

The uninterested look on Jean's face sent chills up Diane's spine. She wanted . . . needed to put the fear of God back into the girl. "Miranda is dead."

An eerie calmness settled over the room until Jean said matter-of-factly, "No she's not. Miranda is alive, and she's going to come back and take me away from here."

Diane felt the blood rush to her face. Her chest tightened, making it hard to breathe as she reached down and grabbed Jean by the hair, yanking her up from the ground so that they were nose to nose. "It's time to teach you a lesson!"

Victoria made the mistake of grabbing Diane's arm to stop her. She backhanded the bitch and then dragged Jean out the door, locking it securely behind her. The young girl's cries as she dragged her across the hallway and down the stairs filled her satisfaction. It was time to show Jean what life was all about.

It had been raining nonstop for hours.

Miranda sat quietly in the hotel room wondering what to do next. She reached for the flyer on the nightstand and took a good, long look at Jean's picture. Her real name was Lara McMann. Her brother had been taken, too, but Miranda had no idea where the boy could be. She sat on the edge of the bed and stared at the phone.

She should call the hotline, but something kept stopping her.

Would somebody answer? She leaned over, picked up the receiver, and carefully dialed the number on the flyer. She heard a ring and quickly hung up.

What if the call went straight to the police? She didn't trust the police. She didn't trust anyone. The hotline was probably a setup.

She came to her feet and began to pace the room. She felt like a fool as she raked a hand through her hair. What would she say? What should she do?

How could it be a setup? The flyers had to have been made weeks ago, well before she ever ran from Mother. The flyers had nothing to do with catching her and everything to with helping Jean. She was being paranoid. The honk of a horn, a car door slamming shut, raindrops hitting the roof . . . every sound startled her, made her wonder if this was it, if her time was up.

She went to the window and peeked through the curtain. There were five cars in the parking lot below. Across the street, she watched a man in a raincoat and hat hunch over as he rushed down the sidewalk before disappearing inside a corner market.

Her stomach gurgled.

The sound of squishy, wet footsteps caused her to step away from the curtain until her back was flat against the wall. The footfalls stopped right outside her door. Frozen in place, she hardly breathed, didn't dare make a sound. She looked around the room, trying to decide what she could use against an attacker if someone crashed through the door without warning.

They were coming after her. She could feel it.

And then footsteps sounded again. Whoever had been at the door was walking away.

Her gaze returned to the phone as she swallowed the lump of fear lodged in her throat. If she dialed the number and no one answered, she would have to leave a message along with the motel's phone number where they could call her back. The thought of telling even a recorded voice where she was staying caused a cold sweat to cover the length of her body.

What was wrong with her?

She was exhausted . . . hungry and exhausted.

After standing in the dark for too long, she decided to rest for a moment before heading out to find a pay phone. She walked quietly to the bed, curled up on top of the mattress, and thought of her mom and how she wished she were with her now.

THIRTY-SEVEN

The next morning, Faith, Beast, and Rage met at the command post in her parents' backyard to see where things stood. "So far," Faith said, "we've had no luck locating a tattoo artist named Fin. Tina, the girl I talked to on Watt, said she recognized one of the men in my painting as being 'in the business,' which tells me we might be on the right track." She looked from Rage to Beast. "What else do we have?"

"I've got a name and a location of someone who may be involved in the sex trafficking business," Beast said. "His name is Patrick and he works out of a liquor store. I've been keeping an eye on the place, but there has been no unusual activity."

"What about the partial license number?" Faith asked.

"So far no match with that make and model."

"Besides the fact that we didn't have an entire number," Rage chimed in, "these guys could have changed out the license plate, for all we know."

"I think I'll turn over the license number and blurry pictures to Detective Yuhasz. It can't hurt."

"We need to find ways to keep your story in front of the media," Rage said.

"Yeah," Beast said. "I say we keep the pressure on these guys . . . keep their faces in front of people."

Jana walked in with a tray of bagels and cream cheese. Her brother's four-year-old daughter, Dacotah, was at her side, looking around with curious eyes.

"Mom said you all need to eat something," Jana announced.

Beast jumped up to help her and set the tray in the middle of the table.

"What are you doing with Dacotah?" Faith asked. "Are you looking after her today?"

Jana looked down at the little girl, all round-faced and dimpled-cheeked. "Bri and I are going to the mall to shop for a few items for the baby's room. She's in the house talking to Mom."

Dacotah was a shy little girl, but that didn't stop her from making a beeline for Beast, who had just returned to his seat on the couch they had brought in the other day. Dacotah only had eyes for Beast as she showed him her Barbie, which was in two pieces.

"Broken arm," Beast said. "Want me to help you fix it?"

Dacotah nodded, then watched closely as Beast expertly twisted the plastic arm back into Barbie's empty arm socket. "Good as new," he said as he handed the doll back to her. She smiled and then climbed onto the couch and wriggled around so she was squished right up next to him, her legs sticking straight out.

"That's odd," Jana said, "considering she doesn't warm to too many people."

Chilly air rushed inside when the door opened and Bri stepped inside. "Have you seen—oh, my." Without another word, Bri walked gingerly around the table in the center of the room, cautiously making her way to where her daughter stared up at Beast, clearly fascinated by the gentle giant.

"Um, come on, Dacotah."

"Look! He fixed my doll, Mommy."

Bri forced a tentative smile as she made eye contact with Beast, gesturing for her daughter to come along but keeping her distance at the same time, as if she were afraid he might reach out and take her hostage.

It was clear to Faith, judging by Beast's demeanor, that Bri's actions were something he'd dealt with many times before.

"Well, we should go," Jana said before she looked at Faith, "but I wanted to let you know that we're getting more and more tips every day. I sent at least a dozen calls on to Detective Yuhasz. Mrs. Perelman called again. She's still having vivid dreams. She said she would call again if she had anything to report." Jana paused. "Oh, and I did have two hang-up calls on the hotline this morning, which was unusual." She shrugged.

Faith tried to keep a hopeful attitude. "Thanks for sifting through it all."

Jana went to Faith and gave her a squeeze. "Not a problem. Hang in there."

Faith sighed. She knew firsthand that all the hoping and wishing in the world couldn't make it so.

Bri had a heck of a time getting Dacotah to leave Beast's side. Finally Beast stood, towering over Bri. They both watched the little girl slip her hand into his as if they were communicating by osmosis. Beast proceeded to walk Dacotah back to the house, with Bri following behind and Jana waddling after them with a smile on her face.

When Beast returned a few minutes later, Faith was looking over the list of H&M clients for the dozenth time, hoping one of the names would leap off the page at her. She and Rage had hoped to find a client with notable wealth, but nobody on the list stood out. They had condensed the list to the wealthiest clients, which left a grand total of twelve people. A rapper who lived in a big house in Los Lagos, a dentist from Rocklin, and a couple of doctors in the Sacramento area. When Beast had arrived this morning, he'd said he'd put all dozen clients into his database and they all came out clean—no criminal record or any record of wrongdoing.

"Here's an interesting e-mail," Rage said. "You two need to take a look at this."

Faith went to where Rage was sitting and hovered over her shoulder. Beast did the same.

"Someone is demanding a ransom for the return of Lara and Hudson," she said. "They want fifty thousand dollars delivered to a particular spot within Placer County, not to be designated until right before drop-off."

Beast grunted.

"No police," Rage said as she continued reading.

"Is there an IP address?" Beast asked.

"Nope. Nothing. I checked. It's a foreign IP address. Somebody is probably using some sort of proxy server or something." There was a long pause before Rage said, "So, what do you guys think?"

"Send a message back asking for more information or proof that they have my kids," Faith said.

Rage typed a quick reply, letting the sender know they received their e-mail and wanted proof. She hit "Send."

Beast shook his head. "I don't like it."

"What do you mean?" Faith asked. "There's nothing to like about any of this, but at least it's something." Her heart beat fast against her ribs. She thought of Corrie Perelman and how unstable she seemed, but it wasn't helping her calm down. Desperation, she realized, tended to highlight her emotions. Having her kids snatched away made every decision feel more urgent. There was no way she could let this go without checking it out. How would she sleep knowing she might have lost the one opportunity she had to find her kids?

Her mind was made up.

"More than likely it could be someone trying to cash in, or worse, it could be a trap."

"You think someone really wants me dead?"

"Yeah," Beast said. "I think that's pretty obvious. The scar around your throat is proof of that. I'm sure whoever is behind the attack doesn't like seeing you on TV every other day, either."

Rage looked up from the screen. "Was the nail salon incident on the news?"

Beast nodded. "That's how I knew what you two were up to yesterday. Faith's image is all over the place. They showed clips of both of you leaving the police station. I'm sure whoever is in charge of these goons was thrilled to see that you had a hand in rescuing a few of their girls and shutting down one of their businesses all in a day's work."

"What about you?" Faith asked. "Where were you yesterday?"

His eyes glimmered. "Don't worry about me. I'm just gathering information, and I'll let you know if anything checks out."

Ding. Ding.

Rage read the incoming e-mail out loud. "They doubled the ransom to one hundred thousand dollars. This will be their last correspondence. Faith is to drive to the Mark White Neighborhood Park in the city of Roseville on 504 Sixth Street. She's to go alone and then sit at a park bench and wait for further instructions."

Beast shook his head. "It's not a good idea."

Faith looked into Beast's dark eyes. "I can't just shrug it off, figure it all for a scam, and go on my merry way. What if the men who took my kids were just minions and have suddenly realized that they can make a few bucks? Not one of us knows the truth. What if they really do have my kids or they know of their whereabouts?" She looked at the clock and then at Rage. "How much time do I have?"

"You're supposed to be at the Mark White Neighborhood Park in one hour with the cash."

"Slow down," Beast said. "Think about this for a moment."

"There's no time. I will not ignore their request. I have to check it out."

"It's too risky."

"I'm sorry, but I'm going." She peered into Beast's eyes. "If it were your daughter, you would do the same."

"Fine," Beast said. "Then we're going with you."

Thirty minutes later Faith was in her Camry driving toward Old Roseville to Vernon and then making a left on Sixth Street. Trees lined the road, their branches dancing in the wind. She pulled to the side of the road and suddenly in her mind's eye she saw Lara dancing, too, as Faith videotaped her. Her small arms raised above her head, swaying along with her body. Her crystal-blue eyes filled with joy. Faith reached out, too, extending her arm until her fingertips brushed against the windshield, the moment fading . . . gone, only trees. The knot in her throat traveled downward, like swallowing a jagged rock.

Had it really been only weeks ago that she'd held her children in her arms? Weeks that now felt like a lifetime—two lifetimes. Her insides twisted. "I will find our children, Craig, just as you would have done had you been the one to survive." She inhaled. It should have been Craig sitting here now. He would have already found Lara and Hudson. He was strong and smart and always calm under fire. He would have had a plan and known what to do.

But he wasn't there, which meant she was her children's only hope.

The anger she'd felt since first coming out of that heavy fog of grief sat on her shoulders, poking and prodding. She'd never been an angry person. No road rage or simmering resentment had ever lurked within. She'd never understood angry people and the way they exploded like a volcano when they erupted . . . cruel words bubbling from their mouths, sending bits and pieces of wrath and pain into the air, affecting all those standing too close. In this very moment, though, she felt all their pain in one fell swoop.

"Are we there?" Rage asked from behind her seat.

"Yes," Faith said.

"Where's Beast?"

"He drove around to the other side. I'm going to the bench now."

She climbed out of the car, inhaled the damp air as she walked to the trunk, and grabbed the duffel bag filled with cash. She shut the trunk. The wind had picked up, whistling in her ear. The ground was wet from recent rains, the air moist and cold against her skin. Reaching into her pocket, she gripped the pistol.

Was Beast right? Was this a trap?

She looked around, did her best to tamp down the fear, refusing to panic. *Stay calm. Keep walking. One step at a time.*

The park was small, and it was empty—named after Officer Mark White, who was shot down while trying to apprehend an armed suspect inside the Roseville Police Station. *So much sadness in the world,* Faith thought. Her legs wobbled a bit as she walked across the grass. No sooner had she taken a seat on the bench than she thought she heard a noise. A loud crack sounded somewhere to her left.

The snapping of a tree branch? Or something else?

The wind and the shadows were playing tricks on her.

Crack.

There it was again. She jumped to her feet, pivoted toward the sound. As soon as she did, there was a thump, thump, thump behind her and then a hard tug on the strap of the duffel bag. She turned the other way.

BAM!

Something hard and solid hit her squarely in the forehead, sending her reeling backward. On her back, stretched out flat on the wet grass, her vision blurred as she watched two shadows run off, duffel bag swinging.

"That way!" she heard Rage yell.

Beast was right. She'd been set up. A sharp pain sliced through her head.

"Furious! Are you OK?"

Faith opened her eyes and found herself looking at Rage. Rage helped her sit up and then move a bloody mat of hair out of Faith's eyes. "Crap," Rage said. "The bump on your head is already the size of a Ping-Pong ball. You're too stubborn for your own good. You should have listened to Beast. If you're going to find your kids, Furious, you're going to have to use some logic and"—she squeezed her fingers together—"a little bit of patience would also be nice."

Faith touched her forehead and waited for the dizziness to pass. "I know. You're right."

"Look what I found," Beast said as he headed their way. The duffel bag was strapped over his shoulder. In his right hand he held one skinny teenage boy by his shirt, holding him high enough from the ground that the kid struggled to find footing. The other boy was being dragged along on Beast's left side, knees skidding across dirt and leaves.

"These two thought their ransom idea would be an easy way to make a few bucks," Beast said.

Rage rose to her feet and plunked her hands on her hips.

"They think I should let them go," he went on. "But I thought I'd let Furious decide."

Feeling a little better, Faith pushed herself to her feet and took a couple of steps toward Beast so she could get a good look at the boys. The one on the left looked a few years older than the other boy. His hair was long and straggly. He had big ears and a bad case of acne.

"You think this is all a funny game?" Faith asked.

"We saw you on TV and then went to your website and saw that you were offering a reward." He used his chin to gesture at the other boy. "It was his idea."

"It was not!" the other boy cried. "I didn't want to do it, but Matt told me it wouldn't be a big deal."

"Matt," Faith said. "Did you hit me or did your friend?"

"I did, ma'am."

"Shoot him," Faith said, handing Rage her gun, hoping to scare the boys. "Twice. Once for hitting me and again for calling me ma'am."

The kid made a squeaky noise as he squirmed and tried to get loose. He was scared now. His face paled. Beast had no problem keeping the boys firmly within his grasp. "What about his friend?"

"Kill them both."

They started to cry, and Faith was glad for it. She wasn't serious about having them killed. She took the pistol back and told Beast to do whatever he wanted with the boys.

Faith headed back for her car.

Her shoulders shook, and she stopped suddenly before slowly sinking to her knees as she realized today was not the day she would feel Hudson's and Lara's arms around her. She would not bury her face into the crooks of their necks and breathe in their sweet innocence. Today would not be that day.

Thunder boomed in the distance.

The first drop of rain hit Faith at the same time she felt Rage's arm slide around her shoulder and pull her upright. Together they walked the rest of the way to Faith's car. Rage helped her into the passenger seat and without a word took her keys, walked around to the other side, and climbed in behind the wheel. She looked at Faith as if she might say something, but no words came forth. Instead she turned on the engine, kept her eyes on road, and drove off.

THIRTY-EIGHT

As instructed, Richard Price parked his car near the water fountain outside Aster's ten-thousand-square-foot house overlooking Folsom Lake. This was his first time he'd ever met the big boss at his residence. He looked into his rearview mirror, straightened his collar, and said confidently, "I want out."

And that was the truth.

He knew his chances of being let go were slim, but he'd always had a way with negotiating, especially if he agreed to give him a large share of his past earnings. Knowing that Aster was more careful than most and would never take him out at his own house, a place where he and his wife entertained and his children played, gave him the confidence he needed to go through with it. If Aster refused his request, he would walk away knowing his time was limited. But he wasn't worried. In the event that happened, he would leave tonight. Papers were in order: passport, new ID, everything he needed to make a new life for himself on a faraway island.

One thing was clear. He couldn't do this anymore. He wanted absolutely nothing to do with the human trafficking business. The moment he'd hung up the phone yesterday after Patrick called to tell him Aster wanted to talk to him first thing in the morning, he'd known what he needed to do. Instead of going into the office, he'd spent the day at home making videos and documenting everything that had gone on over the past five years. When he was finished, he'd ended up with a fifty-page Word document that he filed in a private Dropbox account. He'd also printed out a copy along with enough documentation to fill two binders with the names of the men in charge in addition to photos, any and all known addresses, and phone numbers for every trafficker he'd met along the way. He also included a list of names of their highest-paying clients, which included bankers, businessmen, lawyers, and political figures.

On his way to El Dorado Hills, he'd stopped at the post office and sent the hard copy to his sister in Florida, asking her not to open the file and to keep it in a safe in case he needed it in the future.

He'd talked to an old friend and high-powered criminal defense attorney. They had a telephone conference set up for next week to discuss the possibility of turning himself in. He wondered how Aster would feel about that.

The clouds were dark and swollen but had yet to break open. Only a misty drizzle covered his windshield. No need for an umbrella. Richard climbed out of his car and made his way around the side of the house to the pool as instructed.

A dog barked, making him tense. He hoped Aster didn't have guard dogs running around the property. He followed the stone path until he came to a long, rectangular pool surrounded by marble statues and healthy palms imported from the Canary Islands, no doubt.

Aster sat within an outdoor kitchen area complete with rustic ceilings and lots of old-world chandeliers hanging over a dining table and chairs. There were tarps laid out and scaffolding where work was being done. Patrick, the same man Richard had seen last time he'd met with Aster, was there, too, leaning back in his chair a few seats down from the boss. Something about him annoyed the hell out of Richard. Where did Aster find these guys?

Richard tugged at the tie around his neck as he joined them at the table. "You have a beautiful place here. What a view."

Aster merely smiled. "Have a seat, Richard."

He pulled out a chair and took a seat.

"I called you here today because I wanted you to know how badly you fucked up."

Richard felt the blood rush to his head. "How so?"

"Remember Faith McMann?"

As a matter of fact, he did. She was the reason he could no longer sleep at night. Knowing he was responsible for her husband's death and her children's kidnapping didn't sit well with him. Nobody was supposed to die. The wife and kids were never to be involved. He'd fucked up in more ways than one, but Aster didn't need to know the particulars of how it all went down.

"It wasn't Craig McMann who took my money," Aster said.

Shit. Richard straightened, trying to cover the dread seeping into his veins. "I know."

"You knew that Joe Henderson stole from us, then pointed the finger at his partner?"

"Yeah. Joe was the guy I'd been doing business with. When I asked him about the two million dollars, he assured me it wasn't a problem and that he'd look into it."

"And so did you?"

Richard shifted uneasily in his seat. "Of course. But Joe kept giving me excuses until I sent my men over to rough him up and tear apart his house to see what they could find. That's when the rat bastard blamed everything on his so-called friend." *Rat bastard* was putting it mildly. A sheen of sweat formed on his forehead. He knew that Faith McMann and her kids were simply victims of circumstance, but he'd hoped to keep it from Aster. *Shit.* Things weren't unfolding here today as he'd hoped.

"How did you find out?"

"You should know better than most that I've got friends in all the right places, including the brother of an FBI agent working the case."

Richard said nothing.

"So what do you suggest we do about this?"

"I think it would be best if we got those kids back to their mother."

Aster stared at him for a moment as if to gauge whether or not Richard was serious, which he was. Then Aster smiled, a wide grin that revealed straight white teeth. He lifted both hands in the air as if surrendering. "Just hand them over? Sorry, big mistake. Here's your kids, lady."

"Yeah, something like that," Richard said. "I could make arrangements. Nobody would know any of us had anything to do with it."

The grooves in Aster's face deepened. "Don't be a fucking idiot. Those kids are worth half a million in the international market. If they weren't worth so damn much, I would have killed them already. Until it's safe to smuggle them out of the country, I'm keeping them under the radar. And another thing . . ."

Richard kept quiet, waiting for the pompous ass to continue.

"One of my men was shot in the leg by a friend of Faith McMann's, an ogre of a man who was recently snooping around the liquor store on Del Paso. Coincidence?"

Richard sighed.

Across the table, Aster's sidekick Patrick didn't say a word as he picked up the firearm from the chair next to him and calmly attached a suppressor to the muzzle.

In the kitchen window, Richard saw the faint outline of Aster's wife as she put water in a vase. She smiled and gave a quick wave before sauntering off.

He felt safer knowing Aster's wife was only a few feet away. "I want out," Richard said, tired of Aster's intimidation tactics and subtle threats.

Aster smiled. "Who doesn't?" He waved a hand toward Patrick. "Patrick, do you want out of the business?"

Patrick nodded.

"See? We all finally agree on something."

"I'll finish what I'm working on and then I'm out," Richard went on. "I'll give you fifty percent of my earnings for the past year."

"Very generous of you," Aster said, "but the answer is still no."

Patrick moved his hand so that it sat atop the gun.

Richard pushed himself to his feet. "Why don't you think about it?"

"I have," Aster said before nodding at Patrick, who then stood, raised the gun, and fired a bullet into the middle of Richard's forehead.

Stunned, Richard wondered if he'd really been hit. He felt nothing more than a sting, and then blast off, his body went cold and his legs folded beneath him as an image of his sister receiving the package he'd sent flashed within his mind. His last thought before he hit the ground was that he should have included a note wishing her a happy birthday.

THIRTY-NINE

Faith lay in bed wondering if Craig could possibly have had anything to do with money being laundered . . . or stolen for that matter. The notion didn't compute. She wouldn't allow her mind to go there. She slid out of bed. She needed to get back to the client list, find a link to the men who took Lara and Hudson. She turned on her computer.

Twenty-three new messages: mostly condolences from well-meaning strangers who wanted Faith to know she was in their prayers, but also an e-mail from a young man who was offering help if she sent money first. For her convenience, he took PayPal.

Overall, the response to her plea for help in finding her kids was awe inspiring. One hundred thousand people had liked her Facebook page and were keeping a lookout for Lara and Hudson. Small groups had been formed in Yuba City, Grass Valley, and Elk Grove. Complete strangers were doing what they could to raise awareness and help find her children. Her case was gathering national attention.

She gingerly touched the knot on her forehead and prayed someone out there would give her a lead that would guide her to her children. The squawk of a blue jay prompted her to look out her window. She noticed the rope swing hanging from a branch. The last time she'd sat on the swing, Craig had pulled the rope back as if he were going to let her fly through the air, but instead he twisted the rope around and surprised her with a kiss that made her toes curl.

She inhaled a shuddering breath at the thought. She missed him so much it hurt to think about him. She had yet to mourn Craig. Until she found Lara and Hudson, she couldn't allow emotions to get in her way.

As she did several times a day, she stared at the picture of the tattoo she'd painted. She said the name Fin aloud. Angel had said Fin was a tattoo artist who branded girls with a family name or symbol. She and Rage had visited every tattoo place in the area. Nobody had ever heard the name. Not only had she asked Dad to pass the name on to Detective Yuhasz, she'd Googled the name and come up empty. She rubbed the back of her neck. There were so many unanswered questions, so many loose ends.

The rich aroma of coffee brought her to her feet, but it wasn't until she glanced at the clock that she remembered she was supposed to meet Rage and Beast at their house. If she hurried, she would make it on time.

After brushing her teeth and pulling back her hair, she dressed quickly in jeans and a T-shirt followed by a hooded sweatshirt and sneakers. She grabbed her cell phone and backpack and made her way downstairs. As she hit the landing, she heard what sounded like quiet sobs coming from the family room. She walked that way. Mom sat on the middle of the couch, slouched over a photo album, her shoulders quivering.

Faith took a seat next to her. Mom had always loved to make photo albums. She would include scraps of fabric and use colored pens and markers to decorate. The album in her lap was from three Christmases ago. Hudson and Lara were sitting on Santa's lap; they had no idea that Grandpa was the man behind the long white beard and red-and-white outfit stuffed with pillows.

Mom looked at her and wiped her eyes. "Oh, Faith," she said when she noticed the knot on her head and the discoloring around her eyes.

"It's OK, Mom."

"No, it's not. Look at you. You have enough problems without having to see me fall apart."

"I love you, Mom." Faith wrapped her arms around her, and for a moment in time they simply held each other tight.

———

Little Vinnie opened the front door before Faith could knock. His head nearly hit the top of the door frame. Faith had to crane her neck to look him in the eye.

"Charlie and Sally . . . I mean Beast and Rage," he said with a wink, "will be back shortly. They went for a quick run around the block."

Charlie and Sally? She'd never thought about what their birth names might be. Beast and Rage just sort of made sense. She shook the thought away and asked, "Should Rage be running in her condition?"

"I don't think you want Rage to hear you talking like that. Ever since she was diagnosed she likes to pretend nothing has changed. And that means starting the day with a morning run—doesn't matter how exhausted she is or whether or not she can hardly push herself out of bed. I guess running helps her get out some of that pent-up frustration she has within. Who am I, or you," he said, pointing a finger at Faith, "to tell her how to spend her last months on this earth?"

He had a point. And yet the idea of Rage dying at such a young age didn't compute. Yes, she looked pale and exhausted most of the time, but she had a spark to her. She brought energy and life to a room. "Did she get more than one doctor's opinion?"

"She did."

Faith could tell by the way he wouldn't make eye contact that he didn't want to talk about it, either. He gestured toward one of the chairs tucked under the square table pushed against the wall. "Have a seat."

She pulled out a chair and did as he said.

Little Vinnie plopped down on the couch, then leaned forward and grabbed hold of the rifle sitting on the coffee table and started wiping it down with a cloth. "This here is a twenty-gauge shotgun. My son said you were going to the shooting range."

"Yes, that's where we're headed, but that gun looks a little out of my comfort zone."

He chuckled. "Don't worry. This is my baby. We've got all sorts of firearms for you to try out." He lifted an eyebrow. "Ever shot a rifle before?"

"I've been practicing shooting a pistol. As far as rifles go, I've only shot one once, when I was younger. My dad was a commander in the army. He's also a hunter. He used to take us shooting, but it was my brother who had the skills and even competed."

He put the gun down, wiped his hands on his pants, and then reached for the bottle of whiskey, taking a swallow right from the bottle. He held it up in the air, offering it to her.

"No, thanks."

He made a slicing gesture across his throat. "Those bastards did that to you?"

She nodded.

"Beast is worried about you."

"Why is that?"

"Thinks you might be a bit of a loose cannon."

She figured he was referring to the Taser incident. "Me? Ha. That's sort of calling the kettle black—don't you think?"

He shrugged. "From what I'm hearing about your situation, you'd have to be a little crazy to begin with to go after these guys, let alone try to stop them."

"They're everywhere and yet nowhere to be found," she said.

"Seems like it."

She stood, crossed the room, and looked at the pictures lining a shelf. She picked one up. It was Beast, a woman she assumed was his wife, and their daughter—an adorable little girl wearing a flower-print dress and a big smile.

Her insides kinked.

"He hasn't been the same since. Doing all he can to help someone like Rage, and now you, gives him a purpose."

"What about you?" Faith asked. "What gives you purpose?"

"Charlie does."

"Charlie . . . hmm?"

"That was his name before his wife and daughter were killed. Charlie gives my life purpose."

Faith set the picture back on the mantel at about the same time the door flew open. Rage marched inside and nodded hello to Little Vinnie as she made her way across the room to the kitchen, where she poured herself a glass of water and guzzled it down.

Beast entered next, hardly spared her a glance. He took the bottle of booze from the table in front of his father and disappeared inside a room connected to the kitchen. When he came back, he gave his dad a pat on the back and said, "Guns ready?"

Little Vinnie nodded.

He looked at Faith. "Ready to rock and roll?"

Shooting practice was interesting. Mostly it was loud and intimidating, but holding a gun and shooting at a target had felt better than Faith had imagined. That power she'd always been afraid of was no longer something she feared. Watching Rage had been a turning point. There wasn't anything that girl couldn't do. It was hard to believe she was sick at all. She had more stamina than Faith and Beast put together. Faith knew Rage didn't sleep well and yet she'd taken a morning run and then managed to shoot a pistol, an AK-47, and a twenty-gauge rifle with amazing accuracy. "Is there anything you can't do?" Faith asked her as they put their guns away and then cleaned up the brass.

"Yeah," Rage said. "I can't cook."

"That's not true," Beast said as he hitched the gun bag over his shoulder and started off toward his truck. "She made Dad and me the best turkey dinner I've ever tasted—stuffing, cranberry sauce from scratch, mashed potatoes, and homemade bread."

"What about the pie?" Rage asked. "Tell her about the pie."

"OK, it's true. She can't bake worth beans."

Rage punched him in the ribs, making him grunt.

Before Faith climbed into the backseat, her phone vibrated. It was Jana. She hit "Talk" and said hello.

"Faith!" Jana screeched into the receiver. "You're never going to believe this. We've had an uptick in calls over the last twenty-four hours. I try to answer many of the calls, but most of them are sent through to the answering machine. I happened to pick up the last call, though. It was a young girl. I think she might be legit. She sounds nervous, but she knows something and she wants to meet with you."

"Hold on." Faith explained to Beast and Rage what was going on, then she put her sister on speakerphone and asked her to tell her everything she knew.

"I got a call on the hotline," Jana began, her tone calmer. "She said her name was Miranda. She sounded young. She talked fast and sounded scared. She wants to talk to you about a girl named Jean."

Faith didn't understand, but she held her breath and listened.

"Miranda told me she'd been held captive at a farmhouse for the past eighteen months. There were other girls there, too, including a ten-year-old girl named Jean. After managing to escape, Miranda returned to Sacramento, where she found one of your flyers. She said the girl in the picture, Lara McMann, looked a lot like Jean."

The beat of Faith's heart kicked up a notch. "Did she leave a number?"

"No. She doesn't have a cell phone and she didn't want to say where she was calling from, but she's willing to meet you at Candy Heaven on Front Street in Old Sacramento. I told her I would be happy to pick her up, but she only wants to talk to Jean's mother, which she believes is you."

"And you think she's legit?"

"Yes. And as you and I discussed, I asked her to describe what Jean looked like. She knew the color of her eyes, talked about how small she was for her age, and even mentioned the tiny scar on Lara's chin." There was a pause before she added, "It has to be her, Faith."

"When does Miranda want to meet?"

"Right now."

"What does she look like? How will I know it's her?"

"She said she's seen you on TV and knows what you look like. She'll find you. Oh, and she wants you to come alone."

"Do you know why?"

"I think she's seriously scared, Faith."

———

Dark clouds and a cold afternoon drizzle hadn't stopped people from visiting Old Sacramento, a historic site along the Sacramento River. As Faith headed across L Street, she kept her gaze straight ahead and her right hand curled around the pistol in the front pocket of her sweatshirt. If a thug were to pop out of the woodwork at any given moment, she wasn't sure she could handle a firearm. How would she find her stance and lock her wrists before being shot down?

Couples walked along the covered sidewalk window-shopping while a mother tried to maneuver her stroller around them. A jogger ran past, startling her. Her breath caught in her throat. Her palms felt sweaty. The wind caused a loose shingle on one of the shops to sway to and fro. Straight ahead was Joe's Crab Shack, and to her left she could see the sign for Candy Heaven.

Standing on the corner of Front Street and L, she stopped and looked around. She had a clear view, but she couldn't see anyone watching her. Nobody stood out.

Two kids ran out of the candy store. Once again she was startled by the sudden noise. For the first time since her sister had given her the news that a girl named Miranda had called the hotline, she wondered if she'd once again made a terrible mistake. What if the same men who'd been watching her were using the girl as a ploy?

She could be walking into a trap.

The same men who had attacked them in their house and killed Craig could have found one of the flyers she'd posted and set her up. Before she could abruptly turn around and walk back the way she came, someone grabbed her arm. "Faith McMann?"

Faith swiveled about, her grip firmly around the gun, her finger ready to pull the trigger. The girl standing before her wore a baseball cap pulled low over her eyes. Straight white hair was tucked behind her ears. "Are you Miranda?"

"Come on," the girl said. "Let's walk. I think I'm being followed."

Faith started to look over her shoulder.

"Look straight ahead. Act natural."

"How do I know you don't work for the men who took my children?"

Miranda glanced her way but didn't slow her pace. "You don't."

In a heartbeat Faith realized she had no choice but to trust the girl. "Is it true? Have you seen my daughter? Who has Lara?"

"They changed her name to Jean. They also tattooed her arm with the letter *H*." As she walked, Miranda pulled her coat, along with her shirt, down over her shoulder to give Faith an idea of what she was talking about.

Faith kept walking. "Where are we going?"

"We'll find a place to hide and hopefully lose them. Where are you parked?"

"My friends are in a truck close by. I can call them."

"You were supposed to come alone."

The clouds overhead broke open, and within seconds a light drizzle became a downpour.

"I was with them when I got the call," Faith said as she pulled her hood over her head. "In order to make your time frame, I had to bring—"

A shot rang out. The bullet hit the metal sign next to Faith.

Faith ducked. A woman screamed. People dodged past them, running into the shops and restaurants for cover.

"Run!" Miranda said and that's exactly what Faith did. People still on the sidewalks were either frozen in place or ducking behind benches and wooden trash bins.

Faith did her best to keep up with Miranda, running on the street, bent over as she ran, keeping her head low and staying close to the cars parked at the curb. The rain wasn't letting up. Soaked through, Faith tripped as she rounded a corner, but she managed to catch her balance in time to see Miranda cut a sharp right into the parking garage.

They sprinted to the back of the garage and hid behind a Ford Escape, both catching their breath as they waited to see if anyone followed them inside.

No sooner had they ducked low behind the SUV than two men stopped in front of the garage entrance. Seconds later, they split off, leaving one lone man to walk into the garage.

Faith pulled the pistol from her pocket and got into position so she would be ready to shoot if she had to.

Miranda's eyes widened at the sight of the gun.

The clack of the man's shoes echoed off the thick cement walls. Faith held still when the tip of a dark shadow came into view. Another few feet and he would see them both. Faith steadied her wrists and held her breath.

A young couple walked into the garage, chatting away as they headed for their car, oblivious to the danger lurking nearby. The gunman turned and walked back the way he came. As soon as he exited the garage and disappeared farther down the street, Faith put the gun away. Then she pulled out her phone and called Beast.

"Where are you?"

"I'm with Miranda. We're in the parking garage next to Joe's Crab Shack. There are two men with guns. One of them is close by."

"We heard a shot. Is anyone hurt?"

"We're fine."

"We'll be right there. Stay put."

When she got off the phone, she told Miranda as much as she could about Beast and Rage and what was going on. Sirens sounded in the distance. They stayed low behind the SUV and waited.

"Earlier you asked me who has your daughter," Miranda said quietly.

Faith nodded, waited for her to go on.

"Jasper, a boy who worked at the farmhouse, told me that the operation was run by the mafia."

"Where is he? Can I talk to him?"

"He's dead."

Beast's truck pulled into the garage, engine rumbling. The rest of her questions would have to wait. "Come on," Faith said. "Let's get you out of here."

FORTY

Hudson and four other boys, Joey, Denver, Aiden, and Sean, had been brought to a cabin in the woods. Denver, thirteen, was the oldest boy in the room. He was bossy and mean, so Hudson did his best to stay away from him. He had no idea how far they were from home, but his every waking thought was about escaping. They had tried to get out the windows, but the boards covering them were screwed in.

All five of them wanted the same thing—to escape.

They had been making plans since last night, ever since finding a hole to the outside beneath a section of baseboard in the bedroom where they were kept each night. They each took turns digging. Right now it was Aiden and Hudson's turn. As they worked, Denver talked about how the five of them were the lucky ones. He went into gross detail about what the other kids were probably being forced to do to old dudes who paid for sex. Hudson wasn't sure whether or not he believed him. Maybe Denver was only trying to scare them.

During the day, all five of them were led to a large warehouse-type building with cement floors and aluminum walls. That's when they would join together with other groups of boys, where they were all forced to trim cannabis. He'd been doing it for more than a week now. Wearing gloves and using sharp scissors, they spent all day trimming leaves. Sometimes he would get blisters. The scissors they used were chained to the table where they worked. Denver said it was to make sure they didn't use the scissors as a weapon and start a riot. So far, Hudson's steady and fast hands kept him in the mountains instead of on the streets like a lot of the other boys—that is, if Denver's stories were true. More than anything, Hudson wanted to go home.

At the moment, all five of them were back in the tiny windowless room they shared each night. After working from sunrise to sunset, they ate rice and bread and then they were locked in their room until the next morning. There were no beds, only a few dirty blankets scattered across the hardwood floor. At night it got real cold and sometimes they all ended up squished together to stay warm. Except for Denver, who took one of the three blankets and slept far away from the rest of them.

Hudson smiled when he realized the hole was getting big enough that he could probably stick his head all the way outside. He was about to tell the other guys when they heard footsteps outside the door.

Aiden tossed a dirty towel over the hole, covering the pile of dirt. They all looked at one another, then rushed to the middle of the room, plopped down on the floor, and tried to look bored. Sean grabbed a deck of cards and dealt them each a hand.

The door swung open. Hudson rubbed his eyes, feigning drowsiness. When Derek, the guy with the long ponytail, stepped inside, Hudson said, "I'm hungry."

"Too bad. You should have eaten when you had the chance." Derek's gaze roamed the room, his head angling in curiosity when he noticed the lumpy towel in the corner of the room.

A bug skittered across the floor.

In hopes of getting Derek's attention, Hudson jumped up, squished the bug with his thumb, and then put it in his mouth and chewed.

The other boys laughed.

Derek grimaced. "You are one seriously deranged kid."

"Thanks," Hudson said, still chewing.

More snickering.

"You boys won't be laughing for too much longer."

Nobody said anything, everyone hoping he would go away, but that would have been too easy.

"The boss's ninety-year-old grandmother needs some help," Derek said. "And it looks like you boys get to do the honors. One of you is going to have the pleasure of cutting back her brittle yellow toenails while the rest of you give her naked body a good scrub with a damp washcloth. Whoever is left gets to pleasure her in other ways. She may be toothless, but she still has a bite to her and she's as mean as they come." He grinned. "She especially likes little boys with smooth hairless skin."

"I guess that means she likes you," Joey said.

Hudson threw his head back and guffawed.

Derek jabbed a finger in Hudson's direction. "You're a little shit."

"You're a little shit," Hudson mimicked.

"Keep it up."

"OK, I will." Hudson turned around, pulled his pants down, and mooned him.

Derek's face turned bright red right before he charged into the room and slammed him to the ground, knocking the breath right out of Hudson. Joey was smaller than Hudson, but he was a few years older, and he jumped on top of the ponytailed man and started pummeling him with his fists.

Sean had a better idea. He headed right out the door and never looked back.

FORTY-ONE

Back at her parents' house, Faith and Miranda changed into sweats and T-shirt and then dried their hair with a blow-dryer. They were about the same size, which made it easy to find the girl something to wear. After getting warmed up and eating grilled cheese sandwiches and hot soup, Dad ushered Miranda to his favorite chair with the ottoman and handed her a blanket. Miranda seemed to be taking it all in stride, didn't mind everyone staring at her once they were all gathered in the living room.

Beast and Rage sat by the fire while Jana found a seat on the couch next to Mom and Dad. Faith handed her a cup of hot tea. "I hope you don't mind if we all ask you a few questions?"

"I'm fine," Miranda said. "I want to do everything I can to help find Jean . . . I mean Lara."

Mom had passed around mugs of hot chocolate, and Miranda took a sip and then didn't hesitate to tell her story. "Eighteen months ago, my mom and I were living on the streets when a woman named Caroline acted all friendly and offered me a job. I had seen her hanging around my school before and so she was a familiar face. She said all the right things to a girl who didn't have fifty cents to her name. I wanted to let Mom know I was leaving with Caroline, but she said we needed to hurry if I wanted the job. I didn't hesitate to get into her car." She shook her head with regret. "She had bought McDonald's and I ate a hamburger and drank a soda on the drive. I didn't realize until much later that she must have drugged me because when she woke me up we were at a farmhouse surrounded by fields of cows. My head was groggy, and I didn't feel right. Within ten minutes of arriving, it was clear that I wasn't brought there to tutor young girls as I'd been told. I was immediately locked in a room and beaten every day. They changed my name, and if I wanted to survive, I figured out pretty quickly that I had to learn to follow orders. I had to pretend I liked being raped by those disgusting men."

Faith's mom stiffened. Dad placed a hand on her shoulder.

Miranda looked at Faith. "Should I stop?"

Faith shook her head.

"If it makes you feel any better," Miranda told Faith's mom, "in the trafficking world, Lara is special, which is good and bad. They're saving her for the right buyer, which is good because that buys you all some time, but bad because once they find a buyer, who knows where she'll be sent off to."

"What do you mean?" Jana wanted to know. "They couldn't take her far without a passport or ID, could they?"

"According to Jasper," Miranda said, "these people can get anything they need at any time. There's nothin' that money can't buy. But while I was at the farmhouse nobody touched Lara. The worst thing that's happened to her so far is the letter *H* they tattooed on her arm."

"Thank you for that," Jana said. "Do you know what the *H* stands for?"

Miranda shook her head. "Me and the other girls figure it has something to do with the main boss's last name. But that's just a guess."

Miranda took a sip of her hot chocolate before she continued. "The woman in charge insists on being called Mother," Miranda said, "but I've since learned that her name is Diane. I tried to escape the farmhouse more than once, but I was caught and punished. I was ready to give up on living when Lara was brought to the house. I could tell she needed me, but the truth is I needed her."

Faith entwined her fingers and before she could open her mouth to ask the most important question, Miranda said, "I don't know where she is. As I said, I was drugged when Caroline brought me to the farmhouse, and every time I came and went after that I was blindfolded." With her gaze still on Faith, she said, "I'll do whatever I can to help you find her. I told her I would get her out of that place, and I will not break my promise."

"How about Hudson?" Jana asked. "Did you happen to see a little boy who looked like Hudson?"

Miranda shook her head. "I'm sorry. Other than the two young men who worked on the farm, I didn't see any other boys."

Rage spoke up next. "I know you said you were drugged when you were brought to the farmhouse, but how about before you drifted off to sleep? Did you see anything at all? Any buildings or road signs?"

Miranda thought about it for a moment, then set her mug aside and straightened in her seat. "I do remember seeing a sign on the highway. We were on CA-99 headed south. I remember thinking that we were going in the same direction my mom and I had taken when we took a Greyhound bus from Sacramento to Lodi."

"I'll go get a map," Dad said. When he returned, he smoothed the map out on the coffee table where everyone could take a look.

"What about sounds?" Beast said. "Did you hear any sounds when you were coming or going?"

Miranda closed her eyes as she tried to think. "It always felt as if we were on a downhill slope as we left the farmhouse. The tires were definitely moving over gravel and dirt—not pavement. Toward the bottom of the long drive there was a dip, and that's when I would always hear sheep. Lots of sheep. A few times I heard motorcycles in the distance."

"Motorcycles?" someone asked.

"Yeah, it sounded like a lot of them." There was a pause before she added, "The last time I left the farmhouse, Jasper, the boy who was driving, stopped about halfway down the drive. His window was rolled down and he stopped to talk to someone, maybe a security guard or something, which was weird because that was the first time I remember stopping along the way."

"What about the men who were shooting at you and Furious?" Rage asked. "Do they work for that witch at the farmhouse? Any idea who they are?"

"No. I only know they killed Jasper, the guy who tried to help me get away. Jasper never told me a name, but he did say they would come after us. And he was right."

———

Late that night everyone was asleep except for Faith. It had taken some convincing, but Miranda had agreed to stay with Faith and her parents for a while. She was sleeping upstairs in the bedroom next to Faith's. Tomorrow, she and Miranda would take a drive, head up CA-99 and see if anything spiked a memory, a sign or maybe a familiar-looking building that might lead them to the farmhouse.

Unable to sleep, Faith decided there was no time like the present to exercise and build up some strength, figuring a workout might also help her sleep. First she stretched; then she did planks and sit-ups. She worked up a sweat and was about to take a quick shower when she saw a beam of light shoot across the backyard.

Alert now, every muscle tense, she watched from the upstairs window, careful not to let whoever it was see her. As far as she could tell, there was only one beam of light, which hopefully meant one person.

She put on her sneakers, slipped a sweatshirt over her head, then grabbed the gun and headed downstairs. Before making her way through the kitchen door that led to the backyard, she snatched the flashlight from the top drawer next to the refrigerator.

The moment she stepped outside, the bitter cold hit her like a slap to the face.

Careful not to make a noise, she walked across the lawn, heading in the same direction she'd seen the figure go, which was toward Dad's workshop. She probably should have woken Dad up, but she'd been afraid that whoever was there might run off before she had time to figure out who was snooping around. Something told her that if the men who had attacked her ever came around, they wouldn't send one lone man to wander about the backyard in the dead of night.

As she rounded the corner, she was surprised to see the door to the workshop opened. She and Dad had been keeping the door locked at all times. She hadn't heard a crash or a bang. Standing outside the door, she listened until she heard the sounds of footsteps at the back of the room near the bathroom. That's when she stepped inside, gun in her right hand, and flashlight in the left. When the intruder stepped out of the bathroom, she shone the light in his face and said, "Don't move or I'll shoot."

He raised both hands.

A tool belt was fastened around his waist. The beam of his flashlight was pointed at the ceiling. A dark cap was pulled over his head. Dark circles framed bloodshot eyes. His nose was red from the cold, and the lines around his eyes and mouth were deep.

"Joe?" The last person she'd expected to see was Craig's partner, Joe Henderson. "What the hell are you doing here?"

"Did you have your pool fixed lately?" he asked.

Fury caused her eyelid to twitch. He must have been to her house and seen that the money was missing. She refused to let on that she knew where the money was. Better for him to think someone else had found it. "Why do you ask?"

He sighed. "I'm going to level with you."

It took everything she had within not to shoot him. "I'd really appreciate that, Joe."

He started to lower his arms.

"Keep your hands in the air."

He did as she said. "A few months back, I inherited a large sum of money. I had to hide it from my wife . . . so I hid it in your pool equipment at the other house."

"You mean the house where your good friend Craig lived?"

"I'm sorry."

She waved the gun wildly at him. "Do you think I'm a fucking moron, Joe?"

"No. No. Of course not."

His eyes darted around the room, looking for a way to escape, no doubt.

"Don't even think about running. I'll shoot you," she said, venom lining her voice. "I might even enjoy watching you die."

He opened his mouth to talk again.

"Shut up! That money you hid at my house is the reason Craig is dead. Where have you been getting all this money, Joe?"

When he didn't answer, she stepped closer and raised the gun so that it was pointed at his forehead.

"Don't shoot. Please don't shoot," he said in a whisper. "Craig had nothing to do with any of this." His voice cracked, and his shoulders sagged. "I'm sorry, Faith. I never meant for any of this to happen."

"Where did you get the money?"

"A client needed my help hiding money."

"So you helped him launder money?"

He nodded.

"They never would have killed Craig unless they thought he'd done something wrong. Why did they kill my husband?"

"Because they thought he stole millions of dollars." His head fell forward.

"Did Craig know about the money?" she asked, her mouth dry.

He shook his head.

Guilt and shame for doubting Craig, even for a moment, swept over her in a giant wave. But it didn't last long. Instead, an emotion much stronger than guilt took precedence, a sentiment that had recently become achingly warm and familiar. The anger she'd been tamping down returned in an instant, spitting and sizzling within her veins.

"Look at me, Joe!"

He did.

"Don't pretend you're sorry now, because that's bullshit and we both know it. You're a sorry excuse for a human being." More than anything, she wanted to shoot him dead, then strangle him for good measure. Instead she counted to three and tried to calm herself. "I need information, Joe."

A sheen of sweat covered his forehead. "What do you need to know?"

"I want the client's name. The man you stole from."

Silence.

"It's over, Joe. Give me the name, or I swear to God I'll shoot you down right now, right here." She clenched her jaw.

With both hands still raised above his head, he took a step backward, closer to the sofa that lined the wall.

"Give me a name, and I'll let you go," she told him.

"I need that money, Faith. They'll kill me if I don't return the money."

"That's too bad, Joe. You should have thought of that a long time ago. If you don't give me a name, you're not going to have to worry about them anyhow." She lowered the gun, aimed for his leg, and then pulled the trigger, hitting the wall to his right.

Shit. Not even close.

He fell backward onto the couch, cowering like the chickenshit that he was.

"Listen to me, Joe. That money is dirty. That money is the reason Craig is dead and my children are missing. I have absolutely nothing to lose, and you're not leaving here without giving me a name."

"I never meant for Craig to get hurt," he told her, crying now. "The business was going under. We both did all we could to salvage it. I borrowed against my house. I lost everything . . . my wife, my kids."

Calmly, deadly, she put the muzzle to his head. "I want a name. Now."

He closed his eyes and whispered, "Richard Price."

Richard Price. She recognized the name from the client list. But since he wasn't one of the wealthiest, she'd crossed him off the list. Something didn't add up.

"Faith! What are you doing?"

Wearing pajamas and a robe, Dad stepped inside the command post carrying a rifle.

Faith let the hand with the gun drop to her side. "Don't let him run off, Dad. He's the reason Craig is dead. I'm going to go back to the house and call the police."

Thirty minutes later a row of police cars and unmarked sedans filled the driveway.

Detective Yuhasz, three police officers, and two FBI agents all showed up at around the same time. After Joe Henderson was taken away in handcuffs, Faith was asked to take a seat in the family room and answer a few questions. Her mom offered coffee and tea and after everyone politely declined, she quietly made her way upstairs with a mug and a plate of toast, no doubt for Miranda since they had all decided it would be best if she stayed in her room until everyone left.

"What was Joe Henderson looking for?" Agent Jensen asked Faith.

Detective Yuhasz stood close by.

Dad sat on the couch next to Faith.

"Joe admitted to helping one of his clients launder money. When the business took a dive, he stole a large sum of money from that same client and hid it at my house on Rolling Greens Lane."

"And he thought you had the money?"

"Apparently." Until her children were back in her arms, she refused to hand over the money.

"Anything else?"

"Yes. He admitted that Craig had no knowledge of illicit funds being laundered through the business."

"I have to ask you again. Did you ever come across a large sum of money at the house on Rolling Greens Lane?"

"No," she said, her patience running low, refusing to let him get to her, refusing to hand over what could be her only bargaining power. "Joe hid money at *our* house, the house I shared with my husband and two children. Joe is the reason Craig is dead and my kids are missing. I want to know what you people are doing to find my kids." She looked over at Detective Yuhasz. "What are *any* of you doing to find my kids?"

Detective Yuhasz shifted his weight from one foot to the other while Agent Jensen shoved a hand through his hair and said, "Joe Henderson said you held a gun to his head. Why?"

"What would you do if you saw a man snooping around your backyard in the middle of the night?"

He couldn't argue with that. He shut his notebook and stood.

"Your people confiscated H&M records and computers," Faith said, wanting confirmation that Richard Price was the man she needed to talk to. "My guess is that you knew from the start that Joe was money laundering, which tells me you must know which client he was laundering for. I want to know his name, and I want to know if you've questioned him."

Agent Jensen raised a brow, then looked at Agent Burnett, who nodded.

"Richard Price was the client in question. Being that he was recently found dead on the side of the road, we were unable to question him."

"Murdered?" she asked.

He nodded. "Took a bullet between the eyes."

Forty-Two

As soon as Derek realized Sean had run out the door, he scrambled after him, but not before fumbling with the lock and then shouting at someone in the cabin to help him find the kid. Hudson looked at the other boys. He saw panic in their eyes. Once Sean was found and dragged back to the room, they would all pay for his mistake.

If they were going to escape, it had to be now.

Hudson and Denver had the same idea at the same time and they both rushed to the corner of the room and started pulling at the baseboard with renewed energy and determination. The other boys caught on quick and started helping. The first layer of dirt was hard and packed in there pretty good, but Joey took off his shoe and used it to dig. Pretty soon the dirt was crumbly and loose. Five minutes later, they had a hole big enough for Joey to squeeze through.

A gunshot sounded in the distance, and they all stopped digging. Quiet fell over them. A few seconds passed before they started clawing at the dirt again. Denver was the biggest, and he knew the hole needed to be bigger if he was going to have any chance of escaping. His face was red from working hard and fast. Sweat dripped from his forehead.

The air coming through was colder than the chill inside the room. "Blankets," Hudson said. He jumped to his feet and ran around the room gathering blankets. He grabbed the deck of cards. Hudson was surprised when a pocketknife fell from the pile in his arms and hit the ground with a clank.

Denver looked over his shoulder as he dug. "I stole that today from one of the idiot guards."

They all froze when they heard the men shouting to one another.

"We've got to hurry!" Hudson rushed over to the hole and started shoving the blankets outside to Joey. Aiden climbed out next and then Hudson. Denver was still digging when they heard two men talking right outside the door.

"Come on, come on," Hudson said in a panicked whisper. "There's no more time!"

Denver crawled halfway through the hole before his hips got stuck. He grimaced and pushed.

Hudson grabbed one of his arms and pulled. "He's not budging," he told the other guys, "Help me pull him out."

The other boys came to help. One of them tried to loosen the dirt around Denver's waist while the other kid hooked an arm around his other shoulder. They counted to three and pulled hard.

This time Denver slid out.

They grabbed the blankets and ran as fast as they could. Aiden took the lead, then skidded on his feet up ahead, stopping in front of a dark shadow that Hudson thought was a fallen tree branch until he got closer and saw that it was Sean. He'd been shot in the back. Never had a chance.

Denver knelt at Sean's side and felt for a pulse, then nodded his head. They stared at him for a long moment before someone said, "We have to go or that's going to be us."

Voices in the distance spurred them onward, causing them to scramble and break off in different directions. Denver and Aiden cut to the left. Joey followed Hudson to the right.

It was cold and growing dark.

Hudson focused on the ground, doing his best not to trip on dead branches or pinecones. The men chasing them were much older, which was why Hudson decided to run up the mountain instead of down. He could hear Joey at his side. The kid appeared to be in decent shape. He wasn't breathing too hard.

They needed to keep going. If those men shot Sean, there was no reason to think they wouldn't kill them all.

The next thought that ran through Hudson's mind was, *What would Grandpa do?*

FORTY-THREE

"All you had to do was keep an eye on a few young girls. How hard could that be?"

Diane sat across from Aster and tried to think of some way she might be able to turn this impromptu meeting around. She used to know exactly what to do to soothe him, but ever since walking into his office, she'd felt as if she were talking to a stranger. "How was I to know that Jasper would betray me? He's been with me for many years. I had no idea he'd fallen for the stupid girl."

"That's because you've obviously been neglectful of your duties. Attention to detail has never been your forte. You're too selfish and foolish to mind anyone but yourself."

"That's not true. I used to spend every waking hour watching your every move, figuring out what I could do to make you happy. I gave you everything, and in return, you made me into nothing more than a babysitter."

He came slowly to his feet. She instantly wilted beneath his virility. All resentment melted away as he came to stand behind her, so close she could smell his aftershave. The first touch of his fingertips on both sides of her face caused an electrical current of pleasure to wash over her. She leaned her head back into the palms of his strong hands, wishing he would carry her to the fur rug set before the fireplace and make sweet love to her. Instead she felt his fingers slide down her chin and over her throat, stopping there. His fingers dug into her flesh. The harder he pressed, the more difficult it was to breathe. She struggled to get loose, but he held tight.

"You are to watch over those girls," he said, enunciating every word, "as if they were your own flesh and blood. If you feel as if you can't do your job properly, then you need to let me know so I can remedy the situation. Do you understand?"

She couldn't speak. She needed air. She pulled at his fingers and managed a small nod of her head.

He dropped his hands to his side and told her to get out.

She gasped for air as she stumbled from his office.

Faith stepped out of the shower and peered into the mirror. The knot on her head was purplish gray. Even without the bruises, she hardly resembled the woman she used to be. Thinner, yes, but also . . . hardened. The happily married fourth grade elementary teacher was gone, erased in an instant, wiped clean like the chalk from a chalkboard.

They are everywhere. Hotels, restaurants, truck stops, and regular-looking homes that you pass every day on your way to the post office.

Marion Carver's words kept repeating themselves over and over in her mind. She thought of Miranda. At the moment it seemed she was Faith's only hope of finding the whereabouts of the farmhouse. With that in mind, she dressed quickly, then grabbed her bag and her keys and hurried downstairs, where she found Miranda eating eggs and bacon while Mom ran around the kitchen, making sure she had everything she needed.

"Thanks, Mom," Faith said. She looked at Miranda. "Are you ready to go?"

Mom frowned and pushed a plate of scrambled eggs her way. "Aren't you going to eat?"

"She's right," Miranda said. "You've got to eat."

Faith sighed. The last thing she needed was one more person telling her what to do, but they were both right. She needed to eat. She dropped her bag to the floor, pulled out a stool, and took a bite. After she finished everything on her plate and gulped down the orange juice, she looked at Miranda and said, "Do you think Lara is still at the farmhouse?"

Miranda thought about it as she chewed. "I sure hope so."

Three hours later, Faith and Miranda were still in the car. They had driven on CA-99 from Sacramento to Stockton and now they were on their way back. They had stopped in Lodi to fill the gas tank and grab a sandwich. So far nothing along the highway had stood out for Miranda. There was a lot of flat farmland on both sides of the highway, and truthfully it all looked the same. Trying not to feel discouraged, Faith merged back onto CA-99 from East Lockeford Street headed back toward Sacramento. Fifteen minutes later, Miranda cried out for her to pull over.

Faith yanked on the steering wheel. The tires screeched, tossing up gravel as she pulled to the side. The car behind her honked as it passed.

Faith's heart rate spiked. "What is it?"

"That sign! Andy's Farm. I've seen it before. Turn around! We need to take the exit we just passed."

Once it was clear, Faith merged back onto the highway, then sped ahead and took the next exit and found her way back on the highway going in the other direction. A few minutes later she got off the exit Miranda had pointed out. They drove for a mile or two before Miranda shook her head. "This doesn't feel right."

Faith got back on the highway and took every exit, driving for a few miles before turning around and repeating the process. They were both quiet, but neither of them was ready or willing to give up.

"Do you think I'll ever get to see Christopher . . . you know . . . before I die?"

Beast and Rage had been sitting in a coffee shop on Del Paso Road across the street from Bill's Liquor Store for most of the morning. He looked at Rage, and despite the fact that they had done everything they could to find Christopher's adoptive parents without results, he said, "I do."

"How do you go on day after day knowing you'll never see your wife and daughter again?"

"There was a time I didn't want to go on. I remember waking up that day and thinking 'Peace out, world. I'm done.' I got up, climbed in my truck, and started driving to Nowheresville. I didn't want to live any longer. And for the first time since my wife and child's death, I didn't think about Dad or anyone else's feelings. I only thought about how nice it would be to end the pain and suffering."

"So what happened?"

"I was driving around town looking for the right spot to pull over and put a quick end to it all, and that's when I found you."

Her eyes welled with tears. "Maybe it's time I stopped being so angry."

"Maybe so," Beast said. "It wasn't your fault you were born to parents who weren't capable of taking care of a child or that the man you ran off with made you his own personal obsession. You gave your baby up for adoption out of love. You alone paid the price for everyone else's mistakes. We'll find Christopher, and I will stay on this earth for the sole purpose of making sure your son grows up knowing how very much he was loved by his mother, a compassionate young woman who never put herself before anyone."

"Beast?"

"Hmm?"

"Thank you."

"For what?"

"For finding me and taking me in."

He looked at the girl sitting before him—such a fragile being. Despite her condition and the fury she held inside as if it were her lifeline, she had hopeful eyes and a peacefulness about her that he was sure no one else noticed. He loved her as if she were his own daughter. He didn't want to lose her, but until that day came, he was thankful for every moment she was here on earth. Before he could find a way to express his feelings, since he'd never been good at such things, she grabbed her bag and jumped to her feet. "Looks like our guy is finally taking a ride."

Beast looked out the window. Sure enough, a well-dressed man, clearly not the same guy who worked behind the cash register, exited the store. Dressed in a dark suit and tie, he opened his umbrella, went to the street corner, pushed the button, and waited for the light to change.

"You get the truck," Rage said, "and I'll keep my eyes on him."

A few minutes later, Beast found Rage running on the side of the road. He stopped long enough for her to jump inside. "He's up ahead, in front of the red Prius."

"What's he driving?"

"A black Chrysler 300. New. Speed up or you're going to lose him."

Up ahead, Beast saw the Chrysler weave through traffic. He did the same, then sped up and nearly clipped the back of a car before rocketing through the intersection.

Rage tightened her seatbelt. "Look at him. He took the curb just to get around the car in front of him. He must know he's being followed."

The light turned red. Without hesitating, Beast also drove on the curb and went a step further by cutting across the grassy park area. Thanks to the bad weather, there weren't any people on the grounds.

Rage hung on to the console and said, "Over there. To your right."

No sooner did he see the Chrysler out of the corner of his eye than the driver took a sharp left. Determined not to lose him, Beast sped up and cut between two decorative palm trees, his truck flying off the sidewalk. Tires rattled and horns blared as he cut through traffic, then made a sharp left. They both caught a glimpse of the Chrysler up ahead.

"What's he doing?" Rage asked when she saw the sedan pull to the side of the road and come to a complete stop. She didn't have to wonder for long. As soon as they caught up to him, the driver leaned out his car window, aimed, and fired. Pop. Pop. Pop. The gunfire echoed off the buildings around them.

"Hang on!" Beast said right before he rammed into the back of the car. Both of them lurched forward as metal crunched and tires screeched. With his hands clamped tight on the wheel and his foot hard on the brake, he looked over at Rage. "Are you OK?"

She tugged on the seatbelt tight across her chest. "I'm fine."

Smoke poured out of the back of the Chrysler. The tires spun and then he was off again, taking a sharp right back onto a main road.

Rage held tight while they weaved through traffic once again. The underbelly of his truck rattled. The light turned red. The Chrysler sped through the intersection, zigzagging through cars and leaving Beast in the dust, stuck behind a long line of cars.

Beast hit the steering wheel with the palm of his hand.

Sirens sounded in the distance.

"Let's get out of here," Rage said.

Beast waited for the cars to move out of his way, then he made an illegal U-turn and headed back for the liquor store. Ten minutes later, he parked on the curb. They both climbed out and headed inside.

"Nobody's allowed back there," the clerk said when he saw Beast walk to the back of the store, tossing empty cardboard boxes out of his way as he made a path. Ignoring the clerk, he tried to open the door to the back room. It was locked. He stepped back. One kick did the trick. The door flew open, smacked against the wall, and hung sideways on one hinge.

There was a chair, a desk, filing cabinets, and shelves all wiped clean.

Rage opened all the cabinet drawers to see if anything at all had been left behind and then repeated the process with the desk. "Empty," she said.

Beast headed back out to where the clerk held the phone to his ear. He took it from the guy and tossed it across the room behind him. "Who was the man that used to do business back there?"

The kid shrugged. "Dude, I have no idea. I just work behind the counter and mind my own business."

Beast pulled one of his bounty hunter business cards from his wallet and laid it on the counter. Then he pointed a finger at the kid and said, "If the man comes back, I want to know about it."

The kid nodded and they walked off.

After driving past miles of endless farmland, Faith pulled to the side of the dusty road and turned toward Miranda. "Does any of this look the least bit familiar?"

Miranda shook her head. "No. I'm sorry."

"It's not your fault." Faith rolled down her window and took a moment to look around. "We'll come back tomorrow and the next day if we have to."

"Motorcycles," Miranda said as she angled her head. "Do you hear that?"

Faith listened closer. "Sounds like a lawn mower . . ."

"No, it sounds like dirt bikes. That's the same sound I kept hearing when I was trapped in that house. We're closer than I thought." She pointed down the long stretch of dirt road. "Keep going," she said as she hit the button and rolled down her window.

Faith drove slowly, listening. The noise grew in volume. Miranda was right. It wasn't a lawn mower, but at least a half-dozen dirt bikes. There had to be some sort of track nearby. They drove another five miles before Miranda gasped and then covered her mouth with her hand. She ducked down low in her seat, squirmed until she was well hidden on the ground.

"What is it?"

"Keep driving. Don't look at the driver when that car passes you. We're too close. We're in trouble."

Faith kept her hands tight around the steering wheel and tried to stay calm. The dirt bikes sounded more like chain saws now. The car coming toward them looked like an old, beat-up Cadillac. Relief settled over her when it looked as if he was going to pass by without any problem. At the last second, though, the driver put a hand out the window to stop her.

She swallowed and slowed to a stop.

He was young, probably somewhere close to twenty. He had dirty-blond hair that fell to his shoulders. His T-shirt was stained. He was crouched low in his seat, which was a relief because otherwise he might be able to see Miranda on the floor in front of the passenger seat.

"Can I help you?" he asked.

"Um, yeah, I sure hope so." She could hear the motorcycles in the distance. "I'm looking for the motocross track. My friend e-mailed me to ask me to pick up her son, and I was told that the entrance was up this road."

"Not this road. You're going to put his motorcycle in that car of yours?"

She laughed. "No, he's just hanging out with his friends and his mom wants him home." She swallowed. "I think I'll drive a little farther up the road and make sure there's not an entrance."

"Lady, there is no motocross entrance. I suggest you turn around, go back home, and shoot off another e-mail to your friend."

"OK, well, if you're sure I can't get there from here."

"I'm sure. In fact, this is a private road." He made a swirly motion with his finger for her to turn around and get lost.

"Thank you for your time."

Grim-faced, he didn't answer, just whipped his car around and headed back to wherever he came from. "I'll see you soon," she said as she made a three-point turn and headed back toward the highway.

"Is he gone?" Miranda asked.

"I can still see his car in the rearview mirror. He's making damn sure that I leave."

"That was Phoenix," she said. "I didn't have to see him to know it was him. I'd recognize that voice anywhere."

"Who is he?"

"He's a trainer. He teaches the girls at the farmhouse how to please a man."

Faith cringed. A part of her, the furious part, imagined going after the scrawny tyrant, ramming her car into his, again and again. Instead she inhaled and counted to three.

"What do we do now?" Miranda asked.

"We go home and come back with reinforcements." The thought that they were getting closer to finding her children caused her insides to buzz with something that felt a lot like hopeful exhilaration.

FORTY-FOUR

Patrick jumped when Aster Williams hit the table with his fists, sending papers flying. "I want you to call that woman and tell her she better stop meddling in my business."

Patrick had never seen his boss this angry before. The veins in Aster's neck thickened, and his eyes bulged from their sockets. If he didn't calm down, he was going to have a heart attack. And then who would be in charge? The thought intrigued Patrick.

Aster picked up a book from his desk and tossed it across the room, knocking over a vase of flowers. "Who the fuck is that gorilla who's been following me?"

"His name is Charlie Ward. He lives in Roseville with his dad, Vincent Ward, and Sally King, some two-bit whore they found on the side of the road."

"Sounds like quite the happy little family. How the fuck did those characters get involved with Faith McMann?"

"After McMann broke a cop's nose, she ended up in detention. She was released under a judge's order that she live with her parents and attend anger management classes, which is where the three of them hooked up."

"That woman isn't letting up, is she?"

The door came open. It was Aster's wife. She wore a fitted, cream-colored dress that hugged her curves in all the right places. She looked at the broken vase on the floor and frowned. "Is that the vase we found in Guilin?"

"I'm busy, honey. I'll get you another."

"Don't treat me like a child. You know how I hate that." She looked at the diamond-encrusted watch hanging on her slender wrist. "We have to leave for the engagement party in the next thirty minutes. I don't want to be late."

The woman belonged on the cover of *Vogue* or *Cosmopolitan*. Long and lithe with perfect bone structure. Aster had no idea what a lucky man he was. "You look lovely," Patrick told her.

"Thank you, Patrick." She lifted her chin and then left her husband's office, shutting the door quietly behind her.

"Why do I always get the feeling you want to fuck my wife?"

Caught off guard, Patrick squirmed in his seat. "I would never think such a thing."

Aster let out an irritating laugh. "Don't worry, kid. I was only screwing around . . . messing with your head." He looked thoughtful for a moment before he said, "We're going to be busy over the next few weeks. It's time to change things up. For starters, I'd like you to round up the youngest kids and move them again, just to be safe."

"Move them farther north?"

"You figure it out."

"What about Diane?"

"I don't trust her. Take care of it for me."

"Got it."

Aster stood tall, stretched his arms. "I've got to go get ready, but I want you to call Faith McMann personally."

"Tonight?"

"Yeah, tonight." Aster picked up a piece of paper on his desk. "Here's one of her flyers. Call the hotline and tell them you only want to talk to the mother of those sweet little kids."

"And then what?"

"Tell her that both her kids are dead and that the party's over." His jaw hardened. "Threaten the bitch. Tell her if she doesn't back off, I'm going to personally kill every member of her fucking family. One by one until they're all dead. And I'm going to make the bitch watch." When he got to the door, he waved a hand at the mess he'd made on the floor. "Don't forget to clean that up before you go."

FORTY-FIVE

The command post in her parents' backyard was packed full. The moment Faith and Miranda returned from their drive, Faith had called an urgent meeting, letting her family know they had located the farmhouse.

Miranda was sure that Jean and Lara were one and the same. If they were lucky, Faith told the group, they might find Hudson, too.

Dad, Mom, Colton, Rage, and Miranda sat around the table in the center of the room.

Jana and her husband, Steve, were seated on the couch.

Beast stood with his back resting against the wall, arms crossed.

Faith stood at the whiteboard, making notes while everyone asked questions or shot out suggestions and ideas.

"Don't you think we should call the police?" Jana asked.

Faith shook her head. "Bureaucracy would slow them down. They would need a warrant. It could take days before they could check the place out. I'm not going to sit here for two days knowing Lara could be inside the farmhouse. No way."

"Even if you wanted to give the police a chance, we don't have days," Beast reminded her. "If whoever is in charge of this operation is on to us, they could move the kids before we can get to them. We must act quickly."

"I don't want to see any of you hurt or thrown in jail," Mom chimed in.

"As soon as we gain access to the farmhouse, we'll call the police," Faith said. "I promise."

"Listen," Dad said. "I've talked with Miranda, gone over the logistics of how the farmhouse and barn are laid out, who lives there and how many people might be there when we arrive. A couple of us will have to scout ahead to make sure we're not walking into a war zone. But for the record," he said, looking at Faith's mom, who was beyond worried, "this is not a mafia compound. It's a farmhouse."

"You can't go with them," Mom told him. "You're not fully recovered. I won't allow it."

"Don't be ridiculous," Dad shot back. "These are my grandkids we're talking about." He leaned over, kissed her on the cheek, and said, "I'm going."

"We can do this," Faith said. "Dad and Beast have military experience. Beast and Little Vinnie, who's on his way, are experienced bounty hunters, both familiar with guns."

"Is this the place?" Rage asked. She had located the farmhouse on her computer using satellite. Surrounded by pines and redwoods were ten acres of land; the main building was hardly visible beneath myriad oaks, but to the left, where trees were sparse, was a barn.

Miranda leaned closer to the screen. "That's it."

"Can you zoom out," Faith asked, "so that I can see more of the area surrounding the farmhouse?"

Rage clicked a button until Faith could see exactly where she and Miranda had been. "The young man in the Cadillac stopped us right about here," Faith said, pointing at the dirt road. "And that," she said, indicating the left of the farmhouse, "must be some sort of motocross track. We could hear the high-pitched noise from the dirt bikes."

Miranda pointed at the long dirt road, partially hidden beneath a canopy of trees, leading up to the house and barn. "This is where there should be a gate to keep visitors out, the area with the security guard."

Colton got to his feet and went to stand behind Rage so he could see the screen better. "There don't appear to be any wires overhead, so that's good. The trees could be a problem," Colton said, "since the truck we'll be using is thirteen feet high and eight and a half feet wide. We could bring the chain saw just in case. We've done it before. It's all a matter of timing and how many men they have guarding the place. We might not have time to cut down a thick branch if things get chaotic."

There was a knock on the door. Everyone looked that way.

"It's Beast's dad." Faith opened the door and introduced everyone to Little Vinnie. Beast's dad had two large duffel bags, one strapped over each shoulder. Beast took one of the bags and helped him unload, setting the guns carefully on the table. "Who knows how to shoot?"

"I've got my own weapon of choice," Faith's dad said.

Jana's phone rang.

Faith recognized the ringtone as being the one they chose for the hotline.

Jana answered. Listened. Then she handed the phone to Faith. "You have a caller. A man who says he needs to talk directly to you."

Faith took the phone and held it to her ear.

"Is this Faith McMann?" the caller asked.

"Yes, this is she."

"I'm calling to let you know that your children are dead."

Every muscle tensed. "Who is this?"

"It's over," he said. "There's nothing else you can do to help them."

"I don't believe you," she said, ready to hang up. "Do you have any idea how many prank calls we get? You think this is funny?"

"Your son was quite the prankster, full of energy, with a funny mole on his right ear. Your beautiful daughter was quiet as a mouse. It's still a wonder that they were brother and sister. They both died quickly. Neither of them suffered."

Faith's legs felt weak as if they might suddenly give out.

"It's time for you to gather your family together, mourn, grieve, do what you must, and find a way to move on."

Faith looked around the room at each family member.

There was a long, drawn-out pause before the caller said, "And if you don't, you'll have to say goodbye to your friends and family— Mom, Dad, your sister and brother, and, just so we're clear, your nieces would be the first to die. Their lives are in your hands."

Click.

Faith stood there, unmoving.

Lara and Hudson—they couldn't be dead.

No. She would never allow herself to believe it was so. She thought of Corrie Perelman and how she refused to believe Samantha was gone. It made sense to Faith because she could feel her children's presence as if they were in this very room with her now.

"Who was it?" Colton wanted to know.

Faith looked at her brother. "They said Lara and Hudson were dead and that if we didn't stop now they would kill each and every one of you, starting with your daughters."

Colton's face reddened, his shoulders tense. "That's bullshit." He went to the table where the guns had been laid out and grabbed a Remington 7615 pump-action rifle and a Glock 43. "Let's do this."

"No," Faith said as she realized how selfish she'd been to allow her family to risk their lives. She looked at her dad, and for the first time she saw him as a man with vulnerabilities. He was a good man, a strong man, but he wasn't invincible. None of them were. "I can't let you do this. I was wrong. We need to call the police."

"Too late," Jana said, "we're in this together." She took the phone from Faith, then waddled over to the bag and grabbed a .357 Magnum. "I like this one." She looked at her husband and said, "I'm not spending the rest of my life looking over my shoulder."

Steve walked up to his pregnant wife and kissed her on the forehead. "Nice choice, but you're staying home with Mom. I'll go with your brother. Keep the gun by you at all times while we're gone."

Dad loaded his LC9 and slid the safety fully into place. He looked at Beast, Rage, and then Little Vinnie. "Are you in?"

Without hesitating, each one of them nodded and then stood, ready to go.

"Your kids are alive," Dad said to Faith. "I can feel it in every one of my bones. Now let's go get my grandkids."

FORTY-SIX

It was another hour before they were all loaded in the back of Colton's truck. Dad, Steve, Beast, Rage, and Miranda. Faith rode in the front cab so she could show her brother the way. According to Miranda there could be anywhere from three to ten adults, including the woman referred to as Mother, at any one given time.

Faith had tried to talk Miranda into staying home with Mom and Jana, but she wouldn't listen. These people had ruined her life, and she wanted to help take them down, especially Diane. Besides, Miranda had made a good point: the fact that she knew the grounds could prove to be invaluable.

Faith looked over at her brother as they drove along Highway 99. "If they harmed my children, I will go after them. I won't stop until they're dead, every single one of them. I'll spend my life making them pay."

"Let's hope it won't come to that."

"I am worried about Dad coming along. Mom was right when she said he hadn't yet fully recovered from his stroke. He's still a little slow on his feet."

"Dad's the last person you have to worry about. If you've ever listened to any of his war stories, you would know that. He saved many lives on more than one occasion."

"I've heard a few," Faith said.

"He used to share them with Craig, Hudson, and me whenever we went camping."

"He used to tell Hudson war stories?"

"I realize Hudson is only nine, but he's a clever boy. This might be the first and only time I would say I'm actually glad that kid is so fearless. I wouldn't be surprised if he finds a way to make contact with you."

Faith prayed her brother was right. People always thought Hudson was much older than his age. He'd never met a stranger. He was adventurous and courageous.

"Do you remember the story Dad used to tell at the dinner table?" Colton asked. "The one where his unit met with heavy enemy resistance and Dad lay motionless on the ground until the enemy closed in. And when they did, he tossed a grenade their way and wounded or killed all of them."

"I always thought Dad was making those stories up. But, yes, now that you mention it, I do remember."

"Mom says Dad has always run in the direction of trouble, never away from it."

It was quiet for a moment before Faith said, "No matter what happens, nothing will ever be the same again."

"No. Nothing will ever be the same. Just don't let what these people did destroy you, Faith. You're a good person . . . compassionate and loving. Don't let them take that from you. When Lara and Hudson return, they're going to need their mom more than ever."

"You agree with Dad, right? That they're still alive?"

"I do. Hudson has a lot of our Dad in him . . . and he's feisty like you. I bet he's giving someone hell right now. And Lara. She's quiet, but she's smart. I have faith in both of them."

Faith inhaled as she gazed ahead at the road in front of them.

Colton's semitrailer wasn't the only vehicle on the long stretch of highway. What were all these people doing in the middle of the night? She glanced up at the full moon. It was Christmas Day, she realized, and yet nobody had mentioned it.

Colton turned off the highway as Faith instructed. She could feel the gravel beneath the tires. They passed the section of the road where she'd asked the young man where the entrance to the motocross was and he told her she needed to turn around and leave. Faith called Rage on her cell phone. "Almost there. We'll stop at the end of the drive and then stick with the plan. If the truck can't make it up the drive, two of us will scout ahead."

"Sounds good," she said.

Up ahead where the open land ended and rows of tall pines and old oaks began, Colton pulled to the side of the road, shut off the engine, and turned off the lights.

Faith opened the door and jumped to the ground. The only sounds were frogs in a distant creek. Moonlight threw shadows across the trees in front of them, making the branches look like long, gangly arms with brittle fingers as she walked to the back of the truck where Colton was pulling the doors open.

One by one, they exited the truck.

Rage and Miranda jumped out last.

The empty fields behind them glittered like silver dust.

Little Vinnie passed out headlamps and three sets of walkie-talkies with a push-to-talk switch to start transmission.

Rage wore a headlamp and used the beam of light to see where to strap a hunting knife around her thigh.

Dad stepped out dressed in full camouflaged gear, including boots and hat. With a rifle strapped over his shoulder and his LC9 ready to go, he stood off to the side and waited quietly for everyone to gather their stuff. It was easy to imagine Dad as a military commander, a force to be reckoned with. The love she felt for him in that moment, knowing he would do whatever he could to rescue his grandkids, caused her heart to swell with pride, filling her with the determination she needed to see this to the end.

"I'll be right back," Colton said before he jogged up the drive, returning thirty seconds later. "Too many branches to bother cutting. The truck won't make it all the way through. We're going to have to do this on foot."

They were all ready to go. Beast and Little Vinnie led the pack with Steve, Colton, and Dad next, and then Faith, Rage, and Miranda following behind. They walked at a good clipped pace, cold air nipping at their faces. Nobody said a word. Gravel crunched beneath heavy boots.

After a while, Beast had them gather around. He spoke quietly. "I still don't see a fence or a gate, but Miranda assured me we're getting close. Little Vinnie and I are going to cut off to the right and see what we're dealing with here."

Steve stepped forward. "Dad and I will go to the left."

"How will we know when it's clear to move forward?" Rage asked.

"I'll use the walkie-talkie to call you," Beast said, and then he took off.

The rest of them stood in the dark, nobody saying a word. The next five minutes felt much longer. Rage tapped her foot. "I don't like this. I say we move forward."

They all agreed.

Single file, they trudged up the gravel road. Colton took the lead. Rage, Faith, and Miranda followed in line. The farther they went, the thicker the trees became and the darker it got. The moonlight struggled to squeeze its way through the branches and give them light. A few minutes later, Miranda stopped.

Faith stopped, too. "Anything wrong?"

"Can you hear the sheep?"

They all listened. "I heard them," Rage said. "What does that mean?"

"We're almost there."

Shouts sounded in the distance and then a crack and a pop.

Faith's heart raced.

Colton was about to take off toward the sound when they heard leaves crunching and Little Vinnie appeared. "Come on," he said, waving his arm. "There's a chain-link fence up ahead. Who has the first aid kit?"

Panic set in. "It's in my backpack," Faith said. "Why? What happened?"

He pointed over his shoulder at the direction he'd come from. "Steve's been hurt, a knife wound. Doesn't appear to be deep, but he's bleeding good enough." He started off again, heading up the middle of the gravel driveway. "You'll find him at the base of a lone redwood."

"Where are you going?" Faith asked.

"To catch up to my son," Little Vinnie told her. "He's headed for the barn. The gate ahead is open."

Faith looked at Colton. She felt suddenly helpless and out of her element. What was she thinking asking her family to put themselves in danger like this? Everything was happening too quickly.

"It's OK," Rage said. "I'll go help Steve. You go with them to the house." Rage took the flashlight and first aid kit from her and said, "Go find Lara."

"Thank you."

Rage ran off, weaving through trees and brush.

Faith watched until she could no longer see her, then rushed to catch up with Colton and Miranda. The chain-link fence was open just as Little Vinnie said it would be. They walked another two hundred feet before reaching a clearing. The barn was large, framed with timber and painted red. To the right of the barn was a two-story house with gabled windows. Staying hidden in the trees, they crept around the backside of the barn, away from the house. Inside the barn they found Beast sitting on a bale of hay talking to the same guy who had stopped Faith down the road yesterday.

Beast had used ropes to restrain the upper half of his body. Duct tape covered his mouth. "He won't cooperate," Beast told the group. "I don't know who he's trying to protect, but they've got him scared pretty good."

"His name is Phoenix," Miranda said.

The boy's eyes met hers, his expression one of surprise before his face turned red with anger. Shouting at her from beneath the tape, he tried harder to wriggle his way out of the ropes.

Worried, Miranda took a step back.

Little Vinnie and Colton walked around the inside of the barn, checking the loft and making sure nobody was hiding in an empty stall or within a stack of hay.

"Dad and I are going to head to the back of the house," Colton said. "See if we can find a way inside."

"Something's not right," Miranda blurted, stopping Colton and his dad from stepping outside.

Faith frowned. "What do you mean?"

"Mother had a habit of leaving lights on at night. If I didn't know better, I'd say she was afraid of the dark." Miranda edged closer to the barn door and looked toward the house. "She knows we're here."

"What do we do now?" Faith asked.

Beast picked the kid up by the scruff of his neck, dragged him to the barn door, and tossed him outside. "Go tell your boss we need to talk."

Screaming mumbled nonsense beneath the tape, Phoenix ran toward the house.

Just as he reached the first step leading up to the porch outside the front door, gunfire exploded around him.

Miranda ran for cover inside an empty stall.

Faith dropped to the ground inside the barn. She could see Phoenix lying on the ground, motionless.

An eerie quiet fell over them.

"A pistol was fired from the top floor," Dad said, breaking into the silence, "and a high-caliber rifle sounded from bottom floor, far left."

"Agreed," Beast said. "There was also a shotgun . . . fired from the window to the right of the front entry."

"We have at least three shooters." Faith's dad looked at Miranda. "Where do the kids usually sleep?"

"Upstairs. Two separate rooms. Far right. Sometimes Mother uses another room downstairs, also on the right side. She keeps the doors locked."

Little Vinnie pulled a handful of firecrackers from his front pants pocket. He looked at Miranda and said, "We need a distraction."

She nodded and took them from him. He handed her a matchbook, too. "I want you to throw the firecracker toward the front of the house. After it goes off, count to three before you light another one and toss it. Repeat the process until you run out."

"Got it."

"Beast and Little Vinnie will go around to the left of the house," Dad told the group. "And Colton and I will go around the right and try to find a way inside."

"And you," Dad said, handing Faith Colton's walkie-talkie, "sneak around to the back of the barn outside where you can see the back of the house and use the walkie-talkie to let us know if you see anyone leave."

"I can do that," she said, glad to have something to do.

Faith stayed low as she followed Colton and Dad out of the barn, staying close to the trees until the two men broke off to make their way to the back of the house.

Crouched low in the dark, Faith readied her gun and kept an eye on the house. Before she heard the first firecracker go off, an arm came around from behind and knocked the gun out of her grasp.

A dirty palm covered her mouth as the man dragged her backward toward the trees. Frantic, she twisted and kicked.

Her screams were muffled, her struggles useless.

I'm going to die. I'll never see Lara and Hudson again.

Lights began to flicker—the same bright light she'd seen after returning home from the hospital. She's been through too much to give up now. *Fight!*

Rocks and twigs bit into her skin as her captor pulled her along, dragging her through the dark. Reaching out, her fingers brushed over twigs and leaves and then something hard. A rock. She grasped on to it and used all the strength she could summon to turn toward the man and slam the rock into his knee.

Taken by surprise, he grunted and let go of her.

She dropped to the ground. Gasping and sputtering, determined to get away, she scrambled forward, crawling on all fours, pebbles and twigs cutting into her skin.

"What's going on?" a voice asked.

It was Rage. Faith could see the beam of light above her eyes. The shadow of the man stood tall now and he lifted his arms, aiming his gun her way.

"Run!" Faith shouted, but it was too late. A shot was fired.

Her throat clogged with fear, Faith got to her feet. Someone grabbed her from behind, held her tight. "It's me."

"Oh, Rage, thank God!"

Rage went to where the man lay still on the ground. She knelt down and felt for a pulse. "He won't be bothering anyone else."

Faith looked at her and said, "You saved my life."

"OK, yeah, whatever. He didn't hurt you?"

"No, I'm fine."

"Come on, then—we have kids to find."

Another firecracker went off in the distance.

"Steve," Faith said. "Where is he?"

"He's going to be fine," Rage said, urging her onward. "All bandaged up and keeping an eye on the man who was guarding the gate before Beast knocked him over the head and duct-taped him to a tree."

"The men are trying to find a way inside the house," Faith told her. "I'm supposed to be keeping an eye on the house, making sure no one sneaks out. I have no idea where that man came from."

"What's with the firecrackers?"

"They asked Miranda to create a distraction."

Rage found Faith's gun on their way back to the barn and handed it to her.

"I'm out of firecrackers," Miranda told them as they approached. "What now?"

"I'll distract them," Rage said.

"Is there any other way to get inside the house without going through the front door?" Faith asked.

"There is a high window in the basement," Miranda said. "We might be able to get inside that way." She waved a hand toward the side of the house. "Follow me."

Pah-ting! Rage hit the weather vane on top of the roof with a small pistol she'd brought. And then again.

Miranda and Faith left Rage to do her thing. Faith's gaze darted from shadow to shadow. She didn't plan to get caught unaware a second time.

Gunfire exploded from the back of the house. Glass shattered.

With their bellies to the ground, Faith and Miranda crawled across dirt and weeds until they were next to the side of the house. Miranda moved dirt and rocks out of the way, then started pulling loose boards from the earth.

Faith grabbed the end of the last board and used her legs to pull it free. With that done, they both pushed on the window, surprised when it came open.

Miranda shone her flashlight inside. Nothing but stacks of crates and boxes, old bike parts, and oil cans. It was about an eight-foot drop to the ground.

Faith slipped her legs through the window and dropped to the ground without breaking an ankle. Before making it across the room, she heard Miranda jump in behind her.

Faith pulled the gun from her pocket.

"This way," Miranda said. She was about to open the door when they heard shouting and more gunfire. They crouched low, and Faith prayed Dad and the rest of them would make it out of there with their lives.

As soon as it was quiet again, Faith followed Miranda through the door and up narrow wooden stairs. Another door led into a living area, where three couches lined the walls.

The door opened, and before they could turn back a man stepped into the room.

"Dad!" Faith said, rushing toward him. He winced when she grabbed hold of him.

"You're hurt."

"I'll be fine. I'm going upstairs."

Staying low, Miranda and Faith followed his lead.

Dad signaled for them to stay where they were, then headed to the room at the front of the house. Faith ignored his gesture and followed close behind. Every minute or so, she heard a pinging sound when a bullet hit the weather vane. The door to the room was ajar. He brought his firearm to eye level, kicked open the door, and fired off two shots.

Faith winced as she watched the man stagger backward into the wall and then sink slowly to the floor. The gun fell to his side.

Colton came running up the stairs. He squeezed his way between Faith and Miranda, his attention going from Dad to the man sprawled faceup on the floor near the window. He went to the shooter and knelt down beside him. After a moment, he said, "He's dead."

So much death and destruction, Faith thought. *And for what?* She inhaled as she reminded herself why they were here, then turned toward Miranda. "Where are the children kept?" she asked.

Miranda pointed to the door to the left of the stairs.

By the time they reached the door, Beast was coming up the stairs. Everyone was OK, Faith thought, thankful to know they were all alive. The thought that Lara could be inside one of the bedrooms caused her heart to race. She tried a door. It was locked.

Beast gestured for everyone to move aside and then he threw his body into the door, busting it wide open.

Wood splintered and fell like rain around them.

The room appeared to be empty.

Colton signaled to the rest of them that he was going in. With his gun raised, he entered the room first. A shot rang out, and chaos erupted all around them.

Colton stumbled backward.

Faith screamed when she saw the blood seeping through her brother's shirt. It all seemed to be happening in slow motion . . . the woman . . . Colton . . . Beast charged forward, his face a contorted mass of fury as he grabbed the woman and twisted the gun out of her grasp before she could get off another shot.

The woman fought Beast with everything she had, swinging her fist, catching him in the chin. She seemed crazed. Her eyes were wild, ready to fight to the end. When she went for his eyes, Beast swung back at her, knocking her out in an instant.

She crumbled to the ground.

Faith ran to Colton's side, sat on the floor next to him, and held his head in her lap.

"I'll be OK," Colton said, his voice weak. "Go find your kids."

Ignoring him, Faith unbuttoned his shirt, carefully pulled it off him, and used it to stop the flow of blood, thankful to see that it appeared to be a shoulder wound.

Rage pulled her sweatshirt off to keep him warm, then knelt down beside Faith and told her to go find her kids and that she would take care of Colton.

Faith looked at her brother. "Go," he said again.

When Faith stood, she saw Miranda hovering over the woman on the floor, whispering something into her ear as she pulled a string of keys from around the woman's wrist. Miranda sifted through the keys until she found the one that fit the closet door.

Not one peep came from inside the closet, making Faith believe no one could be inside.

She could hear Dad in the hallway talking to the police.

The door opened.

And there they were.

Small children huddled together. It was dark inside and hard to see. Faith's heart skipped a beat as she stepped that way. *Please be there, please be there.*

Miranda looked over her shoulder at Faith and, with woeful eyes, slowly shook her head.

Miranda is wrong, Faith thought. She had to be wrong. Her kids were here. She'd felt Lara's presence on her way to the farmhouse. Nudging her way past Miranda, she looked closely at every face as tears fell. "It's going to be OK," she told the young girls. "Everything's going to be OK." But she wasn't sure she believed it.

Dad stepped into the room, holding his side. When he saw Colton, he went to him.

"I'm OK, Dad." Dad nodded and then looked over his shoulder at Faith and asked, "Are they here?"

Faith met his gaze, tears falling freely as she shook her head. Every part of her felt numb as she knelt down by one of the little girls inside the closet. She couldn't be much older than eight. Her dark hair was tangled, her brown eyes wide with fear and confusion. *Lara,* she thought. *Where's Lara?* She had to will her body not to shut down.

She swallowed a knot in her throat, didn't know what to do or say. And then she saw the necklace hanging around the girl's neck. "That necklace," Faith said as she took a closer look at the gemstone hanging from a chain, a necklace she'd bought Lara on her last birthday. "Where did you get it?" The beat of her heart kicked up a notch.

"Jean gave it to me."

Faith struggled to hold herself together.

"When?" Faith asked, hope springing to life.

"How long ago did Jean give you that?" Miranda asked.

"This morning," the girl said.

"Do you know where Jean is now?" Miranda asked.

The little girl shook her head. "After breakfast they took her outside to a big car and drove away. I cried and cried."

"Are you sure it was Jean?" Faith asked.

"I'm sure. She's my best friend." She showed them both a tiny prick on her finger.

"What is that?"

"Jean made me her blood sister."

Goose bumps covered Faith's arms. Lara had a habit of making all her good friends blood sisters by pricking their fingers with a needle and then rubbing the tiny drops of blood together. The man who had called earlier had lied.

Lara was alive. Faith smiled at the girl. "You must be a very special friend for her to make you her blood sister."

The girl nodded. "That's what Jean said."

Faith stood and went back to check on Colton. Rage was still at his side, talking to him, keeping him calm. Faith was anything but calm. She wanted someone to pay. She walked to where Beast stood and quietly asked him if he would help her with something.

He didn't ask any questions, just did as she asked and dragged Mother out of the room and across the hallway and into the bathroom. The woman groaned.

"I'll only be a minute," she told Beast. Faith shut the door, then leaned over and shook the woman's shoulders until she groaned and opened her eyes.

"Where are my kids?" Faith asked through gritted teeth.

Sirens sounded in the distance.

The woman said nothing, merely smirked up at her.

Seething with frustration, Faith yanked the upper half of the woman's body up and over the toilet until Mother's head hung over the porcelain bowl. She took a fistful of wiry hair and shoved her head inside the bowl, using all her strength to hold her underwater until the woman was clawing and struggling to get free. She wanted her dead, but more than that, she needed answers.

Faith pulled her head up, still unable to come to terms with the fact that Lara and Hudson were not among the children inside the closet. "Where are my kids?"

"They're dead."

Faith dunked her head in the bowl again, using both arms to keep her down.

Water sloshed over the bowl and onto the floor.

She yanked her head upward. "Where are my kids?" she asked again, her voice loud and unrecognizable to her own ears.

Laughter was her answer. A high-pitched sound that rattled Faith's bones.

Beast opened the door. "The police will be here soon. Might want to hurry up in there." The door clicked shut.

"I'll be waiting for you," Faith ground out, close to Mother's ear. "I don't care if you're eighty years old when you get out of jail. Even after I find my kids, I'll be waiting."

"Dead," the woman said through gritted teeth. "They're both dead."

Faith slammed her head against the rim of the bowl and then turned around and walked out, shutting the door behind her.

Beast had returned to the other room. As she headed that way, she heard a noise. She stopped to listen. Between the distant sound of sirens there was no mistaking a tap tap tap as if someone was knocking on a window or door.

She went to the stairs, listened closer.

There it was again, coming from somewhere below. She hurried that way, ran down the stairs, ignoring Beast when he called after her.

Once she hit the landing, she froze . . . listened . . . headed for the kitchen. Windows had been shattered, broken dishes strewn across the floor.

She stopped in front of the man lying in a heap in front of the pantry door where the sound was loudest. He was facedown. Blood puddled at both sides of his body. He wasn't moving, but she still wasn't sure if he was dead. On bended knees, she reached out to feel for a pulse, but Beast and Rage stepped into the kitchen before she could find out. She looked up at them both and said, "Is he dead?"

"He looks dead to me," Rage said. "What are you doing down here?"

Tap. Tap. Tap.

"Did you hear that?" Faith asked. "Someone's inside the pantry," she told them. "Listen."

Five seconds passed before they all heard it again.

Beast grabbed the dead man by the waist and dragged him out of the way so they could open the door. Faith rushed inside. The pantry was narrow but deep. Shelves on both sides were loaded with neat rows of canned food.

The farther inside she went, the lower the ceiling became. About eight feet in, she had to stoop over to move forward until she reached the very back. Nothing but shelves stacked with bags of beans and rice.

Tap. Tap. Tap.

There it was again!

She dropped to her knees, began moving the food out of the way, tossing bags of rice to the side.

"There's a small door back here!" she shouted back at Rage and Beast. "I need the keys that Miranda has!"

"I'll be right back," Rage called back, and Faith could hear her footsteps pounding against the stairs somewhere overhead.

Rage was back in under a minute.

"The police are here," Beast said.

"Out with your hands in the air," she heard a loud voice call out through a bullhorn.

"Go!" Faith said. "Get everyone else out, too. Don't give them any reason to shoot. I've got this."

The first key didn't work. Neither did the second, third, or fourth. "I'm coming," she said to the person on the other side of the door, hoping whoever was inside could hear her.

Her hands shook.

Please, God, please.

She was more than halfway through the keys. She inserted the next one and heard a click. Her heart pounded against her chest. The small square door came open. Daylight from the kitchen spilled inside the tiny room where one small girl, thin and bony, was curled in a fetal position.

"Lara? Is that you?"

A whimper sounded.

Overwhelmed with emotions, Faith felt her arms and legs shake at the thought that the child inside the tiny room might be her own. She could literally feel her children's warm bodies close to hers, see them, hear their voices in her head.

Faith crawled inside, trying to make sense of what she was seeing as her eyes adjusted to the dark. "Oh, honey," Faith said as she wrapped the frail body in her arms. "You're safe now." She held the girl's shivering body close, rocked her as they both cried.

"Faith," a voice called out moments later. "Where are you? It's Detective Yuhasz here. I want to help."

"In here," Faith called out. "We need an ambulance."

Between the two of them, they got the girl out of the windowless space and into the kitchen, where Detective Yuhasz scooped her into his arms. He looked from the small, thin face to Faith's exhausted one, his expression one of disbelief.

Faith wiped her eyes as she nodded, doing her best to stay strong. No, this poor helpless child who so desperately needed to be rescued was not Lara.

"It's her," Faith told the detective, her voice nearly inaudible. "After all this time. Samantha Perelman is alive."

With Faith at his side, Detective Yuhasz carried Samantha from the farmhouse to the ambulance that had just pulled up outside. The place was lit up with spotlights as detectives and agents gathered evidence and taped off sections of the house.

Faith's dad had gone with Colton and Steve in the first ambulance to arrive.

After the EMTs took over and the detective had a few words with O'Sullivan, he turned to Faith as she was about to head off with Beast, Little Vinnie, Rage, and Miranda.

"I'm sorry Lara and Hudson weren't here," the detective told her, "but this gives me hope that we'll find them."

She nodded, unable to find her voice.

He gestured toward his vehicle. "Why don't you drive with me to the hospital? I've got a call in to Mrs. Perelman, who will be meeting me there. I thought you might want to come along."

"You go ahead," she said stiffly, not quite sure of what she was feeling—sadness, happiness, regret, and loss all mixed into one. She needed a moment to herself. Time to think and regroup. "I want to give my mom and sister a call. I might see you there."

Faith caught up to her friends, thankful for their silence.

They walked at an even pace to the end of the drive where her brother's semitrailer sat off to the side of the road. Beast had gotten the keys from Colton, and he climbed in behind the wheel.

They drove home in silence.

A full moon, big and round, followed them most of the way, and all she could think of was that this was her first Christmas without her children since they were born. In that moment, anguish ripped through Faith's insides, beating on her ribs and pulling at her heart, until the agony escaped like a wild beast trapped for too long. The low whimper erupted into a noise so pitiful that it took both Miranda and Rage to hold her, calm her, and talk her through the torment within until she was able to tamp it all down where it belonged, leaving only a tiny light to hop about, the same flickering light she knew was there to remind her that this was only the beginning.

Epilogue

Two Days Later

Standing within her parents' kitchen, Faith took a good, long look at her family. Battered but not beaten, Dad was fine, but that didn't stop Mom from coddling him, making sure he had everything he needed.

The bullet had been removed from Colton's arm. He was recovering at home with his wife and two daughters.

Steve was still in a hospital room at Sutter General in Roseville with Jana at his side. The doctors assured them he would be up and about in no time. He was a hero. According to Little Vinnie, if Steve hadn't shown up and taken care of a third gunman at the gates, Beast would have taken a bullet to the head. Instead Steve had wrestled for the gun. He got the weapon, but he wasn't fast enough. Before Beast could take the guy out, the man took a slice out of Steve's leg.

A total of thirteen children had been saved from captivity—five under the age of twelve. Seven more girls had been locked in a downstairs bedroom, gagged and bound. And then, of course, there was Samantha Perelman.

They had spent the day after the shootout being interviewed by Agents Jensen and Burnett. Thanks to Dad, they were all allowed to walk away without being charged with any crimes. After speaking to an attorney, Dad had spoken for them all, pleading self-defense and making it clear that assault had been their only option since a felony was being committed and the assailant struck first, opening fire and killing a young man before they could call authorities. When their assailants no longer posed a threat, they stopped firing back and called the police.

Diane Weaver, the woman in charge at the farmhouse, and the man Beast had fastened to the tree were the only two thugs to survive. Both had a long criminal history and would be spending some time in prison on charges of child endangerment and trafficking.

Faith was about to walk outside to get fresh air when someone turned up the television. Every local news station hovered over Corrie Perelman as she exited the hospital.

"How is your daughter doing?" the reporter asked.

"She's suffering from malnutrition and dehydration, but the doctors are expecting a full recovery."

"Is it true she'd been taken by human traffickers?"

"You'll have to talk to the authorities about the details. I'm only concerned with my daughter's health and that she's back home where she belongs." She started to walk away, but then stopped and turned to the reporter she'd been talking to and looked straight into the camera lens. "I want to thank Faith McMann for finding my daughter." Mrs. Perelman stood straight and tall, no longer resembling the anxiety-ridden woman of a few days ago. "This city, this world," she went on, "needs more people like Faith McMann. She refuses to let these horrible, soulless criminals take our children. Despite everything she's been through, she hasn't let up. If anyone out there knows anything at all about the whereabouts of Lara and Hudson McMann, please call the authorities right away. I'm begging you. And, Faith, if you're watching, you need to know how grateful I am for your kindness and for giving me my life back. I'm forever indebted. God bless."

The room fell quiet.

Faith made her way outside, where she took a seat on a bench overlooking the expanse of oaks and willows. Her chest felt tight, her breathing shallow. Her emotions were all over the place: grateful for the rescue of thirteen girls, glad for Corrie Perelman but still simmering with anger. Because in the end, nothing had changed—her husband was dead. Her kids were missing.

It took all she had to rein in her fury and keep it bottled up until the appropriate time and place—and that time would surely come.

Rage had followed her outside and took a seat next to her. "Are you OK?"

Faith looked into her eyes and said, "I have to be. For my kids."

"They're lucky to have you," Rage said.

As Faith thought about how fragile life was she reached over and patted her new friend on the leg. "And I'm lucky to have you."

"Where do we go from here?" Rage asked, staring straight ahead. "How does anyone fight something so limitless and never ending?"

"We keep doing what we've been doing," Faith said. "We make our voices heard. We get the community involved. We talk to individuals, businesses, and law enforcement until we're blue in the face. And we never let up. We hit the streets and the truck stops and the darkest corners of our city where these monsters feel most comfortable and we point fingers, or weapons, whatever it takes to make them talk."

"And if they refuse?"

"We shut them down and move on."

The door to the house opened, and Beast stepped outside. "You two ready to go to the range?"

Faith stood. And beneath an overcast sky, one step at a time, one breath after another, she walked onward across the soft, green grass.

Acknowledgments

I can't say enough wonderful things about Alan Turkus, my very first editor, who worked with me on the Lizzy Gardner series from beginning to end. Thanks for everything, Alan. You will be missed.

JoVon Sotak, Charlotte Herscher, Tiffany Pokorny, and Jacque Ben-Zekry. Your hard work is greatly appreciated.

My husband, Joe, for being my rock every step of the way.

Cathy Katz, Ruth Cole Cunningham, Morgan Ragan, Brittany Ragan, Joey Ragan, Jesse Crowder, Dillon Yuhasz, Sam Johnston, and Megan Tandberg for editing, reading, brainstorming, and sometimes just listening! Thanks!

ABOUT THE AUTHOR

Photo © 2014 Morgan Ragan

New York Times and *USA Today* bestselling author Theresa Ragan, mother of four, lives with her husband in Sacramento, California. In 2012, she signed with Thomas & Mercer and has sold 1.8 million books. Besides writing thrillers under the name T.R. Ragan (including the Lizzy Gardner novels *Abducted, Dead Weight, A Dark Mind, Obsessed, Almost Dead,* and *Evil Never Dies*), Theresa also writes medieval time travels, contemporary romance, and romantic suspense. *Furious* is the first novel in her new Faith McMann suspense series. To learn more about Theresa, visit her website at www.theresaragan.com.